Headhunters

Anton Marks

Why Headhunters?

SCAN ME

RUNNYMEDE ESTATE

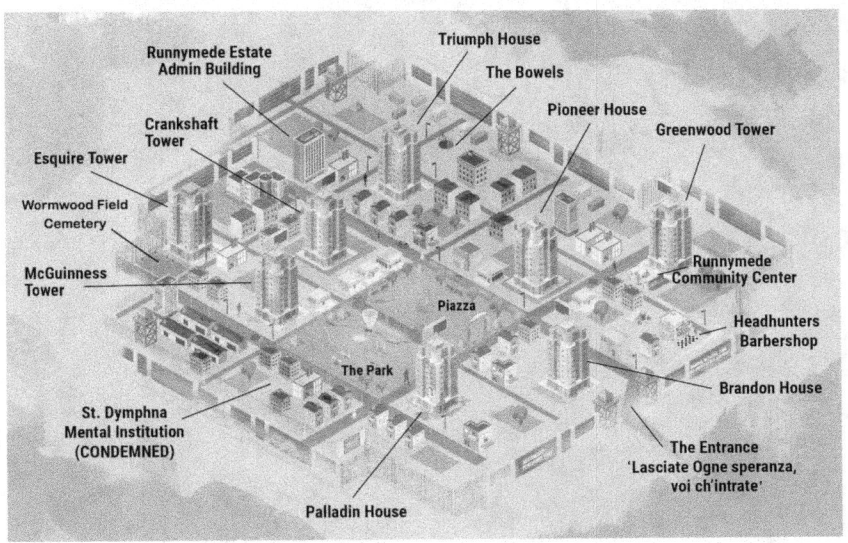

Chapter One

No tree, it is said, can grow to Heaven
Unless its roots reach down to Hell.
Carl Jung

There were six of them pursuing him, and Zach Ellison was running for his life. They were snapping at his heels, crazy in their eyes and murder on their minds, sprinting after him full tilt with knives and machetes swinging. If he counted the stragglers who couldn't keep up the pace, eleven psychopaths wanted to dismember him.

And no one knew why. Not really.

The notorious drug-pushing 'R' Team Clique were in thrall.

A higher power was pulling their strings.

Evil incarnate.

He'd seen them pushing their poison on numerous occasions on the estate, but he stayed out of their affairs. This attack, along with others he'd had to endure in the past, formed a pattern that defined his life.

This was his life.

A slip, a trip or a miscalculation in his movement, and they would be upon him like a pack of wolves.

It was a life that he had fought against in the beginning, but eventually was forced to accept.

This was to be his destiny, and he was prepared for it. At least that's what he told himself.

He may be without weapons, but he has a quick mind and even quicker reflexes. His strategy - and something he had trained for - was to use the brutish architecture of Runnymede Estate, his home, to his advantage.

His mentor Hortense saw to that.

She saved his life.

Zach didn't know it at the time, but Hortense had hired and paid for two of the best Free-Running experts in the UK to train him. And over two years, fractures, broken bones and scraped skin, he realised two things. One, he healed quickly, and two, he was a natural at parkour.

The old lady knew he'd do well.

Now she was gone, and he didn't know if he could do this alone.

But he had to.

Zach kept up the relentless pace, blocking out the howls and screeches behind him.

He hurtled down a corridor, the doors of the flats he passed a blur, his trainers rhythmically slapping on the concrete, and his pursuers baying for his blood; the memory of Hortense was in his head.

Yuh know dem can't ketch yuh bwoy but let dem try. It's good practice. Use it.

It didn't feel like practice.

Ahead of him, a tangle of shadows undulates on the floor,

ceiling and walls. More of the R Team Clique gangsters stepped into the sparse light.

How did they know he'd be heading that way?

They came at him screaming, ahead and behind, anticipating blood from a trap sprung. Zach kept running into the jaws of death.

The snarls and grins turned to incredulity as Zach suddenly changed direction.

Two lunges.

That's all it took.

Two lunges, and Zach was hurling himself up and over the barricade that protected the corridors of the flats from the elements and propelling himself into midair. He was free-falling from two storeys up.

For a fraction of a second, he felt weightless until his eager fingers grabbed the stalk of the tall street light, five metres away and adjacent to the corridor he had leapt from. It bent slightly with his weight as he nimbly corkscrewed all the way down to street level.

Zach was on the move as soon as his trainers touched the asphalt.

He would run until his lungs exploded before he let them get the better of him. He needed answers beyond what he already knew.

Zach was the main character in this waking nightmare, a role he did not choose for himself and could neither comprehend the part he had to play in it nor why it had to be him. All he really knew was he had to survive.

He had a bigger purpose.

Being told that he was important felt good in the moment. Even his parkour training had become something he looked forward to, but it was all wearing thin.

Zach wanted to go through this purgatory in peace, but the bitch and her human cohorts wanted him to suffer.

It had been over a month since he had seen Anastasia, but he saw her this night.

The higher power behind this nightmare was resplendent in her horrific glory.

It felt like he had swallowed lead, and his balls had shrivelled to the size of peanuts.

This same visceral reaction every time.

She stood on the crisscross overpass bridges as Zach flew by below a howling mob behind him. She was a tall figure shrouded in the bone-chilling mist that seemed to seep from the concrete. Horns, plaited hair, dark skin, eyes like furnaces, immaculately put together at all times, a mouth filled with perfect teeth that only showed when she spoke because she never smiled. And what about those fucking things that looked like dogs, chomping at the bit as their mistress held them in place.

He had dreamed she had released them on him.

"Leave the tender pieces for me," she called out to them as she released them from their chains.

They never did catch him.

In the nightmare, he was lucky, but in the real world, tonight could be their night.

Behind him, the 'R' Team Clique had his scent again and were relentlessly on his case. They had sold their souls to that demon bitch who was overseeing the possible carnage from the bridge. Some of those kids he knew not as friends but as passing acquaintances, as they hung out on the corner. Selling crack and intimidation hadn't been enough. Maybe this was the only way they could secure their territory. Make a deal with the devil.

They'd been robbed.

Zach knew that if he wasn't faster and fitter than these animals baying for his blood, only a handful of people would know he disappeared or even cared.

Sprinting down Richmond Lane, a prickle of awareness made him slow.

Something was different.

No shit! There were more of them.

No, something about how they were coming at him.

He ran towards a dead end. His pursuers veered off, knowing it was ahead and knowing Zach could easily negotiate it.

And how did they know that?

The wall approached.

Zach timed his leap, scrambled against gravity for a second, grabbed the lip of the wall and vaulted over it. He hit the ground and rolled. He was sprinting away as they broke the corner. Walker, the de facto leader of the Clique, who fancied himself a kind of military leader among drug dealers, had stepped up his intimidation tactics over the months, making Zach ever more cautious of their tactics.

He would stay ahead of him with speed and local knowledge.

Hortense had promised all this would stop, and for two years, it had. Now, the old woman was dead, and days after her passing, the darkness that had engulfed the place he called home. He would not disappear like the others. He couldn't. Not without a fight. There was no way he would leave his Pops alone, grieving after his mysterious disappearance.

No fucking way!

They had both watched helplessly as his mother and Pop's wife rapidly succumbed to cancer. Doing all they could did not make them feel any less guilty. His father blamed himself, questioning if he could have done more, and Zach wondered if the move to this god-forsaken estate had signed his mother's death certificate. He blamed this place for his mother and now Hortense. He'd do anything to make sure his father would not become a victim.

Anything!

Survival would be a good start.

A thought flashed through his mind, so clear and distinct it took him by surprise. Why hadn't he thought of it earlier? Run by the parade of rundown shops and slip into the work site. He'd done that so many times as a shortcut home. He'd definitely lose them there for sure, and a sense of calm overcame him even as his lungs began to burn.

He skidded to a stop at the top of a flight of concrete stairs in the Runnymede Estate maze. Reducing his stride to position himself correctly, he launched himself down the steps five at a time with a practised, continuous movement. He felt light on his feet and sure of his body like the mountain goats he had seen on NatGeo navigating the precarious mountain ledges. At the bottom of the stairs, he looked back up to see the thugs bungle at the top, swearing and making their way awkwardly down two at a time.

Zach kept moving.

He could see the shopping precinct approaching, the imposing structure of the 1940s brutal architecture that threw harsh shadows in his way like he was in a giant game of Snakes and Ladders. He shouldn't be, but he was slowing in anticipation of safety. His chest was heaving, and his thighs were burning with the effort. While the chasing 'R' Clique was hot on his tail, it seemed not to be affected by the chase. He could hear them howling and cursing like they were drugged up or motivated by something else entirely. That same evil something that had a grip on this place. The streetlights flickered, their bulbs hanging above the white lines like alien fruit, and all the shopfronts were boarded up, or security shutters were pulled down. It felt safe, reassuring, and brighter than he remembered a few nights ago. He was pondering that inconsequential fact, his legs pumping, not expecting that, in a moment, his world would change. Behind him, the raucous shouts had diminished. A cold terror rose from the root of his groin to the crown of his head.

He could see them in the distance.

The gang had split up again, doing that prediction shit again. Knowing where he would go and trapping him. They were blocking his shortcut and patiently waiting, armed with machetes, knives, and baseball bats. It was as if the drive had been sucked out of him. His knees weakened, and his stride faltered just as he approached the shutters of the Co-Operative Shop. He was walking by this, his fists clenched, his thoughts frantic and his movements like a puppet.

He was dead.

Fuck!

Zach had to find somewhere to hide inside one of these shops, but they were all shuttered by the business owners or barricaded by the Council. Smashing his way into the laun- derette wouldn't work; they would just come in after him. He stalked past two more places of business as if he knew what he was about to do. The next two shop spaces were supposed to be empty, and at the end was a Fish and Chips shop.

They were already closed, that much he knew.

Zach braced himself; sweat was trickling down his fore- head. He tried to accept that this would be his last stand in the bush-strewn empty lot. They would spill his blood, and that would be that.

He jogged the next few steps, his weary legs taking him reluctantly to nowhere, and ... then ... he ... stopped.

For a minute, he thought he had taken a wrong turn, but no, he was in the right place.

HEADHUNTERS.

No more than a night ago, this plot of land was a fire-gutted, garbage-strewn eyesore that stank of piss and decomposing food matter. Now stood a sparklingly new barber shop, incredibly spacious, brightly lit with a line of pristine leather and brass barber chairs inside, all manned by barbers. Nail stations and some hair stylist chairs were located to the sides, all of which were occupied.

What the fuck?

The hairs on his arms stood to attention.

Zach's mouth hung open as he peered inside, transfixed. The thought of his pursuers had completely left his mind. The glass was so clear that Zach could imagine walking straight through it. It was just a transparent film that wouldn't offer him any resistance if he tried to enter. As his mind processed the conundrum, he saw the most beautiful woman he had ever seen, tall, with dark skin, piercing golden brown eyes, and long flowing golden locks. She was braiding the hair of a woman who had her head back and eyes closed. The hairstylist looked over at Zach and smiled. His whole world had slowed, but his thoughts were just as frenetic as they were when he was being chased. Zach reached out to the door, and the angry profanity approaching popped his bubble of unreality. He quickly pushed the door open into the establishment and stepped inside, expecting the searing pain of a knife or machete to follow, but it didn't. The door closed behind him, and he clapped his back to it in preparation for what was to come. There was panic in his eyes as he braced himself.

Reggae was playing through the speakers.

Three high-definition screens showed abstract audiovisualisers animated to the music.

It smelled of calming vanilla.

"You don't have to do that," a deep voice to his right startled him. "They can't come in."

Zach ignored the voice and tried to wedge his shoulder into the ultra-clear glass. A calmness flooded over him, and for some unknown reason, he began to relax even though his mind refused to accept it. He kept his shoulder to the door, and it was only because he felt no pushback that made him look up and outside again.

His blood chilled.

The gang stood outside looking in. Their bloodthirsty cries had dissipated, their crude weapons hung loosely by their sides, and their eyes were inquiring, but not one of them attempted to come in.

Zach's mouth opened and closed in confusion. He could swear they could hear his hammering heart.

"You believe me now."

The voice came again, but this time, Zach looked over to its possessor.

The older man, with a greying Afro and glasses perched at the tip of his nose, pulled out a flannel from his old-timey tan apron, which displayed an assortment of shiny metal scissors, shears, and razors. Some were snugly set in the big pouch in the front, and others in much smaller pockets on the fringes of his apron. It was almost militaristic, as if he were preparing for war rather than a haircut.

He wiped perspiration from his brow.

"We have a strict policy of keeping our space calm."

Zach looked at him, perplexed, unable to process what was happening.

"Why are they just standing there? Why aren't they trying to come in?"

"I told you, our barbershop is not for them. It's out of bounds."

Zach tentatively leaned off the door, not taking his eyes off the boys outside.

What did he mean by, out of bounds?

It was creepy how they stood there. Zach's eyes slid across the faces that once were feral and bloodthirsty, that now looked confused and defeated. He shivered with an uncontrollable tremor that shook him from the inside.

What the fuck was happening, and what was this place?

One after the other, they walked away as if they had forgotten what they had intended to do. Eyes wide, their pace almost robotic. They came to life again as soon as they were a few feet away from the shop front. They were back to their boisterous selves, laughing, joking, but none of them looking back. They left carrying the murderous rage with them.

Zach crumpled a bit, head down, looking unstable on his feet, breathing hard, his nervous energy emanating off him in waves.

"Water?"

Zach looked up just in time to see a bottle of water arc its way to him. He plucked it from the air.

"Good reflexes," the distinguished man sporting the Afro said. "My name is Sylvester, and these lovely people behind me are part of my team." He turned around and, with a flourish, motioned to the beautiful woman with the long golden locks. "That is Medusa," Sylvester said.

Medusa bowed with her hand on her heart. Zach noticed her long, immaculate nails.

Then Sylvester turned to a well-dressed, little person standing on a stool, cutting an old gentleman's hair with the flourish of a sculptor.

"That is our resident shaper and handyman, Puck."

"Pleased to meet you, young sir, "Puck said, pausing with a smile and gleaming scissors in hand. "You need a cut, young man; come by and see us. It's on the house."

Zach nodded, but Puck's attention was already back on the man in his barber chair. The motion with the scissors was a blur as he worked.

"Now you know us; we are no longer strangers," Sylvester said. "Come visit us again, but I think your father may be worried. You'd better make your way home."

Zach stared at him.

Sylvester walked over to the door and lowered his voice.

"The coast is clear. Trust me."

Zach looked into his eyes and then outside. He composed himself without a word and slowly walked through the door.

"Straight home," Sylvester said.

Zach didn't have to be told twice. He looked back at Headhunters Barbershop almost as if to confirm it was real and scurried away into the enclosing shadows towards Palladin House.

Chapter Two

West London 1945 - End of World War II

In the shadows where I tread, Whispers turn to dread, Planting fear in every heart, Watch it tear them all apart.

Sewing seeds of discontent, Chaos blooms where'er I went, Twist the mind and break the will, Let the fear grow stronger still.

In the quiet of the night, I'll make wrong what once was right, Sow the doubt and fan the flames, Humans playing twisted games.

Sewing seeds of discontent, Chaos blooms where'er I went, Twist the mind and break the will, Let the fear grow stronger still.

The lanky creature, which had a passing resemblance to a human being, was dressed in tails and a top hat, singing the words of his ditty with glee as it moved with uncanny speed and dexterity along the banks of the river. He had unusually long legs, a freakishly long stride.

A grotesque yet graceful gait.

He moved through the swirling fog, clutching a glass jar with a copper filigree design of ancient origin on both ends. A well-sealed alchemical stopper prevents the glowing objects within from being scattered incorrectly. Not that the man with the pallid grey skin of a corpse and a rictus grin splitting his face was worried. The most difficult part of his mission was entering this world, and he had done that. His one job on this 'Jewel' was to plant the seeds contained in his jar. His mistress had given him the honour of being the one to reestablish some control over this precious world.

And he wouldn't let her down.

There had been other attempts, but none had gotten as far as he had.

This Earth plane had a reputation for resilience and stubbornness, repelling numerous attempts to establish a foothold. He slipped through the wound that appeared in the body of space-time. It was a random occurrence in his dark world, yet the Hu-mans waited for him. He slipped through their grasp, but they wanted to unalive him. Not before he planted the seeds.

The ones who called themselves the Protectorate snapped at his heels, but the Hu-man's couldn't catch him. They would try, but they couldn't. At the suitable place, the point of no-source, he would plant it, release the contents. It must be done! It must return to the earth. It had much work to do. Spread the seeds of discontent, it was told. Spread the seeds of discontent.

Hortense Smiley had never darkened the inside of a jail cell or prison in her life. She had been an upstanding Brown's Town Community member in St. Ann, Jamaica. A regular churchgoer at the Wesleyan Methodist. And she was being courted by a light-skinned church brother, who said he wanted her hand but also wanted something else before he said, I do.

So, where did it all go wrong? Oh, so wrong.

England was in turmoil after the war, and it needed help from the colonies to rebuild. The mother country had called, and Hortense heeded that call. She was tested and found to be fit, well, and weirdly gifted. She would work for a department in the Home Office and be able to send triple the amount of money she had initially thought to Mama Gee. The British pounds would set up her family for life, but she may never benefit from it. That was a sacrifice she was willing to make

Tonight, had been her watch—well, her team's watch—and the Department would punish them for their failure. They would not come out and say it directly; that was not the English way, but there would be consequences. The silver-tongued brute had befuddled the guards protecting the portal with its songs. They were trained to combat otherworldly influences and charms, but this somehow bested them.

This grinning, singing demon had been different. He was not listed in their records, and there were no reports of such a creature ever attempting entry. How could she have known a dimensional being with aeons of practice in weaponising its voice would darken her corner of the world? It had tricks the Protectorate had no record of. Their protocols had failed, and someone's head had to roll for that.

All she could do was make up for her team's lapse in judgment and recapture the creature. The van had dropped them off on the main road at an entrance to the river, and her four-person team bungled out, armed and ready. A walkie-talkie test had been conducted in the back of the van, allowing them to stay in constant communication. All four took off running along the river, impeded by wispy fog, moored long boats and wild plant growth off the path. Hortense had the least weight to carry; her crossbow and arrows were on her back, but that wouldn't have made a difference; she ran like a gazelle, nimble and fast. She could keep up this pace for hours.

Another one of her gifts that made her perfect for her leadership role in the Protectorate.

She flew across the uneven riverbank, knowing somewhere ahead in the swirling fog was her quarry. The creature had stayed ahead of her team. She had maintained a visual for the last three miles but was losing the visibility on this fleet-of-foot demon. The fog was getting thicker at this part of the river, and it was difficult for her to remain focused. Something about the encroaching fog that wasn't just interfering with her vision but her perception, too.

Even with her enhanced eyesight and speed, the lanky man, whose black tail, pale skin, and comically long legs were nowhere to be seen. Hortense's frustration was causing her to doubt her next course of action. What if this thing escaped into this dimension, never to be found again? How would it darken the world further? What would she have to do to make amends for this 'crasis!'

Hortense couldn't afford to make those dark thoughts dilute her focus. She had a job to do.

She looked at the tracker called Pete, who was struggling to keep up behind her.

"What you sensing, Mr Hibbert?" She asked. "Him, couldn't just disappear, could he?"

Pete, a young white 'bwoy', with the uncanny ability to perceive traces of a person's essence left behind in the physical world, was being overwhelmed by the creature's signature. He was always booted and suited, and tonight was no different. Breathing heavily with a bowler hat under his arm, his green eyes were taking in the seen and unseen.

"This bloke won't stand still, Ms. Smiley," he said, exasperated. "One minute, I can sense him, and the next, he's gone. I don't know what his intentions are, but he seems to know where he's going. All I can say is he's not far from us."

Hortense keyed her walkie-talkie transmit button twice.

"Any sign of him, Mr Perkins?" There was a crackle, and Hortense's teammate answered. The soft-spoken ex-military man with hyper-physical reflexes was moving effortlessly on the other side of the river, easily keeping up with Hortense's speed. In their pursuit, he had skipped across a thirty-foot-wide river like a flat stone flung at speed along the surface of the water.

Skip! Skip! Skip!

"The target has crossed over to a plot of land adjoining the river, he said. "Lots of weed, grass and god knows what else is in there. After that, I've lost all visual of him."

"Follow him in and disable him if possible, if not keep him under observation ... Be careful, Mr P."

"Understood, Ma'am."

"Margaret, where are you?"

The third member of their team was Margaret Chang. If she didn't want to be found, she could remain undetectable. Hortense knew there were people who could render themselves invisible from an optics standpoint - her science teacher back home would be proud. Margaret, on the other hand, could make all living things perceive her as not being there - telekinesis and brain chemistry.

Blindspot by name, blind spot by nature.

A very useful talent for an agent.

"Margaret, come in."

"I'm here, Ms Smiley," her voice was low but clear. It had a tremulous edge to it, signalling her excitement. There was a background sound that had nothing to do with the connection that was making Hortense's eyes water. "I have eyes on the target," Margaret continued. "It's stationary and behaving very strangely."

"Can you take it down?" Hortense asked.

"I'm not sure..." Margaret hesitated. "I don't want to take the risk. It's generated a greenish orb around itself. I think you need to get here."

Hortense grabbed Pete by the shoulder and peered into his eyes. "I need to get to Margaret's position as quickly as I can. Find us and be careful."

Pete looked at her.

"I'm golden, Ms. Smiley, you go. I'll catch up."

Hortense nodded and spoke into her Walkie-Talkie.

"Mr Perkins, let's go."

Across the river, there was a rustle and a snap of vegetation.

Hortense turned and sprinted away so quickly that a foggy template of her hung in the air for a heartbeat, then dissipated like gentle snowfall.

NONE OF THEIR WEAPONS COULD PENETRATE THE forcefield. Margaret had quickly set up a perimeter, using a new top-secret tool called a Glow Jar to produce light by mixing two chemicals that reacted by giving off a strong luminescence. Six such jars surrounded the area, lighting the scene, interspersed with Viking runestones for containment. The smiling demon was seated cross-legged in the high grass, eyes closed, head tilted up to the heavens, and his thin lips animated. The large vial it had carried protectively under its arm was now open, and the contents - a glowing, steaming, pulsing sack of organic anti-life- were bubbling in a pool of its own broth in front of him. His incantations had a violent effect on it. A dirty olive coloured, protective bubble of energy enshrouded him, thwarting all their attempts at breaking through. It was a metaphysical and physical barrier. It took Hortense no time to decide what her plan of action would be.

"Mr Perkins, set deh dynamite."

The military man didn't need to be told twice. He had everything he needed in his tactical vest and his backpack. He got to work quickly.

"Why here?" Margaret asked, both women stepping back so Mr Perkins could work.

"I couldn't tell yuh, Ms Chang?" Hortense shrugged; the same question had obviously been on her mind. "I have a feeling we will soon find out." She walked away, leaving Margaret to absently watch Mr Perkins put the final touches on his explosive device. In the deepening darkness, Hortense moved through the bush and into a clearing with three large advertising boards extolling the virtues of a new type of Housing development - The Runnymede Estate Development Group - The Future of Housing.

The question of why here, could solve so many questions she had. For now, it was stuck in her craw and would bother her until an explanation made sense.

"Do you think it's a strategy?"

Hortense turned suddenly towards the source of the voice. Her colleague appeared beside her, seemingly materialising out of the thin wispy fog, her talent easily disarming Hortense's defences. Margaret behaved as if her sudden appearance was to be expected.

"Dem do nothing without forethought. Dis is deh first piece of the puzzle."

Hortense nodded, looking away from the advertising boards

planted randomly in the soil. Her focus rested on Mr Perkins' busy preparation in the distance.

"All I know is there is someting about our world that dem love and our team was deh weak link. We let dem in."

Margaret wasn't happy with that assessment from the way she screwed her lips but she didn't respond.

Hortense lost focus for a moment, staring at a point through Margaret and beyond her. Wherever her wandering mind had been, she abruptly reigned it in.

"Ever since that portal appeared in East London, the Ministry of Defence has been fighting to protect the city from whatever wants access into our world. I know what yuh tinking. It was just a matter of time. An yuh right. We may not be at fault, but we are responsible."

Margaret nodded, her features passive, her training second nature, but underneath the calm was a storm of questions that wanted to deny their sole responsibility for this.

"The disciplinary is going to be a harsh one for us."

Hortense's perfect white smile was grim and bitter.

"For us? No. For me Margaret. Me alone is responsible for dis. And me alone will bare deh responsibility as team leader."

Margaret shook her head in denial, words of refusal about to form on her lips, when Mr Perkins called out to them. They hurried back to see the red, flushed face of Mr Hibbert, who had finally caught up with them. He was gawking at the cross-legged demon ensconced in a protective shield.

Hortense looked at him.

"Do yuh want to give your Technocasting skills a whirl?"

Pete adjusted his suspenders and shook his head as if he regretted what he would say next.

"Not on your nelly, ma'am. If you can't crack it then it can't be cracked."

Mr Perkins laughed and guided his colleagues away from the blast area with a gesture.

"Let's get to a safe distance, ladies and gentlemen."

Hortense watched Pete and Margaret walk away to safety, while she stood and took one last look at the creature that had breached the portal. It had not moved from its lotus position, and its frantic prayers continued. The horrid thing, like a pulsing cancerous womb that had been at its feet, had now buried itself. For every throb of that demon seed under the ground, the earth around it became a green transparency, showing the thing taking root in staccato snapshots. She wondered if it knew that seven sticks of dynamite had been rigged around it. She wondered if it knew its mission had failed.

Did it even care?

It must have read her mind because she could suddenly hear it begin singing its ditty.

They'll turn on one another, Brother fights with brother, and as the madness spreads, I'll dance among the dead.

Sowing seeds of discontent, Chaos blooms where'er I go, Twist the mind and break the will, Let the fear grow stronger still.

With every step, the world descends into the dark where light pretends, and in the end, when all is spent, I'll reap the seeds of discontent.

Chapter Three

The Chaos Realm

In all chaos, there is a cosmos
In all disorder, a secret order
Carl Jung

Anastasia sighed in the dim glow of her lair, where the air pulsed with the wails of the eternally damned. Their soothing sounds and the poetic stanzas of grinding teeth were the perfect addition to her contemplation. The walls of her mansion were carved from black stone that wept with an ichor-like fluid, whispering ancient incantations as they pulsed in time with the suffering beyond. The lake of Amorga, a churning, blistering sea of molten souls, roiled outside her windows, its flames licking the void as if reaching for escape. The scent of sulfur and despair hung heavy, a perfume she could not get enough of.

Her Zartegs lay coiled near the hearth, their bodies a grotesque marriage of reptilian scales and sinewy flesh, their breaths a rhythmic growl, deep and resonant. One of them shifted, its amber eyes flickering open from restless sleep. It farted, adding its note of corruption to an already corrupted atmosphere.

She stroked it.

Her focus was on the grand, three-tiered board that dominated the drawing room—a battlefield disguised as a game.

The Eternal Game.

Anastasia ran her claw-tipped fingers over the pieces, each one pulsing with a life of its own. These were not mere tokens; they were beautiful souls, tethered to humans who moved with free will. Seven humans lived on the Runnymede Estate— seven gifted souls of immeasurable worth. Two had already been taken, claimed by her hand. That left five. And the Headhunters had come to protect them.

A sneer curled her black-painted lips. The Headhunters, those wretched agents of balance, thought themselves guardians. They moved unseen, slipping through the veils of reality like wraiths, disrupting her carefully laid plans. Their presence was an infestation, a disease she needed to excise before they could rally the gifted to resistance.

Across from her, the opponent sat in eerie stillness. The Eternal Game was always played with two. Herself and a trapped spirit from whichever dimension she was campaigning against. In this case, the Earth plane. A hooded spectre, faceless, silent, patient. It played its pieces with maddening simplicity, favouring precision over brute force, minimalism over spectacle. This was what unsettled her. She thrived in complexity, in chaos, in layered deception. And yet, the spectre she was against had a strategy and had taken two of her strongest warriors off the board already.

She exhaled slowly, dark amusement flickering in her ember-like eyes. Six days. That was all the time she had to tip the balance irreversibly in her favour before the game's next cycle began, in another place and another time.

Her hand hovered over the board, considering her next move. One shift here, and a human at Runnymede would fall ill. In another, paranoia would slither through someone's mind, turning them against their neighbour. A more aggressive play, and she could force the remaining five out of their homes and hope they fall prey to a Killen beast.

She shuddered delightfully.

There was no such thing as hope, only plans and execution. The sublime beauty of it all was that the Hu-Man's would never suspect the war raging around them. What they would call spells, she understood as the manipulation of natural laws beyond their understanding. And those forces were woven into the very fabric of their estate, ensuring their blindness. To them, life went on as usual. Work, love, and trivial concerns. Cattle were grazing in a field while wolves prowled just beyond the tree line.

And yet, the Headhunters threatened to shatter the illusion. That, she could not allow.

A goblet was placed at her side by one of her valets. The creature was a lovely, grotesque thing with four arms and a face stitched together from forgotten nightmares. The liquid inside shimmered unnaturally, black and iridescent, shifting as though it were alive. She lifted it to her lips, savouring the bitter cold that slid down her throat. Power hummed in her veins, an intoxicating reminder of her dominion.

Her grin widened.

"Let them come," she whispered, rolling one of the soul-pieces between her fingers. A tiny, flickering light trapped in obsidian. The mortal it represented was still unaware, still safe —for now. But not for long.

She reached forward, moving one of her pieces decisively. Somewhere in the human world, something shifted. A tremor in reality. A subtle but precise ripple in the fragile web of fate.

The spectre did not react immediately, but she knew it was watching. Calculating. Waiting.

The game continued.

Chapter Four

Zach stood for a while, watching his father from the doorway. His eyes misted with tears, his heart heavy, and a pall of sorrow suddenly draped heavily over his shoulders. It was too early to be maudlin, but he couldn't help himself.

What had he done with his life?

In his more upbeat periods after his Mom died, he promised his father he would free him from his job. Mr Ellison had worked in the specialist foundry for more than twenty-five years. A place where steel runs like volcanic rivers, where his gloves and overalls are scorched, and he watches the fading glow of metals from sunrise orange to dull gun grey every day.

That promise he never fulfilled.

He was twenty-seven years old, had no real direction in life, couldn't hold down a job and lived in one of the worst estates in the borough. And if that wasn't enough for anyone to bear, the place he called home, the place where his mother lived and died, was evil. And he couldn't protect the only man he would give his life for from its effects. The old Man tucked into the breakfast Zach had prepared for him. Mr Ellison was enjoying his food so much while watching morning TV that he didn't see the tears or the faraway look in his son's eyes. After his Mom had passed, Zach was on the fast track to a lucrative athletics career; he had promised that he'd save his father from the drudgery of meaningless work. Instead, a career-ending injury that he had long since healed from, it forced him into the ranks of the dead-end employed.

Then he met the mysterious Hortense Smiley, and she proceeded to lift the scales from his eyes, revealing his purpose and the hellish world he was trapped in. She had trained and protected, and now, Hortense had passed on; it was his time to be the protector.

But could he?

Even if the supernatural only showed itself in his orbit and his father and the majority of the estate were oblivious to the goings on, he didn't want his dad to be collateral damage. Especially now, with a new player introduced to the game.

Headhunters Barbershop.

"Yuh not eating?" Mr Ellison asked, his fork halfway to his mouth as he caught Zach's faraway look. "You've been quiet, son; come sit with your old man and tell me what's going on."

"Aren't you supposed to be heading off to work?"

"They can wait. Now come sit," Mr Ellison patted the seat beside him. "How's the job hunting going?"

Zach plonked himself down beside his father and flung his arms around his shoulders.

"It's alright." Zach shuffled in his seat, a tell that indicated he was lying. "It's just tough times all around. I'll find something, but in the meantime, online customer service will have to do."

The old man sighed.

"Don't be like me and settle," the old man took a sip of his hot chocolate. "You're a talented boy, Zach. Use your creativity and embrace your other talents."

"I'm trying." Zach lowered his head; a sped-up movie clip of everything he had gone through, everything that his father knew nothing about, flashed before his eyes. He wanted to explain the twilight world he inhabited, which tested not just his wits and sanity but his physical strength. He wanted to let him know the grave danger they were both in, but he couldn't. Zach had promised.

"I 've got an appointment at the Job Centre today, but I'm not expecting much from that." Zach leaned back in his chair and watched his father finish his breakfast.

"Think positive, son. Today is going to be a good day for you." The old man smiled, balled his calloused fist and playfully tapped him on his shoulder. "Chin up."

Zach smiled.

"I'll keep it positive, Dad. I promise."

"I worry about you, Zach." Mr Ellison lowered his voice, his tone questioning. "Sometimes you look like you've got the world on your shoulders."

"You don't know the half of it," Zach muttered.

"You know you can talk to me about anything, right?"

"Of course. Who else have I got to talk with except you?"

"You mean that?" The older man asked.

"Of course, now you better get going or you're gonna be late."

"I get the message." Mr Ellison stood up.

"See you later?"

"Later," Zach said, smiling like it was a foregone conclusion.

. . .

ZACH STOOD STARING AT HORTENSE'S FRONT DOOR, reliving the sadness and panic he felt when he discovered her body peacefully lying in bed, adorned in her Sunday best, her life flame departed, but looking as if she was taking a nap. It was his heavy heart that gave it away, his sixth sense a better assessor of the situation than his five senses ever were. Zach wouldn't be Zach if he didn't use the First Aid skills he had trained in to ascertain if she was really dead.

She was dead.

It took him more than an hour to barely compose himself through tears and some anger. That's when he saw the note on her side table.

No, it wasn't a suicide note that wasn't her style. She loved life but had been blessed with more than most would ever experience. The note stated that she loved him and explained that her time here had come to an end. Then there were instructions on what he should do with her. Seeing her like that was difficult enough, but her dying instructions left him scratching his head.

Not surprising for the woman she was.

Although her instructions were clear, Zach still questioned himself about what he had done and what he was about to do. Zach stood at Hortense's green front door. He stood on a protection glyph, Hortense had drawn from coloured chalk. Its metaphysical power was obvious every time he walked over it. Hortense was a popular woman and she'd been missed striding down the corridors, engaging with dogs, babies and adults alike. Zach was getting the most pressure from the community centre where she volunteered. He had dropped a story about an infectious disease that kept the most persistent away. He had access to her one-bedroom flat day or night, and her place had been his home away from home for over two years. He sometimes slept on the sofa, and he could be assured of the best night's sleep.

Whatever he had been through that day, her flat was a true sanctuary. The place would never be the same without her presence, her voice, and her cooking. Zach looked across the council estate from the seventh floor. A blood red sun dipped behind the grey monoliths that sheltered frightened and desperate people. They once had a home and freedom. The house remained, but freedom was in short supply. Hortense had been dead for a week, and already the dark forces that had dominated the grey corridors, concrete warrens and winding staircases were creeping back to take up residence. His old fears reemerged, and the memory of his paranoia before Hortense's calming presence came back cold and sharp. Still standing outside, his eyes darted around his surroundings furtively. The shadows were encroaching around the sharp, grey edges of the buildings. Coalescing in the tight spaces and hibernating unspeakable things.

Zach's arms prickled from a slight drop in temperature along the corridor. He looked to his right, the neighbours had their lights on in their kitchen, and further along, a hallway light shone through a front door. All the corridor lights were busted, so as the darkness took root, this entire floor would be dangerous for the likes of him. He would report it and hope the Association would act on it, without him having to come in contact with any of their representatives. If they once were human, whatever had taken hold here had transformed them, too. He shuddered, looking over to an unusual pocket of quiet further along the balcony that absorbed the ambient sounds around it. Zach could hear his own breathing, his heart pounding and felt the weight of the clothes on his body. And as before, he was their focus. Zach took out his mobile phone from his back pocket. His iPhone was ensconced in a leather jacket for protection. Tucked into a designer slash on the outside was the front door key. Zach took it out with trembling fingers and looked to his right again to make sure his fears had not manifested into reality. There was nothing he could see with his eyes, but that did not diminish the threat; it just made it unseen. He looked down at the intricate Veve drawn in multi-coloured chalk in the doorway - an otherworldly algorithm protecting the flat from unwelcome visitors of the demonic kind. He guided the key into the lock, turned it, feeling the unusually complex dance of spring-loaded pins, cylinder and bolts and pushed the door open. He had done this hundreds of times, but in this instance, it felt unusual, more secure, comforting. He closed it behind him and stood in the darkness of the hall. Zach breathed in deeply and detected the pervasive aroma of ginger and baked bread. He sighed with relief and switched on the lights as he headed towards Hortense's room. He had closed the bedroom door the last time he was here, and it remained that way. What was he expecting?

The old lady rising from the dead?

Not funny and not impossible. Not by a long stretch. He pushed the door open and looked around the room before his eyes settled on her. Hortense lay there as if she were asleep, and after a week of death, she looked perfect. He didn't need to be a pathologist to know this was far beyond rational explanation. She was a mystery in life, so why would her death be any different?

He thought of her written request, impressed by her cursive strokes of ink on fine paper.

LET MY BODY REST WHERE YOU SEE IT, DON'T MOVE ME, *grandson.*

Don't call the authorities.

Watch over me when you can.

Open my sea-chest, read my letters and documents. Learn more about my past.

When you eventually meet my adopted family, bring them to me, and they will know what to do.

FAMILY, WHAT FAMILY. SHE HAD NEVER MENTIONED A family for the two and a half years they had known each other. All Zach could think was that they would make themselves known when the time was right. He had learned enough from her by now to follow her instructions to the letter. Just because keeping the truth at arm's length was bearable now, Zach wasn't so sure he could keep it up. Something had to give. He stared down at Hortense's closed eyelids and used the back of his hand to touch her forehead. Her skin was cool and dry.

"Why did you have to go, Miss H? I don't think I can do this alone."

He straightened a ribbon on her blouse and left the room, closing it gently behind him.

Chapter Five

In the gloom of Hortense's flat, silence draped itself over the furniture like a funeral veil. Zach couldn't bring himself to let natural light into the space.

It didn't feel right. Not yet.

The TV was playing Judge Judy reruns - Hortense's favourite show, in the background. He sat in her comfortable Easy Boy, his focus not on Judge Judy's snide remarks but on the vintage metal sea-chest he had dragged from Hortense's room to this small lounge. When he had read Hortense's written instructions, Zach had a need to open it, but he didn't.

Not then.

It had sat there for days, gathering the kind of dust Ms H would not appreciate. He rocked, forward and back, the hush told him everything. She was gone. The laughter that used to ricochet off these walls when she teased him about his lack of culinary skills. The soft crackle of vintage Reggae vinyls playing on her old record player, the sounds following her from kitchen to bedroom like the smell of curry goat: gone.

All that remained was a battered steel sea-chest squatting

beneath the bay window, its curved lid stippled with rust the colour of dried blood. Hortense had lugged that box from Brown's Town to Kingston, from Kingston to Tilbury Docks, and finally up the Runnymede stairs. She had chained it shut, locked it twice, and never once invited Zach to peer inside.

Until now.

And still he was in two minds.

You've got to open it sometime, Zee. Why not now?

He sighed. Got up and knelt in front of it. Hortense had made sure it was fully accessible. No padlocks, no need for keys. Zach felt something in his chest unmoor as he placed both hands on either side of the top.

Ready? No, he was not ready. But readiness was a luxury for men who had a choice. He lifted the lid.

Black metal swallowed the little light from the low-wattage bulb, then reflected it back in shards. Letters lay bundled in twine, the colour of molasses. Beneath them: sepia photographs, Java-tin film reels, a tarnished brass compass, the severed fletching of a crossbow bolt, a frayed field notebook, three glow-jars whose chem-lights still pulsed faintly emerald after all these years, and — folded in oilcloth — the crisp white armband with the silver letter P embossed on it. Zach didn't need to rack his brain to decipher what that single letter meant. It marked every Protectorate officer on the portal watch. Zach inhaled. Camphor, gun oil, ginger pomade, dried sorrel: the scent of a life lived on two continents and at least three planes of reality.

He took the topmost letter. Jamaican postage. Thirty-six shillings in stamps. Mama Gee's hand, a river of cursive that slowed only for sorrow:

My child, we are proud of your bravery, but I hear things in the Gleaner 'bout soldiers dying from unexploded bombs and dreams of you working with Duppy and demons. Are you praying every night, my daughter?

A warm tear struck the page, and the ink spidered outward. He wasn't sure if it was Mama Gee's or hers.

HE PICKED UP A PHOTOGRAPH NEXT. NAMES WERE written beside the four figures on the steps of a bomb-scarred Thames warehouse: Hortense front and centre, hands tucked into a greatcoat too big for her slender frame; Pete Hibbert behind her, suspenders proud, bowler askew; Margaret Chang, half-smile vanishing beneath the brim of a trilby as though already practising vanishment; and Captain Douglas Perkins, chin sharp enough to bayonet the wind.

Someone — Hortense, surely — had scrawled along the white border in a fountain pen:

WE RACE THE DARKNESS & WIN, JUNE 1st 1946.

Zach touched each face in turn. He tried to summon their voices, but the photograph guarded its ghosts jealously.

A NOTEBOOK FELL OUT OF A BUNDLE OF PAPERS HE HAD taken up. It looked interesting, so he opened it. The first page bore a single line in her looping hand:

If we fall, let the record stand: we fought demons, so the world might dream in peace.

Below, neat entries:

June 3rd 1946. The Runnymede estate has been newly acquired by Elder G Ltd. Local rumours of a "singing man" in the fog. Unconfirmed.

June 5th. Portal flare predicted 22:12 hours. It's my watch. Lord, steady my hands.

June 6th. We failed. The creature escaped. Sowed something we cannot name beneath the peat—new orders: mop-up, contain-ment, silence.

She had underlined *silence* three times, rending the nib with each stroke.

Zach's fingers trembled. Hortense had told him snatches: the chase along the river, the voice that turned men's bones watery, the dynamite. But this entry sounded like a confession.

THE NEXT ENVELOPE BORE THE RED WAX SEAL OF THE Home Office. He unfolded the parchment.

RE: DISCIPLINARY FINDINGS — OPERATIVE H. SMILEY

It is the panel's unanimous decision that, while extenuating circumstances pertained, responsibility for the lapse in Portal Rigour (Ref: East-E6/1946) rests with the Duty Officer. Opera-tive Smiley is therefore reassigned to Class-B Rural Contain-ment, effective immediately. No term set. Conditions of secrecy remain absolute.

Runnymede: her exile. The estate Zach himself roamed at night. How many times had Ms H cursed the posting? Over fifty years. How many times had she smiled that weary smile and said, *"Some penance not meant to end, son."*

Now he understood what she paid to keep the estate 'balanced.'

ZACH PICKED UP A FADED GREEN MANILA FOLDER WITH the octopus logo of Elder G Ltd. embossed on it. It smelled of cigarettes and a faint whiff of Frankincense. There were tech-nical drawings and reports on the Runnymede Estate project from the 60's. He carefully flicked through the sheets, his fingers dancing to a stop on a typed page that drew his attention.

Elder G Ltd.: Adjoining Works Assessment — Runnymede Estate / St. Dymphna Hospital (1966)

*Under instruction of the Borough, we assessed the proposed Runnymede Estate to be constructed beside the condemned St. Dymphna Hospital for the Distressed Mind (location: north-east fringe, behind the old rail spur). Built 1878–82 in red-brick Gothic Revival by architect **Ada Kincaid** to the endowment of **Sir Reginald Ormsby**, the structure retains a largely stable shell, though interiors show progressive collapse and fractured vaulting; all service tunnels are to be sealed and the shell temporarily braced. The hospital occupies an older barrow field with shallow overburden and variable alluvium (reduced bedrock); therefore, estate blocks should adopt piled/raft hybrids with isolation joints and a minimum **30 m** structural buffer from the hospital envelope. Instrument survey recorded minor magnetic deviation and barometric irregularities consistent with local folklore of a "thin place"; while no mechanism is established, precautionary detailing (shear keys, tuned bracing, vibration limits) is advised, and Kincaid's spiral/chevron tiling— subsequently described in specialist literature as "containment sigils"—should remain undisturbed. Subject to these mitigations, the estate may proceed; St. Dymphna's to be retained as a sealed, braced heritage mass and used as a visual/landscape barrier, with quarterly monitoring for movement and gas ingress.*

A FEW LAYERS OF PAPER ABOVE THAT, FOLDED IN quarters, sat a telegram dated November 1966
   FROM: Margaret Chang — Hong Kong
   TO: H. SMILEY — RUNNYMEDE

—Intel chatter: They're breaking ground on the estate— something stirring in the soil. Old seed waking? Contact me if able. Love you, sister.

THE COLD COCONUT WATER FELT GOOD GOING DOWN. ZACH had taken a break, his mind in overdrive. He placed the empty glass on the table and dug out a creased newspaper clipping from *The Daily Gleaner*, 1945, headline shouting home across the Atlantic:

JAMAICA'S OWN IN BRITAIN'S SHADOW WAR — WOMEN OF THE PROTECTORATE

A grainy reporter's photo captured Hortense in khaki fatigues, chin lifted as though tasting the wind for trouble. The article bragged about colonial daughters defending the Empire from "Unusual threats." A 'We Need You' piece to coax fresh recruits from the islands. Zach smiled despite himself. Hortense had called it *propaganda with nice punctuation.*

Beneath the clipping, another letter: Pete Hibbert's spidery scrawl from 1970's.

Smiles,

Perkins ain't the same since that night. He drinks like a scouser and sings worse. But he says the seed they buried is quiescent. Still, I see it in his dreams. Hope Runnymede's treating yuh kindly.

The ink blurred where a liquid had spilt over it. Zach couldn't tell if it was whisky, tea or grief.

THE COMPASS RESTED IN HIS PALM NEXT, HEAVY AS destiny, with a brown tag attached to it by a string. The glass face was cracked, but the needle still jittered, refusing to obey Earth's poles. The tag read: A demon-finder. Points wherever you don't want to go. Zach set it on the floorboards. The needle quivered, then swung to the north-east corner of the flat — toward the allotments where the old riverbend used to be before builders redirected it. Toward the place, local children whispered of lights in the soil.

He shivered.

BENEATH EVERYTHING ELSE, WRAPPED LIKE A RELIC, LAY an ivory-handled rachet-knife. Zach palmed it reverently. Engraved along the spine in Gothic script:

VIRTUS IN TENEBRIS — *Courage in the dark.*

Hortense had never so much as nicked herself peeling an orange, yet she carried a fighter's blade. He thumbed the steel; it was still whetted to a priestly edge. A slip and blood beaded his fingertip. Funny, how quickly skin remembers mortality. He sucked the cut and tasted iron, salt and sorrow.

HE WAS AFRAID OF THIS. BEING AWARE OF THAT enormous distance between what he thought he knew about her and what the reality was made him worry that he would find out about something that would alter his opinion of her.

He gathered the letters to his heart and read on. In margins, she doodled hymnal bars, formulas for binding circles, Jamaican proverbs, and snatches of English poetry. One very recent entry snagged him:

March 14th 202... Zach's first night of seeing between the cracks. Bwoy got the gift, even if he don't see it yet. Must teach him how to stand in a place till the dark gets bored and wanders off.

He inhaled sharply. She had been preparing him. Every night, they'd walked the estate, and she pointed out the cracks in reality disguised as cracks in plaster. Every joke about his "big eyes" was not a joke at all.

ZACH SAT CROSS-LEGGED, HAVING ARRANGED SOME OF THE contents of the chest like stations of a private pilgrimage: compass north, armband south, photographs west, rachet-knife east, letters at the centre.

He closed his eyes and let the night spool backwards. He saw Hortense sprinting along the river, braids whipping behind like pennons of defiance. He saw her standing before a tribunal, chin high, even as the verdict shackled her to silence. He saw her volunteering at the community centre, humming hymns. He saw the moment she first took his hand when the estate shadows grew too thick, the squeeze that said: *I know the dark, child. Walk with me.*

He gathered the field notebook and wrote beneath her last entry:

I will keep watch.

He whispered, "Rest easy, Captain Smiley. I'll do what I can."

IT FELT LIKE HE'D RELIVED A LIFETIME OF ADVENTURE IN the hours he'd spent with Hortense's memories. He re-packed the chest with care, each keepsake set inside with reverence.

He opened the front door and felt his pupils adjust to the light.

Zach stepped carefully over the intricate *Veve* at the doorway, which protected the home, and onto the landing, pulling the door shut behind him. The steel chest waited inside, humming with the weight of remembered worlds. Outside, the city waited with equal weight, ignorant or wilfully blind.

He began to hum. Not the demon's ditty, but Hortense's favourite Wesleyan hymn, stitched through with Zach's cracked baritone. The sound echoed down the stairwell, thin but unbroken, carrying a promise: the night can sing, and the dawn can answer.

As he descended the steps, he felt like a man, newly apprenticed to the dark, newly sworn to keep its secrets. What those secrets were, he would have to wait and see.

And somewhere, far beneath the soil of Runnymede, something old and patient listened.

While forces beyond his reasoning were planning his demise.

Chapter Six

The Job Centre was no more than two bus stops away from the Estate, but Zach knew the blight that infected the community had stretched its slimy tentacles to the High Street too. You wouldn't know it just by looking, but a pervasive rot had infected everything. The shops in his little part of the world seemed to be doing a thriving business. Not what you would think. There were no empty lots, and most popular food franchises were represented, with two of the five major supermarkets opening in the last year. It was clean and organised. However, what was going on here was much more subtle and insidious. When he thought about it, his head hurt because only he saw it. Zach stepped off the 437 bus and began to walk the short distance to the Job Centre. In a blue Adidas tracksuit and matching baseball cap, he stiffly checked out his environment. This was not the kind of place the 'R' Team Clique would roll through.

Their power base was the estate - the place where the seeds were planted.

That did not make him feel more comfortable. His life was

about survival, and he couldn't walk around with his head in the clouds. He was under siege; he had to be around for his father, the memory of his mother and his girlfriend. Now that Miss H was gone, Maya was the only person he could confide in, and she lived on the other side of the city. He hadn't seen her in person for over a year. He was afraid to leave his father to see her, and he didn't want her coming to see him.

No fucking way.

A WhatsApp relationship had been working, but for how long?

Zach approached the clock tower that announced the beginning of the High Street and shivered. There was a flag of Poland drawn with crayons on one of the flagstones.

He knew who made that doodle, and it felt like a hundred years ago.

The old clock that still told the correct time had become the meeting place for the local drunks, addicts and homeless. Zach knew them well and had a chat with them when he passed by the stores. Alcoholism didn't cherry-pick who it destroyed. VJ was Indian, Larry was born in the UK to Caribbean parents, Michelle was from Newcastle, and the sad list of names ravaged by addiction made him feel helpless. He couldn't make them want to be addiction-free because if he could, he would. Perhaps it was his way of making a difference in their lives by forming a connection with one of the guys. Piotr would drink his cider and laugh at the antics of his fellow drunks, but never really got involved in their squabbles. He loved Bob Marley and had a selection of the reggae stars' T-shirts that he proudly wore around his drinking partners. It turns out he was a lover of old school reggae when he lived in Kraków. When Zach wanted a break from work, sometimes he'd walk up to the clock and sit and chat with Piotr about Poland and his record collection.

Since Hortense died, everything changed. Everything was

going to hell. Zach had not seen his friend for three weeks, nor had he seen the others. They had suddenly disappeared.

The old woman had been the only thing protecting them all. Now she was gone, it was open season. Piotr and his friends had just disappeared. One day, they were here, beer cans and cider bottles everywhere: boisterous laughter and huddled discussions about the minutiae of their existence.

Gone.

All of it.

They had literally cleansed the meeting spot, and now it was as if no one had ever been there, except for Piotr's stamp. A reminder or a taunt?

What if they had just moved on?

The question almost surprised him. It was one that spoke of his naive nature and his belief in the mundane, but he caught himself, chastised himself. This was no coincidence; this was the creeping rot.

Zach walked briskly away, a sudden chill gnawing into his bones. Suddenly, he wanted to leave behind the evidence that he was living in a twisted episode of the Twilight Zone. Most of the small businesses on the High Street had changed. People he'd lived with for almost five years looked the same, but Zach knew they were not the same people he had come to love and respect. It was like they had been swapped with exact copies of the originals. They tried to pass off as the people he knew, but they couldn't hide their mannerisms and speech patterns.

It was all wrong.

How come nobody else could see this?

Maybe they had and were just as concerned, but weren't showing that discontent from their shopping habits; the high street was buzzing. It felt like a battle that he alone would wage.

The big stores seemed not to be affected by the rot. He

could get everything he needed for the home without these creepy clones' weird, small talk and unusual mannerisms. There were real people at the supermarket, and he had made some friends. It was stupid to say, but he felt safe there and promised himself to swing by after his interview.

Zach sat in front of the Job Employment Consultant and asked her to repeat the question. He could have sworn she was asking him to work for a month without pay while he trained. The little he knew about employment law made him wonder if that was legal.

"What about travel? Zach looked stiff in the chair. He couldn't get comfortable. "Won't they pay for transportation at least?"

The consultant shook her head.

That's when Zach's eyes focused just beyond the consultant as he was processing what she had just said. His blood chilled when he saw what could have passed for a spectral presence, but it wasn't. The figure was all in black, with a gaunt white face and raven-black hair pulled into a severe bun at the back of her head, floating through the corridor and into another office.

Zach called her the Headmistress.

And from experience, he didn't 'fucking' stand a chance of getting a job.

They wanted him here where they could keep an eye on him. Break his spirit and break his body. How did she know he'd be coming in today? Zach didn't know who she was or what part she played in the darkness, but seeing her was a bad omen.

"I'm sorry, Mr Ellison, they won't budge on that." She

looked at him intently, pushing her glasses up the ridge of her nose. "What do you want to do?"

What he thought didn't matter; the answer would be a hard 'No'. They wanted him to work for a month with no pay and commute to the sticks one and a half hours each way.

Hortense had explained to him how they would make his work life difficult. They wanted him around the estate. Have access to him. He would play a role, the forces of chaos were uncertain about, but not Miss H. She knew.

"I think I'll give it a pass," Zach said, leaning back into his chair, wanting to get out of there as quickly as possible. "I may have to save some money to cover travel expenses for next time. I'll let you know."

"It's a quiet period," the job consultant said. "I'm sure you'll find something eventually."

Zach believed she meant it.

So this was a bust.

He'd keep trying even if the result was to piss them off. Every month he came here, Hortense believed he was proving to the darkness that they were unable to break his spirit. He felt drained and hungry. As he stood and smiled wanly at the consultant, he decided to pick up some food from the deli bar in the super-market on his way home. As he left the Job Centre and the gloom behind, he looked forward to picking up something to eat and chatting to one of his favourite people. His stomach growling, he headed not just for a full belly but some emotional sustenance.

ZACH WATCHED MARGOT PREPARE HIS FOOD AT THE DELI counter. He had come in at a really quiet time, and that suited him perfectly. Zach couldn't put his finger on it exactly, but ever since Ms Margot McPherson moved to this branch of the supermarket, they connected. He had a thing for being taken under the wings of older women ever since his mom died. Somehow, somewhere, there was a mother figure who would go out of her way to make sure he was fine. Usually, it was a passing contact, but like Hortense - God rest her soul, and Margot, they were more permanent fixtures in his life.

Somebody up there was looking down on him after all.

Margot placed three boxes of food on the counter. She then packed them in a paper carrier bag; they smelled divine.

"I know you won't be cooking this evening, Zachy, so the two bottom boxes are for you and your father's dinner. The top box is for your lunch."

"I don't think I've got enough Margot. Can I owe you?"

She shook her head.

"Are you crazy, boy? You owe me nothing."

She reached over and touched his hand. "I know it's hard times for you both, and you would do the same for me, wouldn't you?"

"Without question." He leaned over the counter and kissed her on the cheek.

From their casual talks, Margot had been through her own tough times, although she didn't often discuss them. Zach was a good listener.

The more they talked about stuff, the more he felt she would be ideal for his father. The old man had been out of the dating game for over five years, since his mother died. He wasn't the matchmaking type. He wasn't much of a romantic either, but he had an overwhelming need to get them together. He'd never done anything like that before. Never felt compelled the way he did to bring two people together like that. Zach had done the right thing.

The embers of love were catching, and although they weren't openly admitting it, he knew they could feel it.

He could.

"How is Mr. Ellison?" she asked coyly.

Zach felt it was strange how she was so formal when talking about his Dad. He guessed it was a generational and Caribbean thing.

"He's good. He loved the cake, by the way."

Her smile was radiant.

Zach looked around for any prying customers, then said.

"Why do we get on so well?"

Margot smiled and then seemed to consider what Zach asked, her eyes scanning the display section with a fleeting glance, then coming up to meet the young man's enquiring gaze. Her smile simmered.

"I never had kids, you know that, right?" Margot asked.

Zach nodded.

"It's not that I never wanted children, but at the time I needed to figure out who I was first." She paused. "Bad relationships." She said as if that explained it all. "One day I woke up and decided things had to change for me, so I left my business and moved to West London."

"Your business?" Zach asked. "I didn't know."

"I'm still processing," she smiled. "But to answer your earlier question, I think a dream, or was it a nightmare, made us click."

Zach laughed but knew deep inside that it was not strange at all.

"I dreamt I was running in the street from these flying black duppies, swooping down onto people minding their business and turning them into dust. I was trying doors to escape from them. Everywhere was closed, and I was panicking, but this one door let me into a coffee shop. Why I didn't hide, I don't know. I just sat at a table watching people die. Someone served me coffee, then someone else slid into the seat opposite, and all that fear I was feeling disappeared. They carried a light inside them that washed away my fear. I was sitting in a coffee shop alone, and I was sad, and someone came to sit at my table, and it seemed like they brought a light with them. I felt better immediately. I wanted to thank them, but they held their head down and kept sipping on their coffee. I couldn't see their face, just their baseball cap. That good feeling kept with me as people died outside, and even when I woke up."

"It made an impression," Zach said.

"It was strange," she said. "Frightening and reassuring at the same time

"But how do you think it made us... Friends?" Zach moved closer, curious to know.

"It was the baseball cap," Margot said plainly.

"The baseball cap?" Zach sounded even more confused.

"When I asked for a transfer from my old supermarket to here, it was a dark time for me. Moving here was a part of my healing process, and my first day here, you came in wearing the same baseball cap I saw the mystery man in my dream wearing."

"Wow!" Zach said, not sure what else to say.

"I took it as a sign. A good one, and I was right." Margot smiled broadly.

The urge to tell her everything was so strong. He wanted to sit her down and explain what was happening to him and the evil that had a grip on the estate. He knew she would listen and be a shoulder to cry on, even if she didn't believe. But, no!

He couldn't risk it. The less they knew of the truth, the better. If he could help it, he wouldn't involve anyone else in this nightmare.

He took a deep, trembling breath.

"Yuh okay?" Margot asked him.

"I'm just glad that crazy ass dream brought us together."

"Me too," she said. "I wouldn't have met either of you otherwise."

Zach nodded.

" I'll leave you to it." Zach looked around to see if he was in the way of any paying customers. "Give Dad a call. You know he loves to hear from you."

She smiled that beautiful smile again.

"I'll do one better," Margot said. "I need my locks washed and tightened. I heard a new barber shop has moved onto your estate. They do everything. I'll come by to check it out after work tomorrow and then come see you both."

Barbershop.

The word seemed to scorch a path through the synapses in his brain. It felt like a brain freeze after an excessively cold Slurpee.

"Headhunters?" Zach said, the memories of the chase and running into the barber shop desperately trying to get away from the bloodthirsty gang members were coming back to him. The shards of memory were piecing themselves back together like a film in reverse. He saw the old guy, Sylvester, opening the door and letting him in, and the gang stopping outside, wandering around aimlessly like he had suddenly disappeared and they had lost their bearings. Surely, they had seen him go into the barbershop, but if they hadn't, they must have seen him standing on the other side of the plate-glass window staring out at them.

They didn't see him.

It all came flooding back in a rush, making him giddy.

The memory of the Barbershop was slippery. It was hard for him to retain it.

Margot was looking at him with concerned eyes.

"Are you sure you're alright?" Margot asked, reaching over the counter to touch his shoulder.

"I'm fine," Zach lied, smiling weakly. "I'm just hungry, I think." He changed the subject quickly. "So what time can we expect you tomorrow?"

Her expression became playful.

"Let me surprise you," she said. "My hair will take a while. Just tell Mr Ellison to have a Guinness punch in the fridge waiting."

"I will," Zach said. "I definitely will."

He bid her farewell, his smile fading as he left the store, his guard up.

Why was the memory of Headhunters' barbershop so elusive?

He'd be wrestling with that for a while. What the fuck was going on?

Chapter Seven

Zach looked up at the logo with a sneering shrunken head, an Afropick stuck in its hair and narrowed his eyes.

This was some crazy shit.

How could it be here? Was he the only one to recognise that this plot of land had been vacant three days ago? Proof, as Hortense would always tell him, that there was no such thing as impossible.

He was no architect, but he was smart enough to know that the dimensions of this place did not add up. Forget about it appearing out of nowhere fully formed; how was it able to be bigger on the inside than the outside?

His eyes wandered over the modern exterior, and he peered inside at the sleek fittings in a deceptively large space. It had saved his life, and yet he still thought he'd turn up here and see an empty lot of land littered with bottles, cans, and syringes.

But here it was.

A business with a Knightsbridge aesthetic in the ghetto.

Who did that?

The design alone made it look and feel out of place. It was not trying to be subtle. How could there be a market here? Most people who lived on these ends couldn't afford the kind of service Headhunters would provide. And you could forget about any clientele, leaving the high street to come to a barber-shop housed on the crime-ridden estate of Runnymede.

Who came up with this business plan?

He didn't need an answer because, in his heart of hearts, he knew there was so much more to what was happening here than met the eye.

So much more.

"Zach, my boy, good to see you." The voice that came from behind startled him. And as he turned, chastising himself for not being more aware of his surroundings, he relaxed some-what. The older gentleman who had introduced himself last night stood smiling.

His name popped into Zach's head immediately.

Sylvester!

He had five cups of Steaming beverage in a corrugated paper tray. His spotless uniform, consisting of a beige leather bib and a white, long-sleeved shirt rolled up to reveal his impressive tattoos, paired with a black tie, made him look like he had stepped out of the 1950s.

"The hot chocolate is yours," Sylvester said, handing him one of the cups. "Let's get inside. You did come to check out the place, didn't you? I was wondering when you'd turn up."

Zach's hot chocolate was comfortably warm in his hands. The smell of cinnamon and hazelnut made his mouth water.

He took a sip.

How did he know his preference for hot chocolate?

Sylvester moved ahead of him to open the door and hold it ajar.

Zach hesitated.

It was a strange reaction even for him.

Stepping through those doors suddenly came with consequences. And not just his differing opinion on barbershop design, but something more profound and life-changing. He was sure many things of great importance had slipped by his attention as if he were blind folded. But not this time. This time, he wanted to make special consideration of this moment.

This was crazy.

Stepping inside, the memories came flooding back.

Zach was surprised by how much he had absorbed when he had stumbled in here. His adrenaline had been off the charts, and his perception had narrowed to such a degree that only the things his panicked mind thought could save him from certain death had been his focus. This time, he could take in the details of this peculiar place. He looked outside again, unable to shake the feeling that he had just passed through a portal that had led him to another world indistinguishable from his own.

"Will you excuse me?" Sylvester said. "We'll talk in a minute." And the man left Zach to observe the frenetic space. And for a moment, he felt lost. He was in a new school again. He was five years old, and his dad had left him in the middle of these strange kids in the playground, where he stood overwhelmed with an unbearable need to talk to his ever-present friend.

His notebook.

Where the hell did that thought come from?

His reaction to this place was nuts. Was it the perfumed smells of hair and skin products that dislodged the emotions and memories? Zach wasn't sure; all he knew was that he was uncomfortable. The kind of discomfort you feel when your secrets are being exposed.

He took a deep breath and looked down. He hadn't noticed it before. Embedded in the glass floor were illuminated boxes arranged in a pattern reminiscent of a chessboard. They displayed sharp-edged weapons—some he recognised and others were wildly unusual. Not the kind of thing you would expect to see in a barber shop, but this was no ordinary hair establishment, that much he knew. Along the white, slightly curved walls on both sides were framed and signed photographs of dead luminaries. Marcus Garvey, WB Dubois, Mary Seacole, and Harriet Tubman, to name a few.

Fakes!

They had to be.

And yet the images seemed to glow from within the boundaries of the wooden frame and glass. Like Alice, it felt as if behind the photographic paper was a world you could enter to meet your idol.

He moved up closer to a picture of Bob Marley, his heart racing. His body was telling him to hold tight as if he were expecting the musician to reach out and touch him.

One Love, Rastaman Vibration to Sylvester, the signature read. Written with a marker pen with boisterous 'b's in his first name and the 'y' like the tail of the devil in his last.

Zach didn't realise he was holding his breath until he stepped back, taking with him a one-drop reggae rhythm that lingered on the fringes of his awareness. He wasn't sure if he'd imagined it or if it was coming from the photograph. That question he would look into if he were ever in the mood to question his sanity.

Putting that idea to bed, something else caught his attention. The shop floor was huge, and so much was going on, but this was calling out to him. A cabinet stood in the curve of Headhunters' layout like a shrine, its curved glass catching the amber light and throwing back ghostly glints. Zach walked over and stood looking at a cabinet of curiosities, which was taller and broader than he was. Inside—resting on velvet, the colour of dried blood—were combs, flasks, pins, and mirrors that didn't sit still. They pulsed faintly. Hummed. Whispered, maybe. Zach leaned in close, drawn by a gravity he couldn't name. Each artefact seemed to carry a rhythm, like basslines buried deep in the earth, vibrating just below perception. His eyes landed on a blackened hair pick, teeth shaped like symbols he half-recognised from a book his grandmother used to read—thick with dust, thick with meaning.

"That's the Afropik of Sekehem," came a voice behind him, low and smooth, like a straight-razor draw. The barber was tall and dark-skinned, his locs tied back, his apron dusted with clippings. "Queen Nyamekye used it to speak with her ancestors. Some say it still remembers them." Zach turned slowly, still caught in the artefact's orbit. "It belonged to a lineage of dreamsmiths," the barber historian said. "The kind who could trace your roots all the way back through the stars."

Zach nodded, his voice slow in coming. "Thanks," he said, and meant it more deeply than he expected. The air around the cabinet felt heavier now, charged, not ominous, but reverent.

For a moment, he was lost in thought until a little boy ran into his leg, making him detach his eyes and breaking the spell. Zach looked down at the cane-rowed little boy who was effervescent with energy.

"Excuse me," he said, the corners of his mouth pulled up into a perfect crescent. "Are you going to be our new AI Simulation tutor?"

"I don't think so. I don't know much about AI." Zach raised his hands in defeat. "I'm Sorry."

The boy shrugged good-naturedly.

"You can learn," he insisted. "We did." He pointed to a group of other children his age and skipped away in their direction.

How could they be learning AI Simulation so quickly, and the building hadn't been here for more than forty-eight hours?

He had to stop being surprised. Headhunters were all about upending convention.

Seven barber chairs were set in a semicircle with comfortable seating around the perimeter. On the tiled floor, decorative lines ran from each of the seven chairs to a central design of a stylised skull. The atmosphere was electric. To say he was surprised by the buzz this place generated was an understatement. But what struck him the most was how safe he felt here. The anxiety remained from managing his own emotions, while an overwhelming feeling of safety permeated the space. Six of the seven chairs were occupied by residents whom Zach recognised. Smiles and conversations were everywhere. It was surreal for a community that had been fractured by such violence and loss to be pulled together by this strange place.

Most of these people were on benefits, working zero-hour contracts, or in part-time work. Zach wasn't being a dick, but he knew these people well, and he couldn't help wondering how they could afford hair treatments, haircuts or tattoos. The questions must have shown on his face.

"We have the resources." Sylvester came up behind him, making Zach turn. The barber had his hands behind his back when he spoke as if he didn't want to spook him. "This community has been through a lot, but they're not alone. They're never alone."

"What do you know of our troubles?" Zach folded his arms and stepped towards him. "Who are you really? Why us? Why now?"

"Good, good questions. Come sit with me."

Zach followed Sylvester to an area tucked away from the rest of the floor plan, hidden by an optical illusion of a wall.

Sylvester walked straight through it, while Zach hesitated, then followed.

The older barber stood at a door that led to the back of House. Just a plain door. Beige paint, scratched metal handle. Zach thought he was being led into a broom closet.

Sylvester opened it and stepped through.

With his heart in his mouth, he followed. There was a noticeable shift in his centre of balance and an overwhelming sense of being lost. His ears popped as air pressure shifted, and a feeling he couldn't shake was telling him he was no longer on the Runnymede Estate. He kept his eyes on Sylvester's back, looking neither left nor right, and when the older man stopped, he stopped. The first door he came to on his right, he pushed open, stood at the doorway, and ushered Zach through.

"What the fuck just happened?" Zach asked, his breathing heavy, a look of exhilaration and fear mixed into his expression.

"You did well," Sylvester said, smiling. "Most humans faint when experiencing dimensional parallax for the first time. Are you sure you haven't done this before?"

Where should he begin?

Zach looked at him blankly, the questions blooming in his head too numerous to express. He took a breath and checked out his surroundings.

Sylvester's office was swanky and neat to an obsessive degree. Framed certificates adorned the walls.

The script was unfamiliar and looked ancient. There were also framed photographs of Sylvester with even more prominent historical figures. The barber saw his expression of surprise but didn't explain. He smiled and slid into an executive leather chair. He positioned himself behind an ornate wooden desk that had scenes of hunters and weird animals exquisitely carved into the wooden frame. The surface of the desk was translucent. A segment of old wood had been embedded in a resin, in all its gnarly beauty and imperfections, lacquered and polished to a brilliant shine.

A sudden feeling of overwhelm surfaced from an unfamiliar place that made Zach's stomach muscles tighten, and a nervous tremor ran through the base of his spine. He didn't feel threatened. This was something else. The unknown. Something he felt a lot around Hortense.

Zach sighed heavily.

How long would he keep lying to himself about what was happening here? Hortense had told him he had a role to play in this. She had protected him and trained him. He couldn't shirk this responsibility. He was here for a purpose, and as much as he tried to make light of it or deny what was happening to him, it had caught up with him, and he couldn't run any longer.

"I know a lot about you, Zachary," Sylvester said. "Hortense was very impressed."

There it is, Zach thought. They are the family Hortense was referring to.

The older man smiled, his eyes were a deep brown with a kind of depth that Zach imagined had seen much and lost much, too.

"Miss H never mentioned you or your business. Ever!"

"She wasn't able. The rules of the Eternal Game forbid it." Sylvester placed both his palms on the desktop.

"Wasn't able?" Zack moved closer to the desk.

"Because of me, son," Sylvester sounded apologetic. 'I told Hortense to keep that from you."

"I know Hortense was forced to be here because of some government operation that went wrong under her watch? But why the interest in me?"

Sylvester leaned back into his chair.

"I know this is a lot to take in, and it would be unfair for me to expect you to accept your situation without some sort of context."

Zach nodded his agreement.

"Sixty years ago, Hortense volunteered to be the estate caretaker after her team accidentally let a Darksider emissary into the Earth plane."

"A Darksider?"

"You would call it a Demon, but a very specific type. They are as old as creation and bring the negative potential to existence, and we, Headhunters, bring the positive. The test that will determine which side of existence - negative or positive- will prevail is called The Eternal Game. Unfortunately, that game is being played here, and we all are a part of it."

Zach stared at him, expecting some facial tick that would appear to indicate that he was being sardonic or even sarcastic.

Sylvester wasn't the jesting type.

"Why me?"

"That's easy, son. You are blessed with heart intelligence."

Zach shook his head and took a deep breath.

"What does that even mean?"

Sylvester leaned back in his chair.

"The human organism has three centres of intelligence. The head, the heart and the gut. Your energies are gathered around your heart. It means you can see things others can't, you can record what you see with honesty and deference. You, amongst all the gifted, can see through the facade that is all around us."

Zach had nothing to say, he understood what the barber was saying. He understood that he was all those things he described, but he did not understand what that meant.

"You are a crucial part of what is happening here, Zach, and Hortense was making sure she kept you safe and prepared. I wish she could have hung on, but..."

He curled his lips and tipped his eyes down to the table, shoulder hunched, then cleared his throat. Sylvester looked back up at Zach, his eyes piercing. "The time for choices is over. At this stage, the only way out of this is through."

"If it will end this fucking nightmare, I'm game." Zach could not control his frustration; his words came out unfiltered.

"Don't be so eager; this will test you to the core."

"Maybe, but I'm tired."

Sylvester nodded.

"I know you don't know me, although it feels like I know you, but you have to trust me if you trusted Hortense. Trusted her instincts. Will you extend that same courtesy to me and my family and reserve judgment for when you know us better?"

Zach considered his words. It was difficult not to like the affable older man with his greying afro and his glasses. Con men were supposed to be convincing, and as much as he wished all of this was an elaborate hoax, every fibre of his being was telling him this was the truth.

His eyes and heart did not lie.

Hortense had been waiting for this crazy barbershop to appear, and he had a role to play in this whole affair. Zach had retreated into himself for a moment, processing what he could, and when his focus returned, Sylvester had his hand on a leather satchel on the table in front of him. It reminded Zach of a saddlebag that some intrepid rider on the Pony Express would have preferred to carry. It smelled of it, too.

"What do you want from me?" Zach asked.

Sylvester pushed the leather satchel over to him.

"Open it," he said.

Zach undid the leather strings that bound the book and opened it up. The notebook had hundreds of blank pages of ancient, veined paper. Zach flipped through the first three pages and quickly withdrew his hand as an arc of static electricity crackled around his fingers, shocking him into alertness. He glared at it, then cautiously proceeded to search through the pages.

"There's a story to be told here, Zachary, and you will tell it," Sylvester said.

"A story? You got the wrong man, Mr Sylvester." Zach swallowed and shook his head.

"The Journal seemed to think otherwise. It doesn't just reveal its pages to just anyone. It wants you to write on its skin."

"Write what? I'm more concerned about staying alive and getting out of this fucking hell hole with my dad."

Sylvester smiled a smile of someone who knew something you didn't.

Zach didn't wait for an answer; he couldn't.

"How is this going to help?"

"This is one of the reasons why you are here, Zachary, to prepare the next unfortunates who find themselves in this position." Sylvester steepled his fingers. "Do you think it was bad luck that you ended up here with your mother and father? There are no coincidences. I don't propose to know the future, but I know you are tangled in the web of destiny, a web you cannot untangle yourself from."

The question came out of Zach's mouth before he could analyse his reason for saying it.

"What if Ms Hortense was wrong? What if I'm not the right person for this?"

"Only Hortense could say. All I know is she believed in you, and we believe in her." Sylvester thought about it for a minute. "The importance of a Chronicler can't be underestimated. Your words and observations will prove invaluable to the next generation of Guardians. If they're to be prepared for what could come, they will need you."

Zach shook his head to clear it.

"You will be under our protection if you decide to be of service. There are forces that will go to any length to destroy you. Without us, it will be a matter of time."

Hortense was a strategist.

Now he understood why she encouraged him to keep a journal. She knew he loved writing and books. Somehow, Zach's passions were part of a solution or remedy to what ailed this place. He couldn't see how. It made no sense to him, but it seemed to make sense to this weird proprietor, Sylvester.

"You know Hortense always talked about what she would wear for her Passover," Sylvester said, looking moist-eyed, the volume of his voice noticeably lowered.

"She had a fancy straw hat with a yellow ribbon stitched through the brim that she adored. Was she wearing that?" Sylvester asked.

"Yeah," Zach said, having mentioned nothing of Hortense's passing.

"It's been a while now, Zachary, and you've done good, now you must allow us to perform the final rites on her body."

Zach nodded dispiritedly, knowing he was carrying out her final wishes but still not feeling happy about it. He sighed heavily.

"When do you want to come by?"

Chapter Eight

A day later, the arrangements were made. Zach had positioned himself outside on the balcony at Hortense's place and had left the front door open. He welcomed everyone who came by, and it was a lot of people. It was heartwarming that Estate came to show their respect and had a sneaking feeling that Sylvester and the crew had something to do with it. She had been a popular figure on the estate, so it should have been no real surprise.

The old lady had touched many lives.

And he was truly moved by the outpouring of love from the community. It was seven in the morning, and still they came. Stay-at-home moms, 9-to-5ers, people on benefits, the long-term sick, and college students left flowers and bungled into Hortense's small one-bedroom flat, saying their final goodbyes.

What would Hortense make of it all?

She was a secretive woman in life and a celebrity in death.

Hortense deserved the adulation, so why did he feel apprehensive? The loss was still raw and would remain that way for some time, but it wasn't that.

The passover ceremony was concerning him.

Sylvester would officiate over a strange ritual, which he wasn't sure if he was invited to. And if he was, could he keep his emotions in check? Lost in thought, Zach was standing outside on the balcony watching the dwindling queue of people solemnly entering the flat, and he was

"How you doing?"

Zach looked around to locate the melodious voice and was surprised to see Medusa. She smiled at him. He had never heard her speak before and was taken aback by the richness of her voice. She was a statuesque black woman with an amazing body built for dance or combat, and she moved like she would be comfortable in both. Her skin was flawless, and she was sporting long, luscious gold dreadlocks that matched her piercing brown eyes. She combined the height of Senegal and the skin tone of South Africa. Even then, there were other subtle touches of nationalities that combined to make up her unique appearance. From how she carried herself, Medusa had no hangups about how she looked or her body. She wore a short black skirt, showing off her long legs - spectacular legs, actually.

There was an iridescent tattoo showing on her thigh, covered partially by her skirt, that he couldn't quite make out but was afraid to run the risk of staring at. Her black blouse was sheer, and her fitted jacket just hid the fact that she wore no bra. He was surprised she would even talk to him after he made an ass of himself by staring inappropriately at her chest the first time they had met. She had pointed it out in a good-natured jibe, but he'd been too embarrassed to see the funny side. He wasn't being pervy either. Yes, she was stunningly beautiful, and she did have nice breasts, but he had been more concerned about the tattoos across her chest. He had never seen tattoos that showed up on dark skin the way these did. It depended on how the light fell on them, whether you would see the iridescent and detailed patterns or not. He also tried to guess her age, even subtly examining her hands, something his Mom had told him was a good way to judge a woman's age, but in this case, he was still left uncertain.

Zach swallowed nervously, emerging from his thoughts

"I'm not sure," he said to her question. "It's been a bit overwhelming. Sudden. Hortense was a good woman."

Medusa nodded with a concerned look on her face. She focused as Zach spoke, and he could feel she was truly engaged with what he was saying.

It felt good.

"You know she spoke a lot about you."

Zach nodded.

"I've heard, but not being disrespectful, she never once mentioned any of you."

"Who would ever believe we existed?"

"Fair point."

"She recognised something in you, a truth that she was willing to stake her existence on." Medusa paused, nodding at the satchel slung around his shoulder with the Journal inside. "I see you've been introduced."

Zach took in a long, withering breath.

"It's alive, isn't it ... the Journal, I mean, and I'm the..." he paused, hoping the word that had slipped out of his mental grasp would return.

"The Chronicler," Medusa added.

"Yeah, Chronicler. I'm still not sure what I'm supposed to be doing."

Medusa hesitated, her mouth forming words, but she made a flourish with her hands to stop herself.

"I tell you what," her words were almost a whisper. "Get to know the Journal some more. Let's send off Hortense, and I'll answer some of your questions then. What do you say?"

Zach nodded slowly.

"Okay."

"I'll meet you inside," Medusa said, lowering her gaze slightly and giving Zach a sad smile.

He returned it and watched her elegantly glide inside.

A thrill of excitement had suddenly gripped his innards. He breathed deeply and tried to stand straighter, pulling his shoulders back. Change was coming thick and fast. The only words of wisdom and sanity in his crazy world would have come from the woman he was about to lay to rest. Zach stared over at the line of people that had dwindled down to about four souls waiting patiently to show their last respects. His gut clenched, and he thought it was the expectation of what was to come, but it wasn't.

His disquiet was justified.

The creepy man from the Housing Association was standing at the top of one of the two staircases that led up to this level. Zach hadn't seen when he had stepped up from the grey concrete step, but that's how these Association boys moved.

They were like wraiths discovering the best routes required for them to travel through shadow and murk. A chill bomb exploded along his spine, and that pleasant sensation in his groin from being around Medusa instantly drained away.

The Housing Association was the nerve centre for the evil inhabiting the Estate and the surrounding areas. The administration building was situated on the north side of the estate. It was a grey, forboding structure. An architectural mausoleum that stood like an antenna transmitting despondency. That thought gave him the chills. If you worked directly with them, you were transformed, and there was no coming back from it. He had seen it happen to people he knew.

Personality change.

Physical change.

All the Housing Association staffers looked slightly emaciated.

Hungry even.

Eyes and cheeks sunken. Skin pallid and stretched slackly over their skulls, like their skeletons had been stuffed into a skin suit as an afterthought. Talking about suits, they all dressed well, but because they were mainly skin and bone, their clothes never seemed to fit correctly.

What was even more unusual was seeing a representative from the Housing Association in the daytime. Creatures of the night, Zach thought and shivered again. Somehow, he felt the truth of that statement in his bones. The man's discomfort was obvious, too, but his voice did not reveal it. His voice was measured and every word precisely enunciated.

"Mr. Ellison?" He projected his question at Zach.

How did he know his name? Zach looked at him without saying a word, hoping he would go away if he didn't engage with him.

The man continued not budging from his position in the shadows and not waiting for confirmation of Zach's identity.

"Mr Ellison," the man continued carefully. "It has come to our attention, since Ms Smiley's departure, you hold the keys for Flat 127."

Departure! The thought blazed in Zach's head. She's dead, you dip shit, just say she's dead.

"And what if I do?"

"Well, if you do, then you need to hand it back to the Housing Association. I can arrange a time for you to come into the offices and present it to one of our consultants."

Zach pictured the foreboding grey building on the north side for the second time and felt spiders crawl up the back of his neck. He heard an echo of Hortense's croaky laughter.

I don't tink so. Dem tek yuh feh a fool bwoy. The key and the place are yours for as long as you need it.

Zach almost smiled, unsure whether he had conjured up Hortense's feisty response or the old woman was whispering in his ear beyond the grave.

"The key is yours whenever you need it back, but you're gonna have to come and collect it yourself."

The words left his mouth before he had the presence of mind to compose them. He was pleasantly surprised. When it came to speaking off the cuff, Zack was shit, but this time the right words had come at the right time.

The man's eyes bugged and his pale skin flushed around his cheeks as if he'd been slapped. He stood straighter at Zach's response, his body tightening as if he wasn't expecting resistance. His features twisted with what Zach thought was frustration or anger, but it did not last. He swallowed nervously, a sluggish tongue moving languidly in his mouth. But no words came out. In moments, he was back to his sombre self. Zach couldn't help but think he had just stifled something ugly from emerging.

The company man stared at him with jaundiced yellow eyes. There was a threat in those eyes. A promise that this was far from being over. The company man nodded and shuffled away into the shadows.

THE FRONT DOOR WAS CLOSED, AND ALL THE WELL-wishers had left. All that remained were the members of Headhunters Barber Shop standing reverently in Hortense's bedroom with Sylvester at the head of the old woman's bed. You would think it would be a tight fit, but everyone looked comfortable, like the space had expanded. The room was filled with the scent of frankincense, and it triggered a whole raft of memories for Zach. It had never been his favourite smell, but he had not only got used to it but prepared the incense for her when she wasn't about. She had a copper receptacle, about the size of a large mug, shaped like a miniature jug. Diamond shapes were cut out of the thin metal all around it. Zach would drop one red-hot coal into it and sprinkle a few grains of Frankincense on top. It would pop and burn, filling the entire apartment with its smell. Uncomfortably, Zach was standing at the foot of the deathbed and was the centre of attention, but he was asked to be there as a significant part of the ceremony. Over his uniform of a pristine leather smock, white shirt, and black tie, Sylvester wore a cassock around his neck, like a priest, with unusual symbols stitched into the fabric that seemed to come alive as the morning sun shone through the bedroom window. The headhunter team stood in silence with all eyes on Sylvester.

He cleared his throat and began to address them.

"We are honoured to witness the transference of the essence of a legendary protector that was our own Hortense Smiley. She served her Earthbound duties, and although human, she became the connection with our kind. She only decided on being one with the universal growth when she discovered a Chronicler. She has made the sacrifice for this plane of existence by protecting its gifted; now it is our time to contribute. We thank you, Hortense, and wish you strength and power for the next phase of the Eternal Game. We would want nobody else representing our interests."

The proprietor uttered a word Zack presumed was like Amen' in most Christian prayers. There was a pause. Then Sylvester took in a lungful of air and started to mouth a guttural chant. He repeated a string of words that carried power. He repeated it over and over as he looked at each one of the gathered, then bowed his head, his words directed to the floor. The alien words carried their sibilance, making Zach's ears tingle. He looked over to a bottle of water on the side table that Sylvester had been sipping on, and the liquid was vibrating in sympathy with the sounds. What had started as a deep, resonant chant from Sylvester had spread to everyone standing with bowed heads. It was melodious but powerful. The words weren't shouted but amplified as each voice added amplitude to the waveform. A waveform that, as far as Zach's amazed eyes could see, was impacting the stuff around him. It felt as if it was building up to something. Zach wasn't the only one who felt that way. Sylvester left the chorus, took three steps to Hortense's body, squeezed her shoulder and said.

"Safe travels, sister. Represent us well." He stepped back and resumed chanting.

Medusa stepped forward, adjusting the pretty bow on the neck of Hortense's summer dress and then whispering something in the dead woman's ear. And so it went until all the members of the Headhunters team had shown their respect. Looking awkward, Zach was the last one to step forward. The chant was continuing around him. He could feel the throaty vibration in his chest. Feel it coming up from the floor. The air itself was being agitated by their voices. Zach looked down at the old woman as if waiting for her to open her eyes, smile and give him her hand to help her out of bed. She didn't need his help - she was as strong as a bouncer, but if he were around, she would ask.

A tear trickled down his cheek.

The chant was relegated to a channel, and the volume was turned way down.

He stood alone.

What would he do without her?

Tears were coming unashamedly. His shoulders slumped, jerking slightly as he sobbed. His insides were husked out, leaving a cold hollowness that wasn't surprising but unexpected.

"Dry yuh tears," Hortense said, and strong arms were around his shoulders. The arms and voice suddenly became Medusa's, encouraging him to step back, but first, he dried his eyes and kissed Hortense on the forehead.

She was still warm.

"Godspeed, Ms. H," Zach said.

He stepped back, and the chants grew louder, the effect on their cramped environment becoming even more pronounced. That hazy effect that hung in the air, that wasn't quite mist but more like light being refracted in odd ways, was settling over the body like a rain cloud. Surprise was reserved for Zach alone. Eyes wide, he watched the spectacle unfold as the chants hit their crescendo. Slowly, the image of what was Ms Hortense within the cloud of obscurity that enveloped her was disappearing, disassembling, atom by atom. In minutes, nothing was left of her but a swirling cloud of granular energy that eventually dissipated. Headhunters respectfully filed out of the room, leaving Zach alone with his thoughts.

Chapter Nine

Zach looked up at the paint stroke patterns on the ceiling of his bedroom and sighed. He glanced over to his MacBook on his desk, and beside it, the odd-looking leather-bound book Sylvester had given him, peeking out of the satchel. It was good to be home, cocooned on his bed, keeping the nightmares at bay. But his usual sense of safety was absent. Maybe it was a consequence of Hortense passing over; he wasn't sure. All he knew was that there was an ice-cold sliver of anxiety poking into the base of his skull. His usual ability to keep the nightmares of outside where they belonged felt somehow different. As if at any moment, the terrors would burst through his bedroom door and into his private world.

His protector was gone.

He took a moment to calm his pounding heart. The nest - a term his dad had coined when he saw him lying on the mess of clothes on his bed, was comfortably squashed and pressed to the contours of his body. Every time he shifted position, a hint of lavender and rose permeated the air from the freshly washed clothes that were strewn over the surface of his mattress. Zach tried to see himself lying in a field, looking up at the clouds drifting overhead.

It didn't work to calm him.

Not this time.

It felt like a day and a half had been crammed into the first hours of the morning. It was just past noon. He had decided to come straight home and not share a glass of brandy with the Headhunters crew who had assembled in the shop. Instead, Zach wanted to come home, spread out on his messy bed and lounge in the familiarity of his bedroom. Medusa walked him home, and Zach was beginning to feel like they didn't want him out of their sight. He was the Chronicler after all - whatever that meant and they were taking no chances with his safety. Later, he would cook something for his old man, but for now, he wanted to process what was happening to him.

Could he?

Sleep usually helped.

His father envied him for how quickly he could fall asleep under any circumstances, but what Mr. Ellison didn't realise was that the magic lay in the makeup of his bed. He rolled around on the washed clothes, which sent up puffs of comforting scents that perfumed the room. The smell of clean clothes made him think of his mom. It always helped to keep him grounded.

Not this time.

He hadn't been in the mood for the last four days to tidy his room, but he promised himself that he would get around to folding up these clothes and putting them away sometime soon.

For now, they were at best extra bedding—at least extra padding for a damaged psyche.

He lay with his eyes wide open, replaying the strange events up to this moment in his mind's eye. Zach knew something had shifted in his life. He had been told it had, and he felt it had. But what did it all mean?

The Chronicler?

Sylvester wanted to see him the next day at the shop. He didn't want to think about it.

"Fool, fool boy!" Hortense would have chastised him.' Yuh cannot run from your destiny.'

The plan had always been to get themselves into a position where they had enough money to pay down on a two-bedroom semi-detached council house. Mom and Dad would share a room, and he'd have his own - until he could find his own feet.

It didn't work like that.

His mom got sick, and all their grand plans went up in smoke. He couldn't think of anything but her recovery and the strange goings on in the estate.

He prayed, and she still died while he watched her agony. His heart was shredded at her passing, and that's when Hortense stepped in. She saved him. The void his mother left couldn't be filled, and Hortense didn't try to. What she did do was reveal the truth to him.

The only escape from this nightmare was to play his role. A role Hortense had prepared him and protected him for. If he wanted to get out of here alive, he'd have to do what was required of him. Not that he knew what that meant exactly, but it would seem he had no choice. He needed to stop fighting the inevitable, or he would be a casualty of this place.

He kept staring at the ceiling, and his mind wandered; a distant rhythmic buzzing was becoming annoying, threatening to break the spell. He did try to smother it, but it was insistent. Soon, the rhythmic buzzing was now front and centre, and he looked over to the source of his annoyance - his laptop.

Zach swung his legs off his bed and leaned into the laptop that was an arm's length away.

Ah, shit!

The pad of his finger smeared the touch-sensitive screen clumsily, and the image of his girlfriend and only confidante outside of the four walls, swam into view.

She didn't look happy.

"You sounded disappointed it was me," Maya Jackson said and then smiled, her annoyance disappearing.

"No, babe," Zach got comfortable on the edge of the bed, grinning. "You know that will never be the case, my dear."

"You're a piss taker Zach Ellison but I still love you."

"I can't blame you," Zach said. "There's so much of me to love. My mind, my body…"

"My broadband cannot take your foolishness this afternoon," her smile mellowed, and her gentle eyes became sorrowful. "How was Hortense's memorial?"

Zach took in a lungful of air.

"Strange," he said simply. "But beautiful. I'm finally believing there is a way out of this, I'm just not sure I'm cut out for what may be coming my way."

"I know you miss her, but you're ready. You may not know it, but I do."

Zach looked at her absently, his thoughts drifting back in time.

Maya was the only person he could share this horror show of a life with. After all, she had been here from the beginning, and he had made sure this wasn't going to be her life, too.

"You know I'm here for you, no matter what. I owe you everything, Zach, and I'll never forget it."

"You owe me nothing, babe. I couldn't see what was coming and let you deal with it alone. I know you're tougher than I am, but you have your own battles to fight." Zach was proud of how he handled that in hindsight, and if he had to do it again, he would. When he found out that he wasn't the only one able to perceive what he thought were supernatural events, he immediately hatched a plan to get her off the estate.

A doorbell rang on Maya's side of the world.

"Give me a minute, Zach, I'm expecting a package." She was so graceful in that wheelchair, as if it were an extension of her. He watched as she disappeared through the door, and in moments, she was back with the parcel on her lap.

"Do you want me to come and see you?"

Zach shook his head.

"Come on, Maya," his voice had a tremulous pitch. "I didn't get you out of this nightmare for you to walk right back into it."

"Wheel back into it," she corrected with a wan smile.

"Funny," Zach said.

"I miss you," Maya said quickly. "We haven't been together for a month."

"And I'm sorry, but I don't want you anywhere near here. I'll come to you as I always do."

"When?"

"As soon as I can. I promise."

She was quiet for a while.

"Is that the book you told me about?" she pointed to the Journal Sylvester had given him. The one that gave him butterflies in his stomach every time he looked at it.

"That's it, I'm supposed to have it on or near my person at all times."

"It looks old," Maya said.

"You don't know the half of it," Zach said. "I haven't messed with it properly. Not yet. But I can feel it wanting to connect with my head. It's hard to explain, but it wants to bond with me somehow."

She didn't realise it, but her voice lowered in a kind of reverence when she asked the question.

"How does it make you feel?"

"Powerful," Zach said." And that's why I'm worried."

"The more you tell me about the slow decline of that horrible place you call home, the more I believe Hortense was preparing you for this."

"So why do I feel overwhelmed?"

"Because it's normal. This isn't the most typical of situations you're facing. We're dealing with something that in the world we grew up in would be classed as insane. Crazy. But it's not. Not at all."

They were both quiet for a while.

"I've been thinking about that Journal and about everything you've told me about what has been happening over the months," Maya said.

"Something dawned on me a few days ago in the kitchen."

"Fill me in," Zach said impatiently.

"Well...have you ever come to a conclusion about something and you're a hundred per cent sure you're right?"

Zach nodded.

"A few times."

"That's how I feel about this. Certainty," Maya gathered her thoughts and manoeuvred her wheelchair into a better position to the camera. "The Journal is going to be an account of the people who live on the estate, the special ones in particular. I think it's going to prepare others who are in the same position you're in."

"Others," Zach asked.

"You didn't think that you were the only one, did you?" Maya asked.

Zach ran his fingers through his short afro.

"You know, I never thought about that."

"That's why you have me," Maya said. "We live in a big world and a boundless universe; there have to be others like you and other places like the estate."

"It makes sense," he said.

"And because of the rules, Hortense would keep talking about how some things needed to be done in a particular way."

Zach thought about it, making funny contortions to his lips as he mulled over Maya's reasoning.

"Who are they?" He asked.

Maya shrugged.

"The opposite side of the coin. You need to watch that YouTube video I sent you about the multiverse theory."

"When did you send it?" Zach picked up his phone and started looking for the errant post.

Maya shook her head disapprovingly.

"You need to make sure my emails get through to you without having to check your spam folder," she said.

There was a mumble from Zach as he continued to struggle to find the video file.

"Did you hear me?" Maya's tone was that of frustration.

"I'm sorry, babe. Yes, I did hear you."

"We're in this together, remember. If I discover anything useful, I must be able to get to you at a moment's notice."

Zach nodded.

" I understand. I found the file."

Maya stared at him, not quite satisfied with his response.

"I'll double-check to make sure you're on my whitelist, and I'm sorry."

"You should be," Maya said with the required level of disappointment that made Zach take stock.

He had to be careful.

The agreement he had negotiated with Maya after shipping her off the estate was that he had to promise that the communication links between them would be open at all times. If he couldn't manage that, she threatened to come back to the estate to be with him. And that couldn't happen under any circumstances.

"So you think they're from a different version of Earth," Zach could barely recognise himself. The man he had been three years ago had transformed into this rugged, slightly cynical, yet open-minded survivor who stood in his place, considering the multiverse theory.

"That's one explanation," Maya said. " But it's a work in progress. The more information I get from you, the better my conclusions will be."

"I love it when you talk scientist," his seductive voice slid into place effortlessly. "Where's that lab coat I like?"

"The one you like taking off," she corrected.

"That's the one."

"You'll have to come over and see, won't you?"

"I will, Wheels. I promise," he paused, sighed and felt the burden of his responsibilities weigh on his shoulders once more.

"If I survive tomorrow, and that's a big if, I'll make some definite plans to come see you."

"You know I love you, right?" Maya said her look was stern.

"I know," Zach said.

"And you WILL survive," Maya demanded.

"I will."

"Good, now relax. I have a physiotherapist session in twenty minutes, and you will call me as soon as it's over tomorrow."

Chapter Ten

This place felt simultaneously alien and achingly familiar. His bare feet sank into soft moss, the kind that glowed faintly underfoot, its light pulsing like a heartbeat. Overhead, trees with iridescent, glassy leaves stretched impossibly high, their branches weaving into a canopy that rippled like water. Moonlight—though there was no moon—bathed the dreamscape in silvery hues.

He turned slowly, taking in the surroundings. It was a sprawling and vibrant garden, yet untamed. Vines crept along stone walls that appeared ancient but unweathered, as if time had forgotten them. Statues stood at intervals, figures frozen mid-struggle: a man wrestling a serpent, a woman shielding her face from an unseen foe, a child clutching an orb that seemed to flicker.

At the centre of it all was a table.

It was simple but elegant, carved from a single slab of onyx and unadorned save for the three-tiered board game atop it. Zach felt his chest tighten at the sight of the game. It was no ordinary one; the pieces seemed to shimmer, their forms shifting slightly when he tried to focus. They all had human form—men, women, and children.

And then, he saw her.

Hortense.

She sat at one end of the table, her hands folded neatly in her lap, her dark skin glowing faintly as if lit from within. Her eyes, sharp and knowing, met his, and for a moment, Zach couldn't breathe.

"Zach mi bwoy," she said, her voice as warm and familiar as the scent of the coconut drops she used to make. "You found me."

Zach leaned on the table and sat.

"Miss Hortense, what you doing here?"

She smiled, and the wrinkles around her eyes deepened with affection. "A question with many answers, child. Some yuh nuh ready fi hear yet."

"I thought you were gone. You—you died. I was there. You were..." His voice cracked.

"Nobody is truly gone, Zachy," she said softly. "It was just time for me to move on to the next stage of this adventure. Death is but a door to another room."

Zach shook his head.

"Where is this place, some kind of afterlife?"

Hortense chuckled, the sound rich and full. "Not quite. My spirit is...caught up, let's say. There are rules here, rules I must obey."

He frowned. "Caught up? What rules?"

She tilted her head, her eyes glinting with mischief and sorrow. "Rules you don't need to worry 'bout. Not yet. Just know my time here is borrowed, and my words must be chosen carefully. Come closer." She gestured to the chair opposite hers.

Zach hesitated before approaching. As he sat, the faint hum

of the board game grew louder, a sound that seemed to vibrate in his bones.

"You taught me how to climb," he said suddenly, his voice soft. "How to move like the world was just another obstacle course. You said it was to keep me fit. To keep me sharp." His gaze darkened. "You didn't tell me it was because of them. The Headhunters."

Her smile faded, replaced by a look of quiet regret.

"If I had told yuh deh full truth, would yuh have believed mi? Or would yuh have called me insane, like any sensible young man would?"

Zach opened his mouth to protest, but closed it again. He didn't have an answer.

She gestured to the board game.

Zach glanced at it uneasily. The pieces had shifted again, arranging themselves into a tableau that felt ominous: a lone figure standing against a tide of dark shapes.

"What is this game?" he asked, his voice low.

Hortense's gaze hardened. "A reflection. A warning. A prophecy, even. It is many things, and nothing at all. But it is much more than a game."

Her cryptic words only deepened his confusion. "Then why show it to me? What am I supposed to do with this?"

She leaned back, her expression thoughtful. "There will come a day, when di world will demand more of yuh than yuh think yuh have to give. On those days, yuh will face a choice—fi run, or fi stand."

"I don't understand," he said, frustration creeping into his tone.

"Yuh will." Her voice softened, and she gestured to the board. "Look closer."

Reluctantly, Zach leaned in. As he studied the pieces, their forms became clearer. There was a figure in green, crouched on a ledge—a figure that looked eerily like him. Surrounding it were dark figures, their eyes glowing red.

And then there was another piece at the edge of the board: a building he immediately recognised as the Headhunters Barbershop - it glowed a brilliant blue.

"You are part of dis game but you are blessed wid choice unlike deh others. Nobody can control yuh actions only you. You are the Chronicler."

Zach's head swam with questions, but before he could speak, the air around them grew heavy. The garden began to dim, the light fading from the trees and moss.

Hortense's expression grew pained. "Mi time is up."

"No!" Zach surged to his feet, panic gripping him. "I still have so many questions! You can't leave again!"

"Mi not leaving mi bwoy," she said gently, though her form was beginning to flicker, like a flame in the wind. "I'm always with you. Always."

He reached for her, but his hands passed through her like smoke.

"Hortense!"

Her voice echoed as the garden dissolved around him. "Remember you have choice, Zach. And remember—yuh stronger than yuh tink."

The last thing he saw was her smile, filled with pride and sorrow.

WHEN ZACH AWOKE, HE WAS CRYING. HIS EYES FLICKED open, and he stared into the fabric of his ceiling. He lay perfectly still, ensuring he felt the heaviness of reality return after revelling in the lightness of a dream. His room was dark, the air still, but his heart raced as if he'd been running.

He rubbed his face, trying to shake the lingering feeling of the dream. But as the seconds passed, the details slipped away, like water through his fingers.

By the time the sun rose, he could only remember a faint echo of Hortense's voice, whispering something he couldn't quite grasp.

Chapter Eleven

Zach stood on the lip of the curb, Palladin House looming behind him and the sharp morning light slanting through the high-rises like a blade. He knew he shouldn't be here, not on his own, not without protection, but he had a feeling he wouldn't be able to do this for some time, maybe never again. It was like he wanted to prove to himself the estate was too far gone for conventional help.

Prove to himself what was to come was necessary.

Runnymede was waking up—joggers sweating, dog-walkers with too-tight leashes, someone burning toast one floor up. Ordinary stuff. That's what scared him. How normal it seemed.

Prove me wrong.

Then came the garbage truck.

It shuddered around the corner like it was limping—an ugly, rusted-out brute of a thing, all boxy lines and riveted steel —military green under the grime. Old Soviet tech, maybe, some Cold War beast dragged back from the dead. Its engine chugged like a coughing lung. Each thud of the tires sounded like bones breaking.

But it wasn't the truck, not really. It was them.

The crew rode hanging off the back. Too tall. Too still. Faces that looked... pasted on, like they'd been peeled off someone else's skull and stretched too tight. Zach could see the seams—hairline cracks near the ears, that uncanny blankness behind the eyes.

Darksiders.

Wearing human skin like a uniform. They hopped down onto the tarmac, their movements jerky and unnatural, like puppets tangled in invisible strings.

He didn't breathe. Didn't dare to.

They moved with slow, deliberate purpose, tossing bin after bin into the steel maw at the back. Then the compressor kicked in with a groan—ancient metal flexing against some unholy resistance. That's when the back hatch opened.

And Zach saw it.

Not machinery. Not hydraulics. Not anything that should've existed. A massive, slick bulk shifted in the shadows inside. Something wet and gelatinous. Something alive. He glimpsed teeth—jagged, serrated, no symmetry or logic to their layout. Tentacles like sewer eels curled around the waste as it slid in, dragging it back. One tendril flicked out, fast as a whip, and snatched a half-torn and leaking bag of food waste, plunging into the contents.

Zach stepped back, his disappointment falling victim to a cold terror.

The thing in the garbage truck blinked at him. *It blinked.*

That was it. That was the moment Zach knew the line had been crossed.

Runnymede was doomed.

Not in the way people thought. The deli down the street, the playground with the chipped seesaw, even the tired little chapel by the underpass—set pieces. Props in a very elaborate lie. And the truth?

The truth had teeth. And it collected the trash.

Zach tasted copper in his mouth, realised he'd bitten his tongue. The Darksiders hadn't noticed him yet. Or maybe they had and didn't care. He hurried back to his flat.

The doorbell chirped three times, and Zach felt a charge of nervous energy leave his groin and settle in his stomach. After his sortie downstairs, he had been dressed and ready for hours. His dad was on an early shift and was glad he was out the door before the circus that was Headhunters Barber Shop came knocking. He hadn't mentioned his new opportunity to the old man just yet. He still thought he was online, helping customers with their car part issues. That conversation would be an uncomfortable one, and he wasn't sure to what degree of truth he could give him. Today, he would decide on how he approached that prickly subject when he spoke to his father again.

Zach took a deep breath, stuffed the journal in his satchel and headed to the front door. Habitually, he looked through the spyhole at the top, showing a shadowy preview of who was on the other side. He saw no one, and for a moment, he thought he might have imagined it. He pulled the door open, and his eyes settled on his feet. The broad grin of Puck welcomed him, all four feet seven of him, standing beside a gleaming white Segway, in his pristine barber uniform, looking up at him.

"Good morning, Chronicler, ready to go?" His chipper tone was jarring that early in the morning, but Zach could feel it wasn't forced; he was actually excited.

Zach nodded.

"Our last engagement did not have one such as you. And that didn't go well for us. But you are here now, and I'm happy," Puck said.

"Engagement?" Zach asked.

The little man shrugged and looked sheepishly at his young charge.

"I'm sorry, but I may have said too much. I'm getting ahead of myself."

"I wish somebody would, I'm still in the dark here."

"Today is the day," Puck said excitedly. "Today is the day. It's scary and exciting, all at the same time." He stopped in mid-flow as if waiting for inspiration to catch up with him. Then he continued. "I don't want to ruin it for you."

"Okay, I appreciate that, I think. But tell me this. Why the first-class treatment? I can make my way to Headhunters on my own, don't you think?"

Puck wagged his finger at him.

"No, no, no." The little man emphasised his point. "You'll never walk on this estate alone again. You're too valuable, Chronicler."

Zach couldn't help thinking that if they were so concerned about his welfare, sending Puck as his bodyguard might not have been the best idea.

Zach had so much to learn about this new world.

Puck gave him a wry smile, his white teeth perfectly formed and evenly spaced. He clicked his heels together, flexed his short, powerful legs, then executed a double back flip and somersaulted almost defying gravity as he landed nimbly on his Segway.

Zach's eyes widened.

"Cool Segway," he stammered, not knowing what else to say.

"Environmentally friendly. Good for moving quickly when needed. Small legs, you see," Puck said. "Can you keep up?"

"I'll keep up," Zach said.

. . .

HEADHUNTERS WAS ALREADY BUSY WHEN HE WAS USHERED inside by Puck. The world outside was going at a snail's pace in comparison to the frenetic activity inside the barbershop. This magical place was not far removed from the barber shops he grew up with. It wasn't just a barber salon ▧ , it was a community centre, a creche, a psychiatrist couch, a Library, a news outlet and now something much, much more. He didn't know where to place his focus. Classic Reggae music played softly in the background, and various groups were performing their sets. On the fringes, there was a table with about six or seven primary school children working studiously on what he imagined must have been homework without supervision. That alone was impressive. Of the seven barber chairs, five were occupied. Three male barbers were chatting away with their customers as they gave them stylish cuts. A headhunter's hairdresser had a woman that Zach knew from the estate, with her head back in a basin, having her hair washed. Then there was the beautiful Medusa, her golden hair neatly bound in a bun, seated like a queen in an ancient-looking high-back wooden chair, inscribed with Yoruba cuneiform. At her feet, seated on a comfortable bean bag, was a young woman having her braids done while she deftly manipulated a Rubik's cube. Zach made one step towards Medusa when he heard his name.

"Zachary," Sylvester called out to him. "You've come just in time, my boy."

Waving him over, Zach made a beeline towards the older man, a half-smile on his lips.

"Mr Sylvester," Zach acknowledged him.

"You look nervous," Sylvester said. "No need to worry about being in here. You're amongst family," Sylvester reassured him.

"All I want you to do this morning is absorb the goings on here. Get a feel for the Journal. Relax, don't fight it."

Zach nodded, still not really sure what he wanted him to do.

"Sit with Medusa and watch her work," Sylvester said. "She's a master of her craft," he paused to think. "This barbershop is filled with wonder, my boy, you just have to know we're to look."

"I'll hang up my jacket," Zach said.

"And I have an 8.30 appointment," Sylvester said. "We'll talk in a few hours. Make yourself comfortable." He bowed, turned, and headed towards his workstation.

"You're here," Medusa squealed, leaving her client and coming over to hug Zach. This woman did nothing in halves. She literally brought him in to rest on her body, with his head on her breasts, and he could feel her smooth contours and tight musculature. She felt and smelled divine. Zach was breathless for a moment.

"Are you going to sit with me?" she asked.

"Is that okay?" Zach had composed himself by this.

"Of course," Medusa said, laughing.

"If I'm honest, I don't know what I'm supposed to be doing," Zach said.

Medusa smiled.

"Listen, watch and learn," she said, stroking his cheeks.

Zach was comfortable on a large bean bag, sipping hot chocolate and watching Medusa make complex braiding look effortless. She was chit-chatting with her young client, who was sitting between her legs. The teenager had four completed 3-D puzzles beside her and was working on a fourth. Zach found himself engrossed with the hairdresser, almost in a pleasant spell if it wasn't for the delicate strains coming from ... somewhere. He patted his back pocket to make sure his mobile was still there and hadn't been producing an auditory illusion, making him think the music was coming from somewhere else.

It wasn't his phone.

He wondered how long the melody that seemed only he could hear had been playing. Then he suddenly knew. His heart racing, Zach unzipped his bag and peered inside.

The Journal played its music of the spheres, and it gently made its presence felt above all the sounds of the shop. It wasn't that its melody was grating on his ears; it was insistent. A heavenly music, that was a perfect combination of harp, kente drums and flutes.

Zach reached for it inside his satchel.

Then he stopped.

Why did he have this feeling that he was on a path of no return? A momentous fork in the road that would define his life from this moment forward. His fingers were close to it, and he thought for a moment if he was doing the right thing. Right or wrong, his mentor did not die, so he could be doubtful about the path he needed to take. He grabbed the Journal and pulled it out of the satchel. It had a heft to it and was warm to the touch, as if its inner mechanisms were generating heat. He gently placed it on his lap, looked down at it, and murmured.

"What do you want from me?"

It went quiet.

Zach opened it to the first blank page and undid the writing implement that was bound to the book's spine. It felt strange, although it was cool to the touch. If the Journal felt old, then the silver-hued pen seemed as if it had been dragged from the future. It was streamlined, more like a projectile than a writing implement, and on touching the skin, it adapted its shape to the contours of his hand. There was no way he would call it a pen.

He suspected that writing was only one of its functions. Now it had a higher purpose. Zach rubbed his thumb over the tip of the scribbler, and a dark smudge like graphene discoloured his fingertip. He stared back down at the blank page and looked over to Medusa, who caught his furtive look and smiled at him.

"Finally," she said, sounding relieved. "Are you feeling it. It wants you to write on its pages."

Write what Zach was thinking. Everyone seemed to understand what was happening here except him. He hunkered down into the bean bag and sighed, his frustration leaving his lips like dragon breath and in its place came an unsuspecting calm.

Then it happened.

Something slipped past his mental defences. An energy that was elated, intelligent and wise beyond human comprehension. A warmth enveloped his body like a shot of Glenfiddich, and with it a flood of alien memories. There was a seamless blending of his consciousness with the intelligence that inhabited the Journal. It was ancient and hungry for knowledge. The intelligence gently took his metaphorical hand and began to guide his thoughts. At no time did Zach feel trapped or smothered by the force, and he felt he could subdue it at any time. He didn't feel the need.

Three apertures opened in the spine of the Journal. Floating out of their miniature enclosures were three silvery spheres, the size of large ball bearings, that rose up in formation to eye level.

Zach looked at them and immediately knew what they were.

Autonomous Data Retrieval Drones.

They had their own mission to complete.

But first, a selfie with the Chronicler.

The trio mapped his features with multi-coloured crisscross beams of light as they busily moved around his face. Once he was mapped and stored in their memories, they cloaked themselves and began their duties, invisible to human eyes.

Zach breathed out, forgetting he had held his breath. He looked down at the Journal and picked up the pen that snuggled comfortably into his thumb and index finger.

His hand moved smoothly across the paper, forming curves, lines, and geometry that he had no direct control over but felt an easy connection with. The scribblers' tip glided over the old paper, leaving sentences and paragraphs that looked like an alien language at first. Zach found that if he varied his focus, he could toggle between the unknown language and English. It was as if a filter had been lifted from his eyes.

He could see ... more, sense more.

His pen strokes were lightning-quick and precise. In no time, he had completed a page, and his hand felt as if he hadn't written anything. Zach's chest rose and fell, his heart pounding as his body tried to compensate for the new experience of connecting with the journal. He was suddenly self-conscious as he came back to himself, breathing evenly. The shop was busy and unaware that the Chronicler had formed a bond with the Journal.

Zach could feel his perception improve, like he had suddenly slipped on corrective glasses and hearing aids. His enthusiasm ramped up a few notches, too.

The Journal was eager to learn using Zach as its vessel and Medusa as its subject.

Zach watched Medusa saying something to her young client, and then she took the thick strands of the girl's hair in her hand and continued weaving. Zach hadn't noticed it before, but Medusa had some delicately designed gold rings on three fingers of her right and left hands. Each ring had a single celestial symbol on it. And on both her wrists, there was a similarly styled bracelet. As he watched Medusa create art on the canvas of a scalp, he began to see for the first time what she was actually doing. The Journal had improved his perception to such a degree, he was able to follow Medusa as she used one tooth of her comb to part the hair into a plait then split that plait into three pieces left, middle, right then close to her scalp she began weaving the young woman's hair and as she did so another shadow pattern was being woven too. This one was a thread of light that was invisible to most but ran through the braided patterns.

The energy was coming from Medusa, being produced from her fingertips and replicating the elaborate cane row pattern she was creating on the young woman's scalp, twist by twist. It reminded Zach of a circuit board, but this one's connections were made from an unknown source. Zach wanted to see the network of energy it had formed close up; it wasn't all uniform in structure, but the detail eluded him. He wanted to see for himself. At that moment, the Journal had its own plans.

Write first and observe later.

In moments, Zach filled four pages of written word and diagrams. He got up and, with his hands behind his back, stepped closer to Medusa, whose hands hadn't stopped plaiting since his little episode.

Not realising she had sensed his approach, she stopped what she was doing and said.

"You can see it, can't you?"

Zach nodded, his voice shaky.

"I can."

"Thank the ancestors," Medusa sounded relieved. "Hortense was right, you are a natural."

"I'm a natural at what exactly?"

Medusa used her head to make a sweeping movement.

"A natural at all of this," she said as if it were the most

obvious thing in the world. "Because your eyes have opened and you have bonded with the journal, let me introduce you to Sheneeka. The young woman sat between her legs, turned her head towards him, and smiled. She had stunning aquamarine eyes.

Zach returned the smile.

"Sheneeka is a very special young woman. She has an IQ of 300 and has a passion for puzzles, as you can see. The world needs her talents, but the others have plans for her. They never want to see her fulfil her destiny," Medusa took a quick breath, her eyes pooling with tears. "There were seven gifted ones on the Estate, and only five remain," she sighed, her chest rose defiantly. "My job is to enhance her abilities as well as protect her against the influence of the others. I merge my gifts with her latent powers, and that allows me to create a protective net as I braid her hair."

Zach tried to absorb it all.

"One murder and one disappearance?"

Medusa nodded.

"Hortense tried to stop it, but she couldn't do it all, and we couldn't come to her assistance sooner."

"She died waiting for you?" Zach tried to modulate his tone, but he couldn't conceal his bitterness.

"And that shame will remain with us forever," she paused, her focus drifting, but her hands still binding her hair. "This time will be different. You have made it different."

Before Zach could ask what that meant, he was compelled to turn to a new page and began writing again.

ZACH WAS THE KIND OF PERSON WHO ATE HIS MEALS IN front of the TV at home or streamed from his mobile when he was out and about. He liked being entertained when he took his meals, and he wasn't sure if that was a good thing or not. What surprised him was that after he'd finished his Tuna Melt, he did not need his latest serialised drama. His new talents and what was happening in the Barbershop were far more engrossing than anything Netflix could provide.

He'd imagined that the rest of the day at Headhunters would involve him flitting from barber to hairstylist like a bee and transferring their knowledge and experience to the Journal, but that wasn't the case. After his meal, the Journal was dormant, and he was watching the barbers work.

"Zach!" Sylvester called out to him just as he was placing the discarded wrappings of his lunch in the bin. He looked up to see the elder barber waving him over. Zach jumped up and made his way to his station. Although the Headhunters' uniform was standard with a few personal touches, the branding remained consistent throughout, except for their work stations. The first thing you noticed about Sylvester's space was his oval mirror. It looked ancient and heavy. Around its edges were intricate designs made from rough crystals set into the circumference of the frame that sparkled as light refracted off them. Zach caught a partial reflection of himself as he approached, and for a minute, he was behind the glass looking at a tunnel that ran for eternity ahead of him. He shivered and shook off the thought while he stood waiting for the barber to complete some deft razor work on a man's short beard. Sylvester shuffled away from his client, who was relaxed with his eyes closed in his chair. The elder barber put his hand on Zach's shoulder.

"You've done well," Sylvester said, lowering his voice.

"Together, we could actually make this thing work. There's one more thing we need to do to make you ready."

Zach nodded, not sure if he should enquire about the severity of his 'one more thing', but as the fear emerged, he felt better about it. Sylvester had a reassuring way about him that would make you walk through fire if he asked you to.

"Don't worry, I'll place you in the Safe hands of our resident Glyphscribe. He will hold your hand and take you through the process pain-free. Trust me."

"Do I have a choice?" Zach asked, but Sylvester smiled.

Sylvester lied.

The first five minutes of the process were painful, but the remainder of about an hour of work was not only comfortable but also amazing, if that was at all possible.

Grafix, the tattooist, was good to be around. He was always smiling, with his slow, deliberate speech. He sounded stoned, but that was just his surfer dude persona. And unlike the other Headhunters, Grafix wasn't as cryptic. So far, Zach had his questions answered. He may not have understood it all - even Grafix had difficulty explaining some things - but Zach finally felt he was being treated as part of the team.

"Do you want to see this bad boy?" Grafix asked, obviously proud of his handiwork. Zach nodded, not knowing what to expect, and watched him take a mirror off a hook on the wall and stylishly twirl it between both hands, then tilted it just enough so Zach could see what had been done. Grafix made sure he saw it from three different angles.

"Wow!" Zach said, genuinely surprised at the look of his fresh new haircut that suited him beyond words. He silently envied men who knew themselves and knew the trends so they could express to a barber what was required to create a cut that was meant only for them. Zach's experience at the barbershop was perfunctory. He left the chair feeling almost robbed most of the time, but never understanding why.

So this was how it was supposed to feel.

He would have never been able to articulate what kind of cut he required in the past, but he had a feeling that with Headhunters, their expertise was such that they could match a style to your face, shape of your head and something more individual.

Something more scientific.

A match to your vibration.

Maya was going to love it. She wasn't the pushy sort, but Zach knew exactly what turned her on outside of intelligence and imagination. Maya Johnson just loved to see her man clean-cut, buffed and polished.

He wondered what she would think of his new scalp tattoo?

Grafix must have seen Zach's broad smile as his mind drifted between the sheets.

"That feeling you're experiencing is the gift a real barber can impart to a hair client. It's a sliver of their energy that can help prepare them for the world outside of the chair. Kinda like an inoculation."

Zach nodded.

"I never saw it like that, but it's true." He shifted in his chair.

"You guys are proud of the work you do here."

"You'd be proud too if you knew our history," Grafix's said.

"A story for another time?" Zach said.

"A story for another time," Grafix agreed.

"I know I've been a pain in the ass with my questions, and I appreciate your patience, but my girl is going to chew my ear off if I don't tell her the significance of this." Zach pointed to the sigil inked into the right side of his scalp below the line of his hair. It was throbbing slightly as he was paying attention to the flowing lines and geometrical shapes that merged into each other.

Grafix rubbed the hairs masquerading as a beard on his chin and looked at Zach levelly.

"It's not that the boss is secretive, he doesn't want to overwhelm you. We've been doing this for a while now, so we've picked up a few things."

"Ok," Zach encouraged him to keep going.

"You haven't been the first, and neither will you be the last. We've had Chroniclers go mad from overload or commit suicide from the responsibility. You seem different, somehow more capable."

Zach nodded and felt it was premature to congratulate himself just yet.

Grafix continued.

"In the next few days, you will really get into the meat of this particular sandwich, and it's going to be both spiritually and physically dangerous. The vibrational protection we can offer you will give you peace of mind, hence the symbolic tattoo etched into your scalp. It will dissipate psionic attacks, especially when you're asleep. Disrupting your sleep cycle by injecting negative psions into the Hippocampus. Bad dreams be gone."

Grafix laughed.

"Thanks," Zach said, sounding unsure of what he was grateful for. Then he sheepishly said, "Now tell me more about the protection against the physical dangers you mentioned. "

Grafix gave a broad smile that almost split his face in half.

"That's a surprise. I will let the boss show you. Just rest assured you'll be working with a legend."

Chapter Twelve

L ater that day, Zach realised how big a deal it was for him to have connected with the Journal. From what he could ascertain, his predecessors had not been as successful as he had been in communicating with the book.

Predecessors with an 's'.

The rest of the Headhunters crew congratulated him with high-fives, handshakes and hugs while he tried to piece together in his head what it all meant. Zach had a feeling that soon he would get many more of his questions answered.

He had merged with the Journal after all.

His questions would have to wait, though, as Sylvester had a line of clients eagerly awaiting his talents. Zach wondered who these people were. Who in their right mind would use a barber you hadn't officially vetted yourself? Unless their word-of-mouth game was strong.

But how? They've only been here for three days.

And yet the residents had come out and were ready to go. A few he recognised from around the way, but the vast majority he didn't know. How did they hear of Headhunters' existence, and more importantly, how did they know Sylvester was any good? The Barbershop had only materialised just over three days ago, and the word was already spreading.

It was either metaphysics or marketing. But whatever strategy they used, it was working. By mid-afternoon, he had drifted away from Medusa and was standing close to a barber who sported a blue mohawk.

Zach had watched a young mother struggle to drag her son over to the empty chair. The boy, no more than seven years old, was thrashing and screaming, the barber chair conjuring some nightmarish image that had him fighting for his life. That was until the flamboyant barber walked up to him with a smile on his face. Once the boy locked eyes with him, the barber made a gesture with his fingers that Zach thought was a greeting at first. Still, he wasn't so sure until the molecules of air around his fingertips formed a shimmering waveform before disappearing.

The boy stopped in his tracks, looking disoriented for a moment until the barber gently ushered him into the barber's chair. The bawling stopped, and in its place were some sniffles and hiccuppy breaths. Whatever had upset him was now forgotten.

The mother sighed with relief.

Zach almost applauded.

He was being swept along by a current in the stream of impossibility that he had no power to influence and didn't know where he would be finally deposited. All he knew was that if Hortense trusted these strange people, he could do much worse than not to trust them himself.

Chapter Thirteen

The Chaos Realm

The alarm echoed throughout the darkened chamber like the archangels were triumphantly sounding their horns on judgment day. Creatures that inhabited the nooks, crevices and the pools of darkness scurried away to even deeper shadow. This place was completely unfamiliar with joy; it was the antithesis of hope. But most revelled in this nature; it was their identity. The very bedrock of this lair was despondency and fear. The demon called Anastasia peered over at the multi-platformed Eternal Game set on the light-absorbing black slab of volcanic rock. In frustration, a muscle fibre spasmed under her blood-red eye. She hoped her spectral opponent, who sat opposite, did not see her lapse in focus. And if she did, so what? Anastasia didn't care. She had the forces of chaos at her disposal to remedy any past miscalculations.

And yet, this unfolding situation made her hounds whimper, and the red flames of her furnaces burned white-hot as they reacted to her rage. The figure of a young man was materialising on one of the squares on the third level of five hundred squares. The levels constantly change and are randomly cranked up from the steamy bowels of her domain, each new level a continuation from the last, but different. The Celestial machinery that gave the Eternal Game its perplexing rules had been here before it all and would be here after it all. The contraption, like a complex conveyor belt thousands of stories high, was below her feet. Manned by thousands of worker bee acolytes, creating variations of the game platforms that even she was not privy to, but over the millennia of playing, she had developed an unrivalled expertise.

So why hadn't she seen this coming?

This!

A Chronicler.

She glared at the spectral figure opposite, the Ying to her Yang. Anastasia could swear there was a smirk on her smudgy features.

This would change everything.

It would do no good to show emotion around her spectral partner because she would use it in her next move. And this was a game of strategy with an infinity of variations and outcomes. Out here in the multiverse of worlds, the game was played with beings who had been given free will by one greater than her. A free will, Anastasia and her kind were tasked to bend and break. But with all things in the universe, a balance must be maintained. The game must be played with two. A balancing force from the world she had her eye on. The Over-lord - may his name be feared- had decreed many millennia ago the rules to this infernal game; it was not her place to question it, but to find creative ways to work it to her advantage. Not every skirmish would produce a victory, this she knew, but this development required ...steps. And she had the exact move that was required for a situation such as this.

War!

Anastasia stood beside the Game, her hip resting on the

black onyx, feeling the vibration and the power that rippled from it. Her attuned eyes could see, and the Runnymede Estate was represented on a crystalline platform. The piece that was glowing bright and that made her feel uncomfortable was the Chronicler. Around him, not as bright as the pieces that represented the dimensional beings who had just arrived and set up camp.

The Headhunters.

But surrounding them were a multitude of her dark pieces, her forces that would overwhelm them in time. Anastasia made the Devil's Gambit move, and aeons of experience made her a master of the game. She moved a piece across three tiles, a dark trail followed it, then circled its new position, pulsing. Anastasia had faced countless spectral opponents over the millennia, and she had even wondered how they were able to master the game so quickly. But this one was unusual. Her spectral counterpart sighed, knowing her next move wasn't possible after Anastasia's play. Her insubstantial hand hovered beside the piece that was the Chronicler, her arm becoming tangible, phasing in and out of visibility, then flesh and blood for a moment as she moved her piece tentatively, one square to the left. Her sigh was like a light breeze that carried dried leaves caught in an updraft.

Anastasia watched her painful uncertainty and grinned.

Chapter Fourteen

The his was different. Puck chaperoned Zach to the Barbershop in the evening for the first time, and the whole roster was different. The Night Shift, as Zach named them, were mostly new faces with a smattering of what Zach thought of as the foundational members.

Of course, he was looking for Medusa, but she was nowhere to be seen. Instead, he noticed someone else in her space.

She was tall with a beauty that didn't require attention— it was a given. She could be a senior, but it was difficult to determine her exact age. Long black hair flowed over her shoulders, and her brown skin had that depth to it—that made you think of First Nation people - Indigenous South American Indians maybe.

He reminded himself that these beings may have a passing resemblance to humans, but they were far beyond humanity.

The woman was working on someone—someone Zach recognised. Amara. A neighbourhood fixture. One of those women who wore pride like perfume, who knew your cousin's real name and how long your mother had been on her feet. But today, Amara looked diminished. Her eyes were closed, her head leaned back in the chair, and where her full hair once bloomed, bald patches now marred her scalp; raw skin showed where clumps of hair had fallen away like dying petals.

Zach wasn't trying to stare. But some wounds pull your attention.

She caught him staring and smiled. She tilted her head and signalled him over.

He swung his satchel around and dug inside for the Journal. The woman watched Zach approach. He shook her hand, held it and was preparing to introduce himself.

"I'm the..."

"... Chronicler,' she finished. "It's an honour and privilege. I'm Maria," she bowed and, without preamble, said. "She's being infected." Her voice was soft but full, like a drum muffled by velvet. "

Zach glanced again at Amara. Her breath was shallow. Her body is still. It was as if she were deciding to continue with the process of breathing.

"Infected by what?" he asked.

"Your doctors call it alopecia areata," the hair expert replied, fingers still working a gentle rhythm across Amara's scalp. "But what you're really seeing is her reaction to negative psionic energy that is pervasive on this estate. It is carving out a home on her scalp, then it will begin to tunnel inwards."

Zach blinked.

His hand was scribbling away in the Journal while his conscious mind attempted to understand what he was being told.

"Will she be alright?" he asked.

"We caught it early," she said, nodding. "Come. There's something you need to see."

They left Amara in the chair, incense curling up around her. The elegant woman led him to the door that led to the back of House. He took a deep breath, knowing what to expect.

Maria opened it.

Zach stepped through—and the world shifted.

It always threw him off. The way reality folded behind that threshold. One second, he was stepping into what should've been a supply closet; the next, he was inside a space that could've housed an airship.

The interior defied logic. Ceilingless yet sheltered. Walls of stone, steel, and light—all changing if you looked too long. Zach's stomach twisted the way it did when elevators dropped unexpectedly. The very air was sentient here.

Maria walked ahead as if it were nothing. Like she belonged in this place that felt like it had no beginning or end. They walked for seconds or possibly minutes.

"This," she said, as they entered a lush corridor of green and gold, "is the Garden."

It wasn't a metaphor. This was a botanical cathedral—alive and aware. Plants twisted into impossible shapes, glowing with colours no earthly spectrum acknowledged. Trees murmured to one another in the rustling language of old souls. Flowers pulsed like they had hearts.

Zach's mouth went dry.

He wasn't a botanist. But he knew enough to know nothing here was native. Or maybe everything was.

The woman reached out, her fingers brushing a translucent vine that shivered under her touch.

"This is *Lumen Vitae*," she said. "It resonates with what's forgotten in us. Reminds cells how to remember themselves, how to communicate better."

She moved deeper into the garden, naming plants as she went, explaining how each one interacted with humans. *Mora*

Visceris, by eating the roots, harmonised discordant frequencies. *Telanthis*, whose petals you rub together and inhale the aroma, triggering forgotten memories and bringing them to the forefront of the owner's consciousness. Each plant was alive and aware of being watched.

Zach kept pace, his boots crunching soft soil that smelled rich, musky and alive.

Insects hummed with weird melodies as plants were being pollinated. She stopped beside a cluster of crystalline shrubs, bowed to them, and murmured some words before plucking several leaves with surgical care. She placed them into a small, shiny gossamer pull-string bag.

"These will help Amara," she said. "It's not just about regrowth. It's about allowing her cells to resume communication."

Zach didn't say anything. He was still processing.

A workstation was set up in the garden with basic chemistry equipment. She ground the leaves with a mortar and pestle that looked ancient. She added drops of something phosphorescent. Then, with a soft whir, she fed the mixture into a sleek machine that blinked awake, reading her intention before adding the ingredients.

The resulting salve glowed orange. It smelled like citrus, thunder, and clean air.

THEY WALKED BACK THROUGH THE GARDEN, BACK through the space that either broke or adhered to the rules of space-time, and returned to the barbershop floor. The door shut behind them like it had always been part of the wall.

Amara hadn't moved. But the air around her had. Thicker now. Charged.

Maria applied the salve with slow, deliberate care,

massaging it into her hair and scalp. Her chant was low, steady. Not a song. Not a prayer. More like a line of code, maybe.

Zach watched, silent.

Minutes passed. Then Amara opened her eyes. She sighed and smiled.

"Wow! I don't know what you did, but that feels so good. The itching is gone."

"I'm glad, but don't thank me yet," Maria smiled. "Let's talk about what you should do next for hair growth."

Zach pulled back as both women talked.

This was an important part of what Headhunters did. The Runnymede community needed a gentle hand and healing. But there was another side to their duties that he hadn't experienced yet. But he knew it was lurking in the shadows and knew he would soon be introduced to it. And Zach knew as night followed day, he was going to hate every moment of it.

IF ZACH WEREN'T AS TIRED AS HE WAS, HE'D BE WORRIED. Unfortunately, he was an expert at discerning the signs of impending bad news. The Headhunters may not be human - the jury was out on that, but they decided to take on the countenance of humans and humans, Zach could read. He was used to seeing the faces of doctors and family after his Mom got sick - he was a teenager at the time and a quick study on the signs of pain. When the doctors discussed her cancer, he could see it. He saw it on his father's face after each test, after every diagnosis, as if his old man was sharing some of the burden with his mother.

They didn't know, but some of that burden was on his skinny shoulders, too.

Paradoxically, the only person who could hide the pain, from him at least, was his mother. She was a masterful liar.

Sylvester and the team, not so much.

At the end of a day that felt almost like a dream. He was in Sylvester's office again, stiffly seated in the only other chair except for his own. Standing in the room were Medusa and Puck, the differences in their sizes dizzyingly apparent.

Sylvester looked over his spectacles, his brown eyes vibrant and alert. He smoothly swung his throne-like executive chair left, then right, then abruptly stopped and leaned forward on the desk.

"Firstly, Zach, I want to congratulate you on bonding with the Journal. I should have had more faith in Hortense; she prepared you well."

Zach nodded, trying to understand exactly what his training consisted of, but gave up.

"This is the moment when things get real," Sylvester continued, looking over at Medusa, who approved of his turn of phrase with a smile.

"What we have seen with our eyes, The Others have felt. They now know you are part of the game, and they will do what they must to destroy you if they have to." He pursed his lips and sighed. "I thought we would have a few more days before they detected your presence, but she took steps to prevent that from happening as it did the last time we clashed."

"She," Zach said slowly, knowing precisely who Sylvester was referring to. "The bitch is real." Zach made a face and sighed heavily.

Sylvester nodded.

"Unfortunately, she's very real. That's her avatar you saw, and to Anastasia, you are sheep. And she's more than willing to slaughter human sheep for the game."

"The game?" Zach said the words with a degree of scorn. "All this is a game to her?"

"The Powers we're up against view your free will as a

mockery of what they stand for. Humans are an aberration across the multiverse and shouldn't exist in their eyes," Sylvester placed both his hands palms down on the table, and it looked like he was about to stand, but he changed his mind.

"Your estate houses seven of what we call Seractut - the flames. In this world, they are able to counterbalance the activity of the agents from the Left Hand Path, whom we call the Darksiders. Restore peace, where they would sow chaos. Without them in the world, humanity would have no hope."

Zach leaned back in his chair and shook his head.

"Why are all the Seractut here, on this estate? How can that be?"

Sylvester smiled like he had heard that question asked many times before.

"Because of the mystical balances and counterbalances that need to be met. Before the Seractut are allowed into the world proper, they must be tested, and this is the way it has been done for your reality."

Puck chimed in.

"They are worried," the little man said. "This plane of reality is so much different from the others we have explored, and the Left Hand Path know that. There is an energy here unlike anywhere else we know of, and we must fight to maintain it, whatever happens."

Medusa picked up where Puck left off.

"When Hortense had you under her wing, she knew what you could become, but wasn't sure you could fulfil it until now." Medusa had been pacing, and her statuesque figure threw a shadow over Zach's chair. Her voluminous hair flowed with her movement like it had a life of its own. Her proximity made him flush. She smelled so good.

"You and your family on the estate are now high-priority

targets for the Left Hand Path. Your father has to exit the estate, or he will be a casualty. That is a certainty."

"Leave and go where? What do you want me to do?"

Sylvester leaned back in his chair.

"We have it in hand."

"How?" Zach leaned forward, his voice raised, his concern unshielded. "He's all I've got. His safety comes first. He doesn't deserve to be affected by any of this; he's been through enough." Zach paused, putting the brake on his catastrophising and calming himself. "What are you going to do?"

"I apologise," Sylvester said. "I may have come across as dismissive, but I do have a plan."

Sylvester reached into a drawer and placed two paper dockets on the table, and a gold and black credit card. He pushed them over to Zach for his ok. He picked them up off the table and examined them dispassionately.

The young man's eyes widened.

"Two all-inclusive passes to Sandals in Jamaica for a month, leaving in three days?" He asked.

Before Zach could ask the question, Sylvester continued.

"I took the liberty of learning more about your father and his lady friend. The first-class tickets are for them both, if you wondered."

For a misguided second, Zach had wondered if it was his ticket out of this nightmare. And he immediately felt bad for succumbing to the thought that this complex dilemma could ever be resolved by running away from it.

"What's on the credit card?" Zach asked.

"Ten thousand pounds for miscellaneous expenses for a month. The holiday package is all-inclusive."

Zach looked up from the items in his hand and stared at Sylvester.

"Thank you," he said.

"Thank you," Sylvester responded. "How do you think you'll sell it to the old man?"

Zach shrugged.

"I have no idea, but I'll find a way."

"Yes, you will because his life depends on it." Sylvester paused and thought for a minute. "When we escort him to your front door, have your story ready."

"I'd better call him then and let him know, he's going to be met."

"Better yet, tell him nothing. Our people will protect him from the shadows. In the meantime, we need to arrange your next steps into your new role as Chronicler."

Zach didn't know if he should take that as a threat or a promise.

"Lady M will escort you home so you can get some rest. I need to introduce you to your partner sometime tomorrow."

"Partner?" Zack asked.

"Partner," Sylvester said without further clarification.

"You're going to need your rest; tomorrow is going to be an eye-opening day."

Chapter Fifteen

There is one main road in and out of the Runnymede Estate. There are five pedestrian exits and entrances. Mr Ellison habitually used two. He had learned to drive in the eighties, but after settling down and having a family, he couldn't justify the cost of maintaining a car. Luckily for him, London had excellent transportation links. You could get to wherever you wanted to with enough time and prior planning. He still missed his car, especially at nights like this, but at least he was much fitter. He breathed a sigh of relief getting off the bus, thankful he had left a group of aggressive drunks, threatening each other and any other brave passengers who complained about the noise and bad behaviour. The Somalian driver was stoic. His focus was on reaching the end of his route without a major incident and returning home to his family. Mr Ellison understood how he felt. If the driver could accomplish that goal by ignoring the occupants of his rowdy bus, then he would.

He watched the Metrobus depart from the bus stop on the main road, its red indicator lights blinking, and wished the driver good luck. Then he turned to the Estate looming ahead of him and shrouded in a mist that was only within its borders. A chill crackled along his spine, making him shudder. He wasn't the inquisitive or superstitious type, but even for him, it was strange how, at night, mainly in the cooler months, the buildings and grounds were shrouded in a gossamer curtain of fog that seemed to leech from the ground. Before Mr Voyt, the groundkeeper who had disappeared under unusual circumstances, explained the reason why this was the case.

"Transpiration, he had said after considering Mr Jenkins's question, expertly shifting a Morris mint to the soft fold of his left cheek. "The architects wanted the flora to be moisture-loving plants like Mosses, ferns and conifers. Some design feature that reinforced the theme of the project." He sucked on his mint. "Anyway, through high transpiration rates, these kinds of plants release water vapour into the atmosphere, so when the moisture-laden air comes into contact with cooler air or condensation, it leads to fog formation."

"Not a good combination for this kind of project," Mr Ellison had stated.

Mr Voyt shrugged.

"For me and you, maybe, but for the architects of this god-forsaken place, they were satisfied with the results."

He always wondered what he meant by that.

Mr Voyt was to disappear three weeks later.

MR ELLISON STEPPED THROUGH THE OLD ARCHED gateway into the estate and shivered again. What was wrong with him? The transition between the roadside and the estate had a tangible demarcation he had never felt before. The hairs on his arm stood on edge, as did the ones at the back of his neck. He wondered if it had something to do with walking from an area of cooler air to the estate, which had a warmer environment. He knew that wasn't the reason. It wasn't just the physical manifestations, because something was going on in his gut, too. It was like his body recognised that he had stepped into another world.

Now that was stupid.

He hurried along the familiar pathway, which would have been a well-trodden track if it were a dirt road and not concrete. Empty cars were situated snugly in their parking areas. Some residents were at home, obviously, but he couldn't see the signs of that. He tried to peer ahead for lights coming through the windows of the high rises, but he couldn't see that far. Visibility was bad, but his eyes were getting used to the mist. Not that it would slow him down. He knew this route like the back of his hand, so why did he feel so odd walking the way he had walked countless times before? He thought about Zach and the call he had made to him earlier today.

"Some friends of mine may meet you as you come onto the estate. They'll walk you home."

"Why?" He had asked. "Is everything okay?"

"I'll explain everything to you when you get home. Don't worry. I love you."

And that was that.

Worry was what parents did. Even if Mr Ellison had no reason not to believe his son was telling him the truth. He just went ahead and worried anyway.

Maybe that's what's on his mind.

That thought lingered until he crossed over onto Gabrielle Street and walked up to the street sign that this morning was in one piece, but now looked like someone with unbelievable strength and a massive, gnarly axe had tried to split it through concrete and tin.

Mr Ellison stopped and shook his head.

"What deh hell is happening to dis estate?"

He knew the answer to that.

The crime rate had risen to unprecedented levels over the years, and it wasn't the kind of thing you would imagine. Young people were dying and disappearing at alarming rates, and there was no clear-cut reason why. The police had regular foot patrols making their presence felt over the five acres of real estate, but it hadn't made a significant difference. The fear remained like a stubborn fog that was ever present, ignored sometimes, but always there to chill your bones and make your heart skip a beat. It was peculiar to walk around with the knowledge that you would not become a crime statistic. On the other hand, if you were a parent, you were constantly worried, constantly vigilant.

Usually, he wasn't worried - his son was no teenager, but tonight was different.

A prickly sensation at the nape of his neck down his back was becoming more pronounced. And so did a feeling of the mist closing in on him.

He hurried on.

At first, he thought the scratching sounds accompanying him were his footfalls echoing off the walls. But there was a noticeable resonance to his steps that he could feel in the ground.

A tremor below him, matching his steps.

No, that couldn't be right.

The unnerving sensation made Mr Jenkins stop. With all his concentration on his feet, he tried to discern what sounds were beneath the concrete slabs. The drumming sounds were directly below him. It had stopped keeping in step with him and had proceeded into the distance. He could feel the vibration proceeding in the soles of his feet.

Unmoving, the old man looked into the distance. The

swirling, almost coalescing mist, like milk, had been gently mixed with an atmosphere of coffee.

He hesitated and didn't know why.

Suddenly, getting home to his son held more significance than ever.

"Your dinner and a hot shower is waiting for you at home, old man," he said out loud and took another tentative step.

Then one more.

And another.

A vibrational tickle at the soles of his feet made him take stock of his next step.

The tremor below him was getting more pronounced by the moment, but thankfully, its epicentre was metres ahead of him. His heart pounding, his mouth suddenly devoid of saliva and a cold chill gripping his gut and spine.

He stopped, immobilised.

He could just make out what was causing the tremors in the distance.

He could just see the churning and shifting earth.

He could hear the guttural, otherworldly screech that made his eardrums itch.

He could hear the glutinous slapping of probing multiple tentacles writhing and, with intelligence, searching for purchase so it could pull itself free from the earth's embrace.

Mr Ellison stumbled back, panic surging through him, his mind unable to interpret what he was seeing. All he knew was his primal, tribal, generational instinct was screaming for him to flee.

Instead, he was rooted to the spot.

His muscles locked, and his eyes fixed.

His rational mind kept screaming, but a part of him, a higher function, held him fast with a morbid fascination for the nightmare squeezing itself into his world. The thing steamed as if its birth canal ran through hell itself. Discerning its amorphous shape was not helped by the mist and encroaching shadows, but his fear heightened imagination filled in the gaps.

A tear dislodged from the pool of his eyes and trickled onto his cheek.

The mere contact of water on his skin snapped him out of his frozen panic. Mr Ellison took two faltering steps back. The creature bellowed, like a thousand human souls trapped in its throat, giving voice to their frustration and agony.

Mr Ellison clapped his hands to his ears, then threw his head down and doubled over. The pain wasn't just in his skull; it ran deeper than that. The sound was grating on his spirit, clawing at an eternal part of him, sapping him of purpose. Thankfully, when the alien scream of frustration or triumph stopped, his head cleared, and his panic returned. Wobbly legs or not, he had to get away from the nightmare that had been birthed from the steaming bowels of the earth in front of his eyes. With an energy he didn't know he had, Mr Jenkins shuffled backwards, turned and started running.

Two strides.

Three strides and he slammed into something.

Flesh and Blood.

He panicked all over again.

The voice was calm and self-assured.

Human.

"Easy, Mr Ellison. We've got you," the voice said. "Zach sent us. Take my arm and we'll get you out of here in no time."

Chapter Sixteen

Zach looked down on the sleeping form of his father, a wave of relief washing over him. He didn't wipe away the tear trickling down his cheek because no one would see. The old man's shoulders were rising and falling gently, his breathing even. He was stretched out in his Easyboy, shattered after tonight's incident and even more stressed after Zach had attempted to explain what he had seen and the brave new world of horror he was now a part of. It was a lot for him to take in, but the old man did. Zach's revelations about what was happening here shook up and dismantled the old man's understanding of the World, and he bravely tried to accept it.

But it was difficult.

The only good thing about this was that his father would forget.

Runnymede would forget. That was part of the mathematics of charm—ancient, subtle, and cruel in its elegance. An algorithm woven into the estate's bones, stronger than steel and older than bedrock, blanketed memories like mist. Screams got lost in static. Blood faded like old graffiti. The Eternal Game,

Sylvester explained, demanded secrecy, and so it was enforced
—not by silence, but by forgetting—only a handful remembered: the gifted, the marked, the cursed. Everyone else woke
up dazed and uneasy, with holes in their memories they would
never have thought to fill. They lived on, none the wiser. That's
how the game stayed hidden. That's how it survived.

Zach had done his best to explain the inexplicable and had
finished the discussion feeling guilty. The old man had been
through enough already in his life, and for him to distort his
worldview with his talk of good and evil, demons, trans-dimensional beings, and parallel universes was asking for too much.

He would forget.

Zach was proud of him for listening and trusting his
instincts. This could have ended disastrously under different
circumstances and with a father who was less involved in his
son's life.

Mr Ellison whimpered in his sleep. For a moment, his body
in the real world acted out his activity in the dream. Zach was
glad the echoes of that terror would remain in his unconscious
for only a short time. He'd be in Jamaica in two days, the
horrors of Runnymede forgotten and luxury awaiting. He
draped a duvet over the old man's shoulder, turned the volume
on the TV way down, and headed for his bedroom.

What would he have done if they hadn't caught him in
time?

He shuddered and felt his knees weaken.

All of this would come to a screeching halt. He couldn't go
on without his father.

He just couldn't.

With that horrible thought discarded, he switched on the
light in his bedroom and made himself comfortable. It was late,
but he knew Maya would be up waiting for a sitrep, as she liked
to call it, so that he wouldn't disappoint. He would usually leap

onto his bed without a thought, but not before he took off the satchel and removed the journal from its innards, placing it reverently on his side table. He stroked it and felt a pleasurable discharge of electricity dance around his fingertips. Zach didn't know why, but he strongly sensed that the Journal didn't want to be covered up. Its unencumbered pages absorbed information from its surroundings even when it didn't have it in hand.

Or did it just need its freedom?

He knew how it felt.

MAYA LOOKED SEXY WHEN SHE WAS DROWSY.

She was out of her Wheelchair and propped up on a bed that looked so comfortable with a fluffy duvet and matching pillows behind her and to either side.

What he would do to be between those legs? Maya had a way of deflecting the harsh glare of the world when he was with her. When he stepped into her world of fluffy pink, stuffed Koala bears and geeky science stuff, he was transported to another world. He was protected from aspects of the world he was not sure he could handle alone. Between the sheets was another world he missed exploring and wondered if he ever would again.

Zach knew she was struggling to stay awake before his features swam into focus on a Zoom call on her end.

"We could do this another time if you want?" Zach teased, knowing he was being sacrilegious.

Maya rolled her eyes.

She was recovering quickly from her drowsiness.

"Nice try, Mister, but no. I want a blow-by-blow account of what's been happening."

Zach raised an eyebrow.

"Blow-by-blow account?" Zach asked.

Maya nodded a twinkle of full wakefulness in her eyes.

"You looked tired, my love," she asked.

Part concern, part sarcasm.

"That means," she continued. "Today was a very, very busy day, I can tell. Spill the beans."

"You're heartless," Zach grumbled.

"I know. Now start talking."

Instinctively, Zach grabbed the Journal and began to spill the beans.

Chapter Seventeen

Chaos Realm

Anastasia sat unmoved upon the Blood Throne, its slick surface humming with a low, sated pulse beneath her. Her eyes, iridescent as oil on water, gazed into the shifting mist that passed for atmosphere in the Chaos Dimension—where direction bent like glass and time sulked in corners. She wasn't watching for anything. Not anymore. Power didn't need to be watched; it was to be witnessed.

Around her, the beetles began their work.

Six of them crawled in synchronised patterns across her scalp and shoulders—black-chitin monstrosities the size of rats, with mandibles clicking in constant, infernal chatter. They weren't summoned; they knew when the mistress needed their skills and *knew* their place in the order of things.

They set about braiding her hair.

Their legs combed her kinky tresses with the precision of war surgeons, and from beneath their plated backs, they oozed a viscous, shimmering secretion—something between oil and sap—that hissed faintly when it met her strands.

The fluid slicked her coils into shape, each braid weaving like a spell of vanity. No mirrors here, but Anastasia didn't need a reflection to understand her image. She was the centre of the grotesque, the jewel on a crown of meat and fire, and her appearance had to reflect that. If her enemies stared too long, they should choke on their awe. If her allies knelt too fast, they should bleed from the eyes.

Even here, especially here, presentation was power.

One beetle clacked as it twisted a final braid, and she hummed low in approval, the sound like thunder curling inside a cavern of bone. A single drop of beetle spit dripped onto her shoulder and hissed through the velvet of her mantle, but she didn't flinch. Beauty was not for the weak.

The Chaos Dimension whispered her name in a hundred hungry dialects.

She smiled, and the throne exhaled blood beneath her.

Her Zartegs were snoring and farting at her feet, exhausted from their usual Trek around the volcanic Lake. The Eternal Game was not far from where she sat, and all the sounds she was familiar with built up an acoustic architecture that never failed to calm her. The groaning and creaking of the self-repairing infernal machine, the murmurs from the legion of operators manning its inputs and outputs, the wails and screams from the workers floating up from the belly of the pit. For her, the sounds of this place were not a distraction but an aid to her process of focus.

And focus she must.

She wasn't the only Inquisitor in the infinite network of realities her kind had contact with.

This dimension had been new to her. There were stories about the Earth Plane and its tenacious inhabitants. She even thought it was the reason why the Hoofed Ones gave her this assignment. Her track record spoke for itself—a hundred and three distinct dimensions, with the destruction of over seven hundred gifted souls.

The real battle for this campaign had begun on the Runnymede Estate, and her strategy was in place, ensuring the conflict would be a foregone conclusion. Yes, there had been surprises, especially how quickly they had acquired the services of a Chronicler. But now she knew, and there would be no further advantages for the inhabitants. The game would be played on her terms this time, and she would see how the gifted hu-mans faced what was to come, even with the aid of the Headhunters in their corner.

The Housing Officers - her soulless stormtroopers that enforced not just order but made sure the estate ran like a well-oiled machine according to the rules of the Eternal Game had been given more freedom to move like wolves amongst the sheep. All that was required for victory would be how she played her hand against her adversary, the spectral being across from her. And if that was to be the deciding factor, then she had nothing to worry about.

The Earth Plane would face unprecedented chaos.

Chapter Eighteen

"We call it the Echo Chamber," Sylvester said, pushing his glasses back up the bridge of his nose and making a grand sweeping gesture with his arms.

Zach had taken in the enclosed space with a sense of awe and incredulity. He was way past wondering about space-time within the walls of the Headhunters building. It was about four times the size of the barbering space, and that was substantial. It was a transparent torus. You could walk around the entire circumference. Complex machines were attached to sections of the material that made up the doughnut shape, and although it breached from outside to in, it was sealed tightly. No matter where he moved, he could still see the focal point that was the dead centre of the structure. And that's where the strange and mundane collided. In the middle of the transparent torus structure was a 1950s barber's chair. He didn't know how he knew what time period it was from, but Zach had a sense he was right.

It was a masterpiece of craftsmanship from a bygone era,

when grooming was an art form, and every aspect of the experience was meticulously crafted with care and sophistication. The chair's frame was constructed from sturdy, polished metal, meticulously detailed with intricate patterns and designs.

Zach had an urge to sit in it and make himself comfortable, but instead, he ran his fingers over the soft red leather and impeccable stitching that formed the quilted pattern of a shrunken head on the backrest and seat.

Even though Zach knew this chair wasn't intended for grooming or the relaxation and comfort of its clients. Nothing of its original function remained. The chair could swivel a full 360 degrees, and a foot-operated hydraulic pump lowered and raised it. To complete this work of art, the footrest was elegantly designed to support the client's legs in a relaxed position, if needed. Somehow Zach imagined its design went unnoticed for its function.

Zach was beginning to realise that acceptance was a good starting point as he navigated this new world. He would never fully understand the inner workings of many things, and only by accepting what he could was he able to prevent himself from going insane.

"What do you think?" Sylvester asked.

"Impressive, mind-boggling, but what is it?"

"While encamped in this reality, the only way our kind can move between dimensions in emergencies is with this. And even under those circumstances, there are rules."

Zach nodded, his stomach queasy and his sense of balance skewed. It had nothing to do with him at all; it was the room and its design.

Sylvester put his hand on his shoulder to reassure and steady him.

"It's constructed from temporal metals mined from Black

Holes. They have an adverse effect on organic matter after prolonged exposure."

Zach's eyes widened.

Sylvester gave a smile and a shake of his head.

"You'll be fine, Chronicler. I wanted you to experience the sensations, the smells, and touch the surroundings for the Journal."

Zach nodded.

"I appreciate it." Zach took a deep breath. "But I think my stomach has had enough."

Sylvester nodded, touching Zach's back with the palm of his hand as he ushered him out of the structure.

"You don't suffer from its effects?" Zach asked as they both walked through the crystalline entrance that had formed on their approach.

"We're affected," Sylvester said. "Our resistance has developed over time, especially if you use it as much as we do."

"And you're going to use it now," Zach guessed incorrectly.

"Not quiet," Sylvester said. "Another member of our team will." He checked his old Rolex. "If there are no adverse temporal conditions in the multiverse," he walked over to a monitor that was part of a console attached to the structure. He looked at the bank of waveform representations, blinked and started looking around for something or someone. One of the Headhunters team popped her head from inside what looked like an equipment cabinet.

"You called Sil?" The older woman hollered back at him.

Zach hadn't heard Sylvester utter a word, but he did recognise the enquirer. She was absent from the barbershop floor, and now he knew why. Her name was Naomi, and he had been admiring her artistic skills with artificial nails back in the shop. He watched her hurry over to them, carrying a strange-looking tool that was a cross between a spanner and a wrench, with

USB connections along its length and capillary-thin pulsing lights running up and down it, like a miniature runway. She had it propped up on her muscular shoulder.

"How does it look?" Sylvester asked, then stopped himself. "Excuse my bad manners. Naomi, this is the Chronicler. You haven't been introduced."

She bowed, took Zach's hand and shook it enthusiastically.

"My pleasure. Truly an honour," she said. "Everyone wants to meet you personally, but once the conflict began, we've all been so very busy."

"I can see," Zach said, looking around.

Naomi smiled and focused her attention on Sylvester.

"We had an energy transference problem, but it's been resolved." She patted the tool on her shoulder.

"The weather forecast looks good, so Anthony should arrive on time."

"Thank the ancestors," Sylvester said, taking off his glasses and using his breath to mist the lenses. They squeaked when he used a flannel to clean them and put them over his eyes. "We're already behind, and the Chronicler needs to get out and about."

"You worry too much, Sil," Naomi said, taking a moment to squeeze Zach's shoulders as if she was making sure he was real. "I have a good feeling about this."

"Your prognosticating skills are always welcome," Sylvester said. "But you know I need dead certainty, not a list of possible outcomes."

"I didn't make the rules, but if the Universe does change its mind, you'll be the first to know."

"Thanks," Sylvester said flatly.

"ETA, minus fifteen minutes and counting," Naomi patted his back. "Chronicler," she bowed at Zach, spun on her heels and hurried off in the direction she had come.

. . .

THE COUNTDOWN WAS AT SIXTY SECONDS AS INDICATED BY an old-school ticker display above the entrance. It made a fluttering sound like birds taking flight every time the numbers formed, adding audio to the tension. Naomi had completed her pre-arrival checks and stood with them, her arms folded, as the Echo Chamber fired up. Zach was surprised they were not alone, but thinking about it, why should they be? Three other members of the Headhunters crew stood nearby watching. Even for them, this was an amazing spectacle. Who knows, they could be waiting for a friend to arrive. The transporter must be a big deal for Sylvester to be here, with him in tow.

Zach wasn't sure why, but he held his breath when the countdown hit zero.

It was like looking into the chest of a titan at its beating heart. The Echo Chamber pulsed, and with each beat, a subtle resonance made Zach's teeth vibrate in sympathy with the chamber's pulsing. The machine was silent except for what he thought at first were whispers. They were everywhere. From behind him. Beside him? Another in front of him, then from below. They sounded human, but he couldn't be sure what the whispers were saying; he had a feeling they were byproducts of the reactions happening inside the heads of the people around him.

How did he know that?

Only then did it dawn on him.

Echo Chamber.

The glassy walls seemed to breathe as light bent, producing the optical illusion of it expanding and contracting like a bellows. The barber chair at the centre of the maelstrom was being caressed by fingers of irregular claws of luminescence, imbued with an impossible iridescence of Starlight that Zach had to shield his eyes from.

It dimmed, and he could make out the outline of the chair

at the epicentre. A dance of light and shadow continued within as the very laws of physics were surrendering to alien forces wrestling it into submission. Strands of energy, like ethereal tendrils, wove an intricate web across the torus's inner surface, intertwining in mesmerising patterns, all at once complex and harmonious like fractal frost. Threads of energy in the hands of a cosmic weaver.

The light show ended abruptly.

There was a muffled sonic or psychic boom he heard in his head more than in his ears. Zach rocked back from the force and looked over to Sylvester for the first time since the Echo Chamber activated the hairs at the back of his neck, still standing on end. From the swirl of energies inside the chamber, the visitor materialised in the Barber chair, its form coalescing from the residual mists of the trans-dimensional journey. Zach blinked and widened his eyes so that he could make out the figure better. It never dawned on him to move closer to the Chamber. He didn't have to; he knew something was wrong from Sylvester's reactions. He saw something through the settling mist that worried him. The older man took a deep, shaky breath, obviously able to see the figure in the barber chair better than he could; the barber's eyes were wide behind his glasses.

"Damn," he breathed. "What did the bastards do to him?"

Sylvester was already hurrying towards the Echo Chamber before Zach could ask if everything was okay.

"Stay here," he said.

Zach nodded, hearing Naomi's frantic voice echoing in the room.

"We need medics down here, now!"

. . .

ZACH'S HEART RATE HAD STABILISED AFTER THE excitement of the last fifteen minutes. While he waited for the medics in full Hazmat gear to wheel the injured and unconscious Anthony from the Echo Chamber, he wrote in The Journal.

It was hungry for words.

A scent, both alien and familiar, permeated the air – a fragrance like jasmine and something else - stardust and cosmic winds? The aroma filled the chamber, mingling with the room's signature scent.

Flowery prose like that would have any editor's red pen all over it in the world outside these walls, but thankfully, the Journal would filter his words and adapt them to its own style.

He kept writing, knowing without knowing this incident was an apéritif to the main course.

Chapter Nineteen

The first thing Zach thought about when he woke up was his father. He felt lighter; such was the relief that Pop's had left the estate. It was strange; before all of this, before his mother's illness, before Runnymede estate, she would have been the memory he instinctively settled on in the morning. Every morning of his school years, she would rouse him. When she passed on, the memory of her, vibrant and alive, had cut a pleasant groove in his memory. He wondered if his mother's memory would fade.

Never.

The trauma of seeing her deteriorate into a shell of her former self would be the first thing he would expel from memory if he could. Unfortunately, the good and the bad were all wrapped up in a joyous, depressing, inspirational, hopeless ball of emotion. All he knew was seeing the Mercedes pull away with Margot and his Dad made what was to come seem bearable.

Zach smiled at the thought, keeping the expression locked on his face even after the warmth of the thought had departed.

Sylvester had been true to his word, and Zach would never forget that.

He yawned; his sleep had been fitful and brief, worrying about what was to come. The swirl of panic in his guts mixed in with an ember of excitement was one reason for his lack of rest, and Hortense was the other.

His dream world had become quite dynamic since she passed. Before then, he remembered nothing of his dreams. Now, he wouldn't class himself as a lucid dreamer, but every night he'd been able to recall snatches of a hellish landscape and Hortense. Always the voice of Hortense, reassuring and soothing him. His guide through whatever level of hell his unconscious was creating. At the thought, his skin prickled and a heap of gooseflesh rose at the back of his neck.

What if it wasn't a dream but a memory?

ZACH WAS DRESSED AND READY WHEN HIS CHAPERONE, Puck, came knocking at the door. It was about seven in the morning, and the estate was rousing from its slumber like a coiled viper. You knew it was going to strike you, but didn't know when.

"Good morning, Chronicler," Puck said in his usual chipper way. "Are you prepared for what the day may bring?"

Zach laughed nervously.

"I'm not sure about that, Mr P, but I will accept what I'm offered."

The little man bowed.

"That is all that can be asked of you," he said sagely, his smile shifting from salutations to his game face. "At your convenience, Chronicler."

He didn't flinch this time.

The title Chronicler was getting easier to accept in his

head; it wasn't so cumbersome as it had felt days earlier, and that was a good thing. He was ready for what could come, or so he thought.

Puck jumped on his Segway and adjusted the straps of a scabbard filled with a wicked-looking scimitar strapped to the LeanSteer Frame.

Wars and rumours of wars.

That was Zach's invitation to close the door and accompany his four-foot bodyguard to the enigma that was the Headhunters Barbershop. He turned to survey the apartment and then checked himself. The leather satchel with the Journal inside, Baggy cargo pants, a breathable tee and a light jacket with his Ollo Sapien on his feet and his Mad Grip gloves in his back pocket just in case. For the next seven days, this would be his uniform. He gently closed the door behind him.

Zach followed Sylvester into the dimensional labyrinthine corridors of Headhunters' back-of-house. It was a constant reminder to Zach of the shop's true nature and that he was a part of something truly remarkable.

They arrived at a dimly lit, no-frills, Spartan quarters, where a man sat with his back to them. The topless man sat in front of a wooden table, working on a 3D puzzle, his fingers deftly manipulating the pieces. Suddenly, he stops, mid-move with the puzzle piece between his fingers, when he turns.

Zach recognised him immediately. The traveller in the Echo Chamber - Anthony. He was looking remarkably well after that ordeal. The warrior's presence was like a tightly coiled spring; his blue eyes were sharp, missing nothing.

Sylvester's deep voice broke the silence. "We have five days, gentlemen. Rest assured, the opposition knows it and will put every stumbling block in your way. The rest of us must spiritually tend to the people of Runnymede Estate, as the war rages around them. To the Darkness, they are collateral damage. We don't believe that."

Anthony grunted.

Sylvester looked at Zach.

"This isn't Anthony's first rodeo, but it will be his most dangerous. Have each other's backs; your lives and the lives of the people on this estate will depend on it."

With a nod, Sylvester left, leaving Zach in the company of the inter-dimensional warrior. The air between them crackled with an unspoken tension as Zach sized up the seated man, whose focus was back to the puzzle.

Zach knew a fighter when he saw one.

Anthony was shirtless and tattooed with arcane symbols running down the right side of his body. He was dark-skinned and had darker scars over his abdomen, his ribs, and his chest. Zach could see a trail of keloid skin repairing itself before his eyes. It was like looking at time-lapse photography of a blooming flower or a crystallising butterfly emerging. Sylvester had warned him that his kind healed quickly, but seeing it for himself was amazing. Anthony's physique was a testament to a life dedicated to the discipline of combat. The muscles of his chest and arms were perfectly defined like a sculpture's masterwork, and his movement exuded a sense of explosive power, like a throttling internal engine ready to release. His broad shoulders tapered down to a trim waist and the sharp ridges of a jacked abdomen. The warrior leaned back into his chair, still ignoring him. Zach watched as his simple finger movements and the flexing of his arm triggered muscles popping on his forearms.

Zach felt his gaze leave Anthony's fit body to a coat hanging on a peg.

He refocused.

Anthony spoke first, his voice low and rumbling. "So you've been chosen as The Chronicler? "he said, rolling Zach's title around in his mouth as if he were tasting it for texture and consistency.

Zach shifted, feeling the weight of the mystical journal in his satchel. "It seems that way. I don't know what I'm doing or what's expected of me. I know whatever I can do to help, I will."

Anthony begrudgingly looked away from his puzzle, twisting his neck towards him. His expression was abstract, as if he wished to be somewhere else. One steady hand held a puzzle piece in mid-air, ready to be placed in the correct position.

His gaze was piercing.

"And what if your 'help' isn't good enough?"

Zach felt an odd heat rising inside of him and gave an internal sigh. It was a unique concoction of tension and fear, a blend that could be explosive if he didn't keep a cool head.

"Life's a bitch, my friend. My help will have to do, won't it? You chose me, remember." Anthony nodded, saying nothing for a while, then said.

"Don't you have any faith in the choice Hortense and the Journal made?"

"Me having faith doesn't matter one way or the other. All I know is Hortense believed, and that is good enough for me."

Zach absorbed the response and suddenly realised, despite feeling attacked, this was a perfect moment for his honesty to show itself. Their budding relationship could do without the bravado; adding some vulnerability to the proceedings wouldn't go amiss.

Zach mellowed.

"I don't know whether they made the right choice or not. Maybe there was someone out there more suited. All I know is Ms Hortense was convinced, and the Journal too. I had a part to play, of course, but I trusted that woman with my life."

Zach grabbed the only other chair in the room, spun it towards him and watched it settle on its four legs.

He sat and continued.

"I've got to believe in something. And I believe, she believed. As shit scared as I am, as lost as I am, I'm even more pissed."

"Being Pissed is good," Anthony agreed.

"I've been trapped here, only surviving because of Hortense's guidance, praying for not just a way out but a way to fight back. I'm on a sinking ship, and I'm not drowning without a fight."

"What we accomplish here in the next five days could mean somewhere in the dimensional realms a civilisation will flourish in peace or destroy itself in war."

"No pressure then," Zach said, shaking his head for clarity. "I can't think about the consequences, I can only think about Runnymede Estate, nothing else."

"Spoken like a true Chronicler."

"Your skill is a second chance for many, the ability to stitch back the fate of unravelling worlds. But why should you care? Your human mind can't comprehend the importance you play in the survival of a myriad of worlds in countless universes. And here you are, uncertain of your role."

"I'm getting a vibe you don't think I can do this, and maybe you're right," Zach adjusted the material of his pants close to the crotch. "But before you judge me, maybe you should improve your recruitment program if you want better results. Sylvester told me that we have no choice but to work with each other, right?"

Anthony nodded silently.

Zach smiled and absently looked again at the black great-coat that hung on the wall. It felt as if it was calling to him.

"What can I say? It sucks to be you."

A ghost of a smile flickered across Anthony's face. "It has taken me some time to break in this body. I like it. I've promised myself I would keep it intact, and so far I have. Unfortunately, the Chronicler from my last mission did not fare as well."

Zach's heart sank.

He hoped his face did not reveal his horror, but he doubted he could conceal it. There was a pause that he had to fill before it made him feel weak and out of his depth, although he was.

"So, what happened to you?" Zach asked, trying to make the question innocuous. "In the Echo Chamber, I mean?"

Anthony's eyes darkened.

"I was tracking a slip—a creature sent by Anastasia. It's like hunting smoke. It had murdered Erik, a friend, and was trying to escape to its mistress. I chased it and it led me into a trap," he looked thoughtful for a moment, his hand unconsciously drifting over a network of scars. "I was stupid, losing focus and letting my emotions get the better of me. That won't happen again."

The words hung in the air, a challenge and a promise.

Zach met Anthony's gaze squarely.

"How is this going to work? What do you want from me?"

"I am your shadow and your shield," Anthony said. "I will not interfere with your duties, but when I order you to do something, you do it without question."

"My duties?" Zach asked

"The Journal will guide you, and you will do what comes naturally to you. Your fight is to open the eyes of the remaining Gifted Ones and record everything regarding the people and the battles we will face. Because of those notes, others like them in other times and other places will stand a chance against

Anastasia's forces. The pen records truths that can shatter lies. Your fight is a different kind of battle." Anthony stood and glided towards a side table beside his bed. "My duty is to keep you alive so you can fulfil your duty. You are untested, while my battle expertise is second to none, but it is worth nothing if you do not respect my authority."

He opened a drawer and took out a pair of battered leather gloves. His hands were large like a boxer's, and Zach wondered why he hadn't noticed their size before now. His palms were broad with no callouses that he could see, and his long fingers rooted into his knuckles like unyielding fence posts in a maximum security compound. He wriggled his fingers into one glove, the skin of his remaining hand cloaked in an umbra of dark energy, a physical manifestation of the raw power he possessed.

His damn coat was thrumming on the hook.

Zach stared at it.

"I see the Journal is prodding you to find out more about my coat?"

"I'm sorry," Zach said. "There's something about it that I can't shake."

Anthony nodded. "We will be working together, so you need to know."

Zach nodded in agreement.

"My Greatcoat is special," Anthony began, standing up.

The coat hung heavy and silent, rain-dark wool mottled with stains that no storm could wash out. Its collar was turned up as if against a wind that only Anthony felt, and the battered buttons gleamed faintly, like tiny stars trapped in the fabric. The shoulders sagged with the weight of battles unseen, the lining frayed where fingers had reached too often into impossible pockets. It wasn't just worn—it was burdened, each thread humming with quiet menace, each fold hiding secrets. And when Anthony stepped near it, the air shifted, like the world itself leaned in to listen.

"It looks like a coat," Anthony said, his fingers brushing the edge of the collar. "But it isn't. It's a key. A bridge between what I think and what I need. Every pocket—" he tapped one of the deep, shadowed folds—"isn't just a pocket. It's a doorway to somewhere I've prepared. Somewhere I've hidden a blade, a shield, a tool, whatever the fight demands."

Zach swallowed, the weight of it settling in. "And where did it come from?"

Anthony's gaze grew distant, as if looking through time itself. "It was made during the last war my people fought, when we still stood guard over the borders of the worlds - crafted by hands that knew how to weave space and thread together. Only one was ever made. The rest... lost when our stronghold fell. Now it's mine to bear."

His voice softened, but the promise in it was hard as steel. "And mine to use, for the cause."

"Damn!" Zach was noticeably impressed.

"Our advantage," Anthony replied, "Because out there," he gestured broadly, encompassing the world beyond the barber-shop walls, "We will need every advantage we can get."

They were silent again, each man lost in thought. Zach broke the silence with a decisive nod.

"Okay. Let's get to work."

Anthony eyed him, a new respect dawning. "Alright, Chronicler. Let's get to work."

Chapter Twenty

The snake of fear curled up in Zach's stomach and tightened around his innards. From his free-running training, he knew that it could be a good thing, especially when preparing to hit an obstacle course. All that was required of him now was to shift his focus away from the task, allowing his autonomous systems to work under his unconscious radar while distracting himself.

The Headhunters Barbershop floor was perfect for that.

While Anthony prepared for tonight's 'Excursion', he sat in the barbershop with his fountain pen and Journal and watched.

The battle wasn't just being fought outside, but in here too. All the beauty stations were full, and so were the barber chairs. Zach wandered over to Puck and silently observed him as he stood on his stool and expertly completed the perfect fade with a snip, snip of his scissors. The young man in his chair looked relaxed, as if he was listening to invisible headphones. Puck reached around to his tool station, all of his shears, scissors and razors glistening, neatly arranged for easy access. Amongst the neatly ordered tools was a small, ancient-looking ceramic pot. Inside, it was a mound of black powder. Puck pinched a portion between his fingers and leaned towards the side of the young man's head, where scalp faded into his black curly hair and blew the dust on it. As if the skin was magnetised and the black dust was iron fillings, it stuck to his skin and formed a set of well-defined archaic symbols that stood out like the lettering was embossed on his flesh. Zach saw Puck close his eyes and briefly mouth a program whose script dissolved into the dust, leaving it to be absorbed by the young man's skin. The boy's eyes popped open, and Puck plucked a double-grip mirror from a hook beside his ceiling-to-floor mirror.

The young man smiled when he showed him his cut from every angle.

"Wicked," the young man gushed. "I love deh style, you even got the EA logo done. I wasn't sure you could do it."

The young man stood up from the barber chair as Puck brushed hair from his client's neck.

"Thought I was too old, didn't you?" Puck said, smiling.

"Not too old, Mr Puck, just not in the know."

The young man reached into his pocket, took out some notes, and tried to hand them to him. The little man blocked his advances.

"While we are here, nobody living on the Runnymede Estate will pay for any service we offer, you know that."

"I heard it, but I didn't want to take the piss. I appreciate it, Mr Puck," he said.

"My pleasure," Puck bowed. "One more thing, Rick." Puck nimbly jumped off the stool. The height difference between him and the young man was stark, but his gaze was unwavering as he stared up into the young man's face.

"Do me a favour?" Puck asked.

"Anything, Mr Puck," Ricky said.

"Leave that knife you keep in your gym bag at home tomorrow. Deal?"

Ricky looked surprised at first, then his eyes went up as he considered it.

He nodded.

"Deal."

Puck shook his hand.

The boy quietly left the shop.

ZACH STOOD BESIDE ZEE, HIS BREATH HELD AS SHE worked. Zee was one of the four female hairdressers on the day shift, along with Medusa, and their skills with braids, dreads, and afro hair were truly amazing. The client, a young woman with high cheekbones and tired eyes, sat silently beneath her touch, scrolling through her phone, completely unaware of the ritual unfolding above her crown. Zee's fingers worked in rhythm with something deeper and older.

Zee tightened the final knot, letting her hands glide over the braid as if sealing something unseen.

"There. It's done."

Zach leaned in slightly, eyes fixed on the design. "That's... incredible."

Zara turned, her eyes gleaming—not just with pride, but with something older, like she carried the memory of a thousand skilled hands before hers.

"It's programming code and protection."

"Protection?"

"Every twist, every parting, carries quantum intention. Vibration. See those spirals?" She pointed to the back of the client's head, where two intricate braids curved and locked into each other like celestial gears. "Those aren't just decorative. They're sigils - universal code that affects the energy of all living things. We've learned to affect reality through the manipulation of hair."

Zach studied the spirals, tracing their flow with his eyes. "And the stars at the crown?"

"They are part of the program language - Astro-Genetic. Particular constellations are tied to her birth. Andromeda, you humans call her A warrior queen. She will take on some of those characteristics."

"But what about the real threats, the things lurking out there?" Zach twisted his head to indicate outside.

Zee nodded her head.

"This isn't about vanity. This is practical protection. Most people don't even know they need it... until it's too late."

His gaze drifted back to the client, still smiling at her screen, unaware of the storm she'd just sidestepped.

"Demons?"

Zach felt stupid saying it.

"Darksiders."

Zee corrected him.

"As you know, some of these evil agents love being in physical form. These flesh and gore entities can destroy your physical body as well as your spirit. They will end you without a thought and feast on your flesh for good measure. But they are easier to manage and dispose of. My family and I are more concerned about the entities that slip in quietly. They feed off chaos. Stir up arguments. Break bonds. They move slowly. Patiently. You won't see them coming, but they're there. Always watching for a crack."

"How do the braids... help?"

"The fractal programs that are the designs of the braids disrupt the energy signature of the wearer. Depending on the Darksider, it can make the wearer less desirable to attack or absolutely repulsive. Your scalp is like the soil— it's an anchor where all the strands of hair act as broadcasting beacons. You humans may not know how to use your power, and so the Dark-siders hate to be reminded of what they are not."

Zach leaned back, letting it sink in. "What if she hadn't come in today?"

Zee's expression shifted.

"She would be collateral damage in this game."

Zach nodded slowly.

Zee continued.

"The Eternal Game has begun. Old things—ancient things —are stirring. If she hadn't come in at least, her flat might have been affected. Maybe not her directly. Maybe her brother. Her mother. Little things would start. Misunderstandings. Restless-ness. Shadows slipping into the corners of their home. And the worst ..."

She let the sentence die, and the silence said more than words.

"You can't save everyone, can you?"

"No, but we can do the best we can, knowing that the energy we weave into our braids never sleeps. It watches, protects. As long as she wears it, she's not a target. Not open."

Zach watched as the young woman stood up, thanked Zee and walked out into the falling light. Her braids shimmered faintly, pulsing with a power she couldn't see but would carry with her.

Zach retreated to his bean bag and watched Zee humming to herself. She reached for her tools, already preparing for the successive crown to be blessed. Zach closed his eyes and let the hum of clippers and whispered prayers fold over him like mist, his world tilting just a little more toward the strange and sacred.

Chapter Twenty-One

Zach put away the Journal in his leather satchel, just as Anthony appeared at the end of the Salon floor.

Here was a man prepared for war.

Anthony wore his black greatcoat that partially concealed his body armour, tactical pants, and boots.

Zach immediately had a new appreciation for what was happening here. Suppose Hortense hadn't broken the spell. He would have been going about his existence, not knowing that the misfortunes that befell him were not just a part of human existence but the residue from an evil that had infested every brick of the Runnymede Estate and would continue to do so if he didn't play his role. He would be cannon fodder in a game that was older than mankind itself.

That thought made him shudder.

Maybe this was where he should be, after all. On the front lines of a struggle, he could not intentionally sway but could influence in other ways. As dusk settled, a tense silence enveloped the Estate. Zach clutched his satchel, and with Anthony beside him, both men stepped into the evening's deceptive calm. The setting sun granted them passage, but he knew it was a treacherous freedom; they were now prey to the night's unseen horrors.

They exited Headhunters, the shop's warm glow retreating behind them, swallowed by the encroaching gloom. Anthony led the way, walking through the shopping parade, his eyes scanning the labyrinthine sprawl of the estate. Zach kept up with him, his heart racing and his senses heightened. Although he had walked these corridors and flyovers many times before, tonight was different.

Tonight, every step had a purpose.

They arrived at the beginning of a concrete gangway that led to one of the eight high-rises that comprised Runnymede's grey, brutalist architecture.

Anthony stopped and looked around before looking back at Zach.

"Where to, Chronicler?" Anthony asked in a husky voice.

Zach had asked that question previously. He had expected the Journal to answer in its mystical way, but Sylvester came to the rescue. He provided him with everything he required, and it was all written into the back of the Journal.

Anthony was staring at him.

"McGuinness House."

Zach mumbled the words, gripping his satchel to his waist and let his feet take him over the gangway, past Anthony and over to the stairs leading down into the looming entrance of Pioneer House.

The estate was a different beast at night; the shadows seemed to throb with intelligence, every flickering streetlight battling to keep the darkness at bay. The residents kept to themselves, unaware that they were in the midst of a mystical war zone. The few people out on the streets were coming home from work or the shops, milling about warily as they headed to their destinations.

They took the stairs together, forgoing the potential death trap of a lift to the piazza level. Both men walked shoulder to shoulder as they headed across the expanse of grey concrete that circled the bottom of the high-rise and led into the foyer of Pioneer House.

Zach pulled away from his minder without warning, making Anthony stop and keenly watch what he was doing.

Zach turned around while he walked away.

"I think I see somebody who needs my help."

Anthony's eyes glittered as he stood in shadow, a physical quirk that was still unnerving, making Zach shudder. His eyes never left him. Zach could feel his gaze boring into his back.

There was no need for him to worry.

"Mrs Monroe, your bags look heavy."

The older woman stopped, looked up at the young man approaching her in the gloom and recognised him immediately.

"Zach? It's been a long time. How's your father?"

Zach took the shopping bags from her before he answered. He hadn't seen her for over three months, and he had missed her. She had been one of maybe six older residents who had always been filled with optimism, despite being surrounded by gloom from the architecture and the sombre spirits of the people. And still, despite all that, she shone.

"Dad's doing well. He's on holiday in Jamaica."

"God bless him, he needed it," Mrs Monroe said, slowing down and then touching Zach on his shoulder to get his attention, staring up into his eyes. "I heard about Hortense when I got back from Barbados. Good woman. My condolences, son. I know you two were close."

"Thanks," Zach said. "We gave her a good send-off."

"I'm glad," said Mrs Monroe. "God rest her soul," she made a quick sign of the cross over her chest. Zach could see her eyes squinting under her fluffy hat. "Is your friend okay?" She asked, using her pouting lip to point out Anthony standing in the shadows.

His guardian's eyes twinkled in the darkness.

Those fucking eyes, he thought.

"That's my friend. He's a bit shy."

Mrs Monroe waved at him.

Zach could make out Anthony's bow from the neck.

The old lady smiled.

Zach had pushed open the swinging doors to the foyer of Pioneer House and shuffled inside. It smelled of dust, dampness, and a chlorine-based cleaning agent. He cleared his throat.

As he walked across towards the bank of lifts, he glimpsed some kids through a set of fire doors, lighting up. Their faces flashed into existence from the gloom as their lighters brought momentary fire.

Mrs Monroe pressed for the lift.

Zach looked at the older woman in her quilted thermal sports jacket, inches from the ground. It was so long, and she was so short.

"Your husband died years ago, and you've got family in the Caribbean. If you don't mind me asking, Ms Monroe, what are you still doing here?"

She gave another one of her warm smiles.

"My grandkids and to help you, of course."

Her answer startled him.

The lift pinged loudly on arrival and opened, wafting out that overpowering cleaning agent.

She stepped inside, oblivious to it, and made some hand gestures for Zach to hand over her shopping.

"You're a good lad," Mrs Monroe said. "Thanks for the help."

"You sure?" Zach asked, handing them over to her, a look of concern on his face.

"I'll be fine, but you must be doubly careful. The estate needs you," she said, lowering her voice until it almost resembled a whisper. "I passed some troublemakers beside the Garden seats on the plaza. They were up to no good."

The lift door juddered to a close, and Zach stood there wondering what Mrs Monroe knew of the war raging around her and the job he had to do.

"NEVER DO THAT AGAIN," ANTHONY GROWLED. "YOU MAKE a move like that, you let me know exactly what's on your mind?"

Zach was a step ahead of Anthony as they headed up a set of broad concrete stairs with a crusty metal rail guard splitting them in two. Beside it, a steep ramp for pushchairs and bicycles wound its way to the top. Ahead of Zach, the atmosphere above the plaza as he mounted the stairs was like a shimmering red welt on the hazy dark skin of the night.

That was the scene before him.

Behind him, he could feel a cold frustration emanating from the man who was supposed to protect him and to do his best to keep the gifted safe.

"You have no concept of the forces at play here and what lengths they will go to see you dead." Anthony continued. "I've been doing this for a very long time, and I've seen it all. If you don't respect what's happening here, you will die."

Zach slowed his breathing, the abrasive tone making him prickly and obstinate. He wasn't a team player; that much he knew about himself. It had nothing to do with teamwork as an idea; he knew he didn't work well with others. His mother would say he didn't like being told what to do, and she knew him better than most. They didn't have to be friends, but a week under Anthony's guidance would be difficult, and he had no choice. If both of them did what was required, even with clashing personalities, they may make it through with their sanity, their life or both.

"I trust your skills, but you have to do what you've got to do," Zach said. "I've got no playbook here, I'm in the dark, trusting my instincts. And if my instincts tell me to help a little old lady, then I'm going to help a little old lady. Do you understand me?"

Anthony grunted.

Zach took the monosyllable as agreement and pressed his point home.

"If you couldn't detect that Mrs Monroe wasn't a threat, then we're both fucked."

Anthony made a remark that came from behind him, and the unrecognisable phrase demanded clarification as far as Zach was concerned. If he was calling him a wanker in another language, he should have the balls to let him know.

The night was heavy with the kind of oppressive silence that only came in the darker corners of the city. The chill cut through the air, making Zach pull his collar higher as he followed Anthony towards McGuinness House. His body hummed with anxiety, something beneath the surface telling him that tonight wasn't going to go as planned. Anthony's gait was slower, more deliberate, as if he, too, could sense the shift in the atmosphere.

They turned the corner, the rusted metal of a forgotten fire escape looming overhead, its shadow stretching across the damp pavement like skeletal fingers. That's when Zach saw him.

A figure stood half-hidden in the narrow alley, leaning against the wall with the casual grace of someone completely at ease in his surroundings. His silhouette was unnerving—tall, angular, with dark curling horns that twisted skyward like a nightmare pulled from some ancient myth. The red glow of a cigarette brightened as the figure took a drag, the ember momentarily lighting up his pale, tattooed face. His sharp cheekbones were accentuated by the ancient glyphs marking his skin that concealed something much older and much darker underneath.

"Stop!" Anthony said in a low voice, his hand already reaching into the inside of his jacket.

Zach froze, his pulse quickening as his eyes darted to Anthony, who was on edge. His usual calm was replaced with an alert tension. His minder had flicked his great coat open and reached inside its folds. Zach blinked.

It was like he was peering into an abyss. The darkness was all-consuming, like a universe within a universe. He couldn't pull his eyes away from it until Anthony's coat closed with his hand under it.

The figure in the shadows chuckled, a sound that resonated with a mocking familiarity. He stepped forward, the dim street-light revealing him fully. His pinstriped suit clung to his slender frame, cut too well for anyone who roamed the back alleys of this cursed place. Thick, curled ram's horns rooted into his forehead, sweeping up and back from a bald head. His sharp eyes fixed lazily on Anthony.

"Anthony." The voice was smooth, rolling off his tongue like silk, but every syllable dripped with disdain. He exhaled a long puff of smoke, letting it curl lazily into the night air. "You look tired, old friend."

Anthony's eyes narrowed. His hand had not left the inside of his great coat since he recognised the man's presence.

"B!" The name was spoken with venom.

Mr. B smiled, revealing too-sharp teeth that glinted like

razors. He took another drag of his cigarette and flicked the ashes to the ground, completely unbothered by the possible confrontation.

"Don't you trust me?" Beelzebub said, nodding toward Anthony. "Surely, you know, nothing you can conjure from your coat will have the power against me." He tilted his head slightly, a gesture that somehow managed to exude both charm and menace. "Tell me, Anthony. Aren't you tired yet? You've been at this game so long... protecting, guarding, chasing this illusion. Sit back, let the forces of chaos reign supreme."

"That's not going to happen," Anthony replied through gritted teeth. His voice was steady, but the undercurrent of hatred was palpable. "We will fight to the last man to maintain the balance despite what you and your treacherous mistress are trying to destroy."

Mr. B arched an eyebrow, clearly amused by Anthony's defiance. He glanced at Zach, who had been standing silent, trying his best to melt into the background, away from the hellish creature's attention. Mr. B's gaze lingered on him, and for a moment, Zach thought he saw something flicker in those black eyes—interest, curiosity, or maybe hunger. It sent a shiver down his spine.

"Ah, the new recruit," Mr. B mused, his tone dripping with condescension. "Not even broken in yet, I see." He waved a hand dismissively, his attention already returning to Anthony. "You always did have a weakness for the lost souls, didn't you? But you can't save everyone, Anthony. Hell, you can't save anyone. Not from me."

Zach clenched his fists, willing himself not to run. He could feel the weight of Mr. B's presence, a suffocating pressure that made his legs feel like they might buckle. But he didn't move. Not yet.

Anthony, however, stood his ground, his hand still in the

stygian darkness of the inside of his great coat. "You may be right, but I will save who I can, when I can. Which is more than you'll ever understand."

The two stood there, locked in a battle of wills, tension coiling between them like a wire stretched too tight. The wind howled softly, carrying with it the distant hum of the city beyond the estate's walls, oblivious to the monsters that moved in its underbelly.

Mr. B's grin widened, and for a moment, his entire face seemed to distort, his features warping into something far less human. "You're as delusional as ever," he said with a mocking shake of his head. "But don't worry. You'll get your chance to play hero. Soon. Very soon."

He took one final drag from his cigarette, letting the smoke spill out slowly through his sharp teeth before flicking the butt to the ground. It sizzled for a moment on the wet pavement.

"Until next time, Anthony." He smiled, all charm and malice. "I'll be seeing you real soon."

Anthony didn't move, didn't even blink, as Mr. B melted back into the shadows, becoming one with the night once more. Only when the oppressive weight of his presence was gone did he remove his hand from his coat.

Zach released the breath he hadn't realised he was holding. "Who the fuck was that?"

"Trouble," Anthony replied darkly, his eyes still fixed on the spot where Mr. B had vanished. He turned sharply, his posture rigid as he started towards McGuinness House. "And he's not done with us yet."

Chapter Twenty-Two

"No!" Zach moaned, swallowing hard, shaking his head, his legs unwilling to take him forward. His short-lived show of conviction brought both men to an abrupt stop, shoulder to shoulder, looking out at the other end of the piazza and the huge blazing bonfire.

Zach clapped his hands over his nose and mouth.

Burning meat.

Burning human flesh.

A pyre.

Something thrashing inside the white-hot interior caught his eye, then it was gone.

A shudder racked his spine, making his body reverberate like a bell.

He could make out three figures with metal pokers tending to the flames as if it were a weekend barbecue, oblivious to the smell. Dozens of pieces of wooden furniture had been stacked high. The shrubbery that had grown there like a forgotten horticultural feature had surely been incinerated to ash. Helping to fuel a conflagration that was crackling and spitting embers into the night sky. Zach could feel the radiated heat making his forehead prickle. A tear trickled from one eye down his cheek, and only then did he realise he was riveted to the spot. Anthony had already begun walking towards the fire and had issued instructions, but Anthony's audio was drowned out by the panic-filled dialogue in Zach's head.

"Did you hear what I said?" Anthony's voice was raised. "Follow close behind me."

Snapping out of his stupor, Zach gave a stiff nod and forced his trembling feet to move. Each step brought them closer to the fire, where the heat rolled out in heavy waves and the stench thickened, clawing at the back of his throat. It was more than smoke—it was the acrid, oily reek of burning flesh and something far worse: fear cooked into the air.

Zach stopped short, refusing to go any further. He turned away from the bonfire, doubling over with his hands braced against his knees, his breath coming shallow and fast. His stomach twisted, but nothing came up. The heat still licked at his back, a cruel reminder of what waited behind him.

Anthony glanced over his shoulder. He saw Zach, saw the tremor in his frame, and said nothing. He understood. He didn't need to speak to know that Zach had reached his limit, for now.

A few steps more, and Anthony could see clearly what the fire was feeding on. The wooden frames—kindling for something darker—had collapsed into glowing piles of ash. But the bodies hadn't. They lingered in the flames, stubborn and terrible. A blackened arm jutted from the inferno, fingers curled like claws, frozen in a moment between escape and surrender. Anthony couldn't tell whether it was reaching out for mercy or fixed that way in death.

Deeper in, half-consumed by fire, a face stared out. Or what was left of one. Skin charred and cracked like scorched parchment, blistered craters where cheeks once held warmth. No eyes. Just sockets. A mouth stretched open in a final scream, soundless and eternal. It looked right at him, then vanished, swallowed by the flames.

Anthony lowered his head and murmured something only the dead could hear. Then he stepped backwards, the fire's heat clinging to him like a second skin, and returned to where Zach stood.

Zach was upright now, hands shoved deep into his jacket pockets, his face slack and still. He stared at the flames, but not *at* them—his gaze drifted somewhere beyond, through the fire and past it, like he was trying to see what lay on the other side.

Anthony stepped beside him. Said nothing. Just stood there in silence, shoulder to shoulder, both of them caught in the quiet horror of what they'd found.

Zach was the first to break the silence.

"What did you see?"

Anthony took his time and considered the simple question.

"I saw the first shots across your bows, and it will get worse. They are saying that they will do whatever it takes and have no qualms about ending innocent human life if it gets them to their objective. That is what I saw."

Zach shook his head in a way that said he understood. He took one last look and turned away to the looming tower of McGuinness House. He pointed towards it.

"Tenth floor, flat 145, a boy named Nathaniel Lane."

Anthony nodded and took the lead.

Chapter Twenty-Three

"Mr Sylvester is so kind to send you around Zach, but I don't think there's a lot you can do," Mrs Lane said, handing Zach a cup of mint tea. The Chronicler accepted it with a smile, his hand trembling slightly and leaned back into the comfy sofa. The horror of the bonfire was seared into his memory, but being here helped to calm the uncontrollable quakes rippling through his body from the shock.

"Are you sure you don't want something to drink, Anthony?" She asked Anthony again.

He smiled patiently.

"No thanks, Mrs Lane, I'm fine."

Anthony was content with his new friend. Ever since they had been invited into Mrs Lane's Front room and sat down, the black and white Albanian cat had locked eyes with the dark-skinned stranger and leapt on his lap, where it retired for the evening. Its ears were pricked up listening to the human's conversation while his new friend rubbed him under his chin.

"Alphonso has taken a shine to you, Anthony?" she said,

sounding surprised." He's not usually the social kind, but he really loves you."

"I have a thing for animals, Mrs Lane," Anthony said.

She nodded.

"I can see, and please call me Elena," she said and sat in a single chair in front of them, crossing her legs at the ankles and clasping her hands on her lap. Zach watched how she wound and knitted her fingers together, then undid them to start again. All her nervous energy was focused on her hands. She was handling the pressure well, but for how long?

Elena was not only attractive but also fashionable, and Zach was taken aback. She had an easygoing smile, and even amidst the shit she was going through, her surface attitude seemed calm. She looked like a model for an environmentally friendly soap powder advert with cascading brown hair over her shoulders, wearing fitted jeans and a slinky, revealing top.

What the fuck was she doing here?

A naive part of his brain screamed the question, but he knew the answer to that.

The answer was what kept every resident of the Runnymede Estate here.

The program.

Zach was glad he was here. Anything that could shield him from the awful realities of the estate was welcome. The two-bedroom flat was cosy and well furnished. Nothing about it was pretentious; everything here had history and was lovingly cared for.

Maybe that's why they both left their shoes in the hallway.

Zach leaned forward.

"Mr Sylvester thought we could talk to the PayDay Loan representatives when they come knocking again. I think we may be able to resolve the situation tonight."

"I've never actually seen anybody," Elena said. "Just

endless banging on the door." Her eyes flitted towards the front door. "I've never answered it once. It sometimes goes on for minutes."

"Has your husband seen anything?" Anthony asked.

"Robert works nights, so he gets my hysterical messages but only sees the end result when he comes home."

"End result?" Zach asked.

"Splintered wood, fist impressions from someone strong and angry banging on the door. And an awful smell."

"They left you a surprise?" Anthony asked.

"All over the door and on the welcome mat," Elena said, the stress of it all showing in her voice. "I've had to keep a bucket of bleach and borax to kill the smell."

"Can I ask something?" Zach said.

"Of course, "Elena nodded.

"What makes you think it's the PayDay Loan people?"

"Nathaniel, my son," she said.

Your son? Zach was about to ask, but his train of thought was dramatically interrupted. The Journal hijacked his nervous system and uploaded a file to his mind's eye.

Nathaniel Lane – The Philosopher's Seed

Gift: Cognitive Synthesis

Nathaniel, age seven, sees the hidden harmony between worldviews. Where adults see contradiction—between African Metaphysical systems, Asian philosophies, European ethics— Nathaniel sees common threads. He doesn't preach. He draws chalk diagrams on walls, asks gentle questions that unpick assumptions, and lets truth emerge where it's most needed.

Impact: The beginnings of a unified human ethic. If his gift ripples outward, it could inspire a world no longer divided by false borders of thought.

"How is Nathaniel?" Zach asked.

"Asleep," Elena smiled. "He could sleep through a storm."

"A good skill to have," Anthony said. "Now, so I'm clear, you owe these snakes nothing."

She nodded.

"I was in arrears before Mr Sylvester came on the estate. I borrowed the money from Mr Hutchinson - the local Payday Loan Provider, but it was becoming hard to pay him after a while, and he started sending people around," she paused, the edges of her lips turned down. "I brought Nathaniel for a free haircut, and Mr Sylvester gave me the money to pay off the loan. I cleared my outstanding amount, and things seemed to get worse."

Zach looked over to Anthony.

"What time does your knocker come calling usually?" Anthony asked.

"I can set my watch to it. Twenty-one thirty and never when my husband is here."

"Twenty-one minutes from now," Anthony said without hesitation. "Zach and I will have a word with your caller. Until then, can I bother you for a glass of cold water and a dish of milk for Alphonso?"

THE FRONT DOOR RATTLED AS WHOEVER STARTED THEIR ritual of hammering began without the slightest concern for whoever the racket disturbed. It was like an industrial trip-hammer had been placed outside with a consistent and powerful pounding action driven by steam or something else entirely.

Zach stood in the protective shadow of Anthony, who stood stock still behind the door, his hand close to the handle as if he had been frozen in place. His great coat had been flung open, and Zach looked briefly into the void, seeing Anthony's hand disappear into the inky blackness. They had sent Elena to her bedroom and locked Alphonso in the front room.

They had both waited in the tiny hallway for about five minutes. All kinds of crazy thoughts were rifling through his head in the quiet, and soon after a couple of minutes or so, his frenetic mind and pounding heart steadied. Even when the pounding began, he still maintained a semblance of calm as he deep-breathed, but who was he fooling? Zach was wired, and it felt great.

"When I open the door," Anthony said, his voice harsh and gravelly. "Count to fifty before you attempt to step through onto the landing. You got me?" He swivelled his neck around to eye Zach.

"I got you," Zach said.

IF HIS SENSES WEREN'T SO SHARP FROM THE RUSH OF adrenaline, Zach could have easily missed what happened next. But he saw it all.

Anthony pulled the door open with his left hand, releasing it to continue its arc from its own momentum. His right hand was already in the folds of his jacket, and three vicious-looking knives came out between his fingers with the blurred movement of his hand. He disappeared out of eyeshot, and that's when the piercing scream ran a cold finger down Zach's spine. He couldn't help himself.

Zach stepped back.

Even though he knew he was safe where he stood in the hallway, that inhuman scream made him question his safety anywhere.

He took another step back.

The sound of struggle drifted through the open door from the concrete corridor outside. The slap of flesh hitting concrete, the scrapping of claws or talons struggling for purchase on it and the rapid.

Pop! Pop!

The sounds were like gunshots. Zach could see the light show that accompanied the sounds of the miniature explosions reflecting off the dull surfaces in the darkness outside and bending into the hall where he stood.

What the fuck was happening?

Anthony had said count to fifty, but he had maybe got to nine. His panic-soaked perception was useless as a means of judging duration; he could have been here for twenty seconds or two minutes.

Who knew?

Whatever it was, he needed to be through the door, doing God knows what to help or be a bystander and 'Chronicle'. He would think about that after he'd bullied his nervous system into taking him through the door and outside to the corridor. Seconds merged into tens of seconds, and he found himself two steps outside the door, his Chronicler awareness absorbing what was happening.

The smell hit him first.

The rank stench of uric acid and sulfur, the by-product of something whose diet was alien and nasty.

What next came into his awareness was Anthony in his true element and the creature he had trapped.

Zach wasn't new to monsters.

How could he think that and keep a straight face?

It was, unfortunately, true.

The vermin that had oozed their way through the cracks between the hellish reality that used the estate as its thoroughfare was nothing in comparison to this. Anthony had his knee in what could be its throat; the knives he had pulled out of his multidimensional jacket were now glowing with an otherworldly bluish hue, skewering the creature through its flesh and anchoring four of its five legs into the concrete. It was thrashing wildly, its two tails thumping the ground indignantly, and its snout caged. Zach thought that would stop it from waking up the neighbours until he saw a mouth stuffed full of sharp jagged teeth brimming from a muscular jaw. The chronicler agreed that a mouth cage was the best option.

"You decided to join me?" Anthony quipped.

Zach wondered if this was the same sullen and taciturn warrior he had met days before.

"I thought you might need some help."

Anthony laughed.

Now this was becoming surreal.

"Do I look like I need help?" He grinned.

"I guess not," Zach said, keeping his distance and controlling his disgust as a foul smell exuded from the thrashing creature.

"This is a Crognot, and it was banging on the door and shitting on Elena's welcome mat. If she had opened up to look, it would have entered and ripped the whole family apart."

Zach swallowed, and it seemed to help settle his stomach.

"Will they send another?"

"No," Anthony said, reaching into his spooky jacket and taking out what looked like a jagged 3D snowflake the size of a golf ball. He slapped it on the skin of the creature, and it reacted by bucking in place and making grunting, growling sounds. In one fluid movement, Anthony stood up and moved back two paces.

"Shield your eyes," he said to Zach.

The Chronicler lowered his head.

He knew something was about to happen, but the bright incandescent flash that turned night to day and a sound like

166

sizzling bacon without the mouth-watering smell still caught him by surprise.

He looked up at the creature and watched as its body began to disassociate into a cloud of swirling hot embers. It seemed as if it never existed except for a sooty outline on the grey concrete. And he wondered if it had ever existed.

Anthony walked back over to where the body had been pinned and retrieved his knives.

"Do you want to give Elena the good news?" he said.

Zach thought about it.

"Yeah, I'll tell her."

And there was that unnerving smile again from Anthony.

"Just don't mention the Crognot."

Chapter Twenty-Four

Zach didn't think he could sleep. His thoughts were pinging, a mile a minute in his skull, and his body was thrumming with excess energy.

This was nuts.

He should be an exhausted heap on the floor, but he was so wired that he came up with an explanation for it as soon as Anthony dropped him off at the flat. He had taken a shower and then prepared himself one of his famous ham and cheese sandwich specials and a cup of hot chocolate. He sent a text message to his old man in Jamaica before he retired to his bedroom. He was cross-legged on his messy bed, the Journal in front of him and his thoughts on the contradiction of being energised after everything he'd been through tonight.

He polished off his sandwich and was thinking of making another one.

That was something else he noticed.

His appetite had grown, and not just for food. He thought of Maya, sexy, half-naked and pissed he hadn't called her yet.

Damn, he wished he was between those thighs, but he had a job to do.

Zach looked at his Journal nestled beside his leg and stroked the leather cover. It kissed his fingertips with a gentle discharge of static electricity.

"You're doing all this, aren't you?"

He picked it up, undid the clasp and opened it. The Journal's pages seemed to murmur as they came apart, and as soon as he cast his eyes on the pages, the alien script blurred, then formed into handwriting that he could understand. He wished his cursive was as neat and flamboyant as the finished writing on the pages, but it wasn't. He was relieved that his chicken scratch had been converted to this elegant calligraphy, especially if it was to be seen by others.

He didn't want to leave a bad impression.

Zach turned the pages to his last entry and skimmed the incident with the Crognot. His storytelling skills weren't bad, but for the life of him, he couldn't remember exactly what he had written and how he knew the things he knew. On the last written page, there was a sketch of the Crognot and a list of its vital statistics, including ways to repel or kill it.

Not the kind of knowledge he had hidden away in his subconscious. The Journal was adding relevant details, information that he was unaware of. Zach guessed it was able to absorb information through him, wherever he was, from the people talking, documents, books, and maybe even psychically. It would make it an invaluable tool to whoever had access to it when they needed the information the most. Although the journal wasn't complete, could he use the information that was already on the journal's pages?

Time will tell.

All he knew - and this was anecdotal evidence but the

Journal was improving his stamina, his appetites and his mental clarity.

Maya would appreciate that.

He placed the Journal in its place on his night table, grabbed his laptop and fired up Zoom. In moments, he was looking at his girlfriend, arms folded, glaring at him in a silken nightgown that had ridden down her right shoulder, showing one delightful breast that, luckily for him, she didn't notice was exposed. Zach swallowed, knowing the signs and fully aware he needed to get ahead of this before they wasted time bickering.

"I miss you," Zach said, the words coming out uncharacteristically smooth and genuinely sincere.

Damn!

He had caught himself off guard.

Maya melted, and Zach glanced over at the Journal and grinned.

Chapter Twenty-Five

The next day, Zach arrived at Headhunters just before lunch. Medusa had picked him up from home at Palladin House. He was forbidden to walk the estate alone, and Anthony wouldn't be awake until the sun went down. So the statuesque Medusa had babysitting duties thrust upon her. He was never made to feel like an inconvenience, though; he would even go as far as to say she enjoyed being around him. With her characteristic strong hug, a kiss on the lips, and a twinkle in her beautiful, golden-brown eyes, they walked and talked. Zach tried not to look over at the area where last night's bonfire was scorched into his memory, but he couldn't help himself. The route they took back to Headhunters did not go anywhere near it, but just the proximity alone made the memories reignite. Medusa had detected his furtive looks and immediately understood how he must be feeling. She congratulated him on last night's mission with another kiss. He tried to say that his involvement was minimal, but she wouldn't have it. Medusa wanted to hear the details over coffee during her break time.

They arrived at a busy shop. She opened the doors for him, and Zach slipped into the barbershop, allowing Medusa to prepare for her next client.

"Well done, brother!" Came a congratulations from Puck in the distance, and then came a boisterous round of applause.

Zach nodded, grinning sheepishly. After their adulation died down, they all bowed in unison. He could feel the respect radiate from them, and it made his spine tingle. Zach wondered if the clients in the chairs knew what was going on. Whether they did or not, they were basking in the show of admiration.

He touched his heart and returned the bow.

That was not the end of it.

Zach had a feeling that he had better get used to this kind of attention. Whether he was used to it or not, it would be given.

He was sure of that.

He couldn't help the goofy smile that appeared on his face as he wandered over to the space he called his own. Zach had taken over a little alcove that served as his observation point, where he would sit and watch, allowing the Journal to translate what he saw into detailed text that would be downloaded onto the page through his hand.

The uncomfortable stool and a small table had been removed.

There was a massive beanbag, two small tables on either side, with burning aromatic candles that smelled of vanilla, and a foldable table he could adjust to a suitable height to put the Journal. Zach made himself comfortable and let out a sigh as the giant beanbag absorbed him. He felt the smiling eyes watching him as he made his space his own. It didn't take him long to remove the journal from his satchel and begin his observation. It was interesting how his body reacted to the Journal's prompting. First, it came as a sense of mild yearning and eventually a sense of passionate interest, such that he could watch paint dry without being paid or bribed. It felt like a genuine need to know, but he knew the Journal had manufactured it.

While the Journal had found something from the minutiae of the Barbershop's daily functions, Zach glanced at the three robot vacuum cleaners that worked in the background to keep the floor spotless and free from hair. Zach was wondering why he felt so interested in what these disk-shaped AI units were doing when one of the barbers that Zach hadn't spoken to but acknowledged many times came over with a tray of steaming hot chocolate and a small plate of sultana cookies.

"Thanks, man," Zach said.

"Compliments of the boss." The barber looked over to Sylvester's space, which was empty. Two clients sat waiting.

His attention came back to the cleanbots.

Zach stood up with hot chocolate in one hand and a cookie between his teeth and decided to follow them. Although these little workers had blended into the background of day-to-day operation, he knew they must have a docking port to empty their load and to charge up; he'd just never thought about it. Now he was compelled to look at them; he didn't know why.

The Journal led the way, manipulating his nervous system for the benefit of the bigger task.

Zach's focus was on the little cleanbot that had completed its circuit and was about to recharge. The robot zipped through foot traffic, clinging to the walls, and its sensors picked up any obstacles that would impact its journey for a recharge. Trying to follow it along the length of the forward-facing portion of the barbershop was proving difficult. It was a busy afternoon, and there were staff and clients everywhere. The robot's memory functions had a major advantage over Zach's brain cells as it calculated its optimal route by disap-pearing out of the shop into the back-of-house through a literal hole in the wall. Zach hesitated, knowing he had access to the area that played Tetris with his senses. He was never a weed smoker in High School, but he let a girl he fancied coerce him into smoking a ganja spliff laced with LSD - called Beast on the Street. He only took two pulls, but that was enough for an out-of-body experience, disorientation, a brain filled with cotton wool and a severe case of the munchies. Beyond that door, explained by Sylvester, were confined bubbles of time and relative dimensions in space that reminded Zach of his misadventures in High School. He had always been escorted into this area, but the Journal was insisting he take the leap.

"Fuck it!" He sighed and turned the knob, felt the warm tingle on his palm on the door and pushed his way in. He had his eyes closed when he stepped inside and pulled the door behind him with a touch alone. He didn't know if it was his imagination, and he hadn't felt it the first time he had come through here, but for a second, he felt his essence fragment like his atoms wanting to go in separate directions, but at the last minute, he decided against it.

Feeling for his balls first, his ass next, then his knees, he opened his eyes and saw the cleanbot scurrying merrily down a passageway that extended as far as the eye could see. Without thought, squashing his fear of being lost in here for eternity, never to be found, he hurriedly followed. The smart thing would have been to observe his surroundings so he could retrace his steps, but something told him that would be no good. So instead, he kept his eyes on the disk-shaped robot as it trundled along to points unknown. Eventually, it slowed down, spun on its own axis as if it was getting its bearings and slid smoothly into a recess in the wall. Not far from it was a doorway for humans or anything looking like a human. Zach guessed that behind the door would be the docking bay for the bots. He stood looking at the door with no markings, just a number, and he knocked.

No answer.

He knocked again.

This time, he heard a muffled response from behind the door. The voice got louder as it approached from the inside, and he was still unable to make out what was being said until it was cracked open.

"Come in, come in," a shrill female voice said. "The Chronicler, what an honour, come in."

The older woman who stared back at him looked like she had just hopped off a lightning bolt. Her white afro stood on end, neat around her temples but chaotic further atop. Her face was smooth, and her eyes were bright and wide like owls. But there was something about her presence that radiated wisdom, age and joy.

Or maybe it was her white lab coat.

She shot out her hand.

"I'm Dr Carmalita, everyone calls me Dr Karma."

Zach took it, expecting an electric shock from her energy, but instead, the hand pump was warm and firm. He wondered if he would ever be as vibrant as the doctor in his advanced years.

"Pleased to meet you, doctor. I hope I'm not disturbing you."

"No, no, no," she said with enthusiasm. "You're welcome anytime. If you can risk your life for these poor people, then I can give you whatever you need."

The doctor waved Zach to a chair, and he stepped into what he would call a laboratory, although he wasn't a hundred per cent sure that was its function. It was hinting at some of the things you would see in a lab, but he wasn't sure. A weird-looking computer monitor, something that looked like a microscope, a robotic arm, machines whose function he couldn't even guess at and three docking bays for the cleanbots. For some reason, he couldn't get his head around the dimensions of the room.

"You followed Sigma 1 down here, didn't you?"

"Yeah, I did," Zach said. "The Journal seemed to think there is something it can learn here. Something you can show me."

"Amazing! Amazing!" Dr Karma said.

One adjective was not enough to describe the doctor's excitement; it required at least two of the same.

"I envy you," the doctor said. "Envy! For millennia, we've had access to the Journal, but we've never been allowed to study it. And here you are, the Chronicler, connected to it, as if it were nothing." She clapped her hands together.

Only when the doctor clapped her hands together did Zach understand why he was here. Well, at least he thought so. He didn't reveal his discovery; he sat and opened the journal, resting it in a clear space on one of the doctor's workbenches.

"So tell me, doc, what do you do here?"

"I thought you'd never ask," Dr Karma exclaimed, beaming. "This is important work."

"We are talking about the same thing, right?" Zach answered his own query. "The hairs that the Cleanbots are collecting on the Barbershop floor."

"Yes! Yes! Yes!" Dr Karma said.

Zach looked at her blankly.

The doctor smiled, being familiar with that look.

"Most people see hair as merely a biological afterthought, a mere evolutionary decoration," Dr. Karma began, her voice a blend of warmth and gravity. "But in reality, it's a sophisticated quantum network, an antenna of sorts, entangled with the very fabric of the universe."

She leaned closer, her voice dropping to a conspiratorial whisper. "All hair has this property, but particularly kinky hair," she continued, "This has a unique structure, a spiral coil that acts as a powerful conduit for quantum energies. These aren't just dead cells, Zach. They are teeming with life, vibrating with energies unseen."

Zach nodded, feeling the build-up of tingling energy at the back of his head as the Journal used him as a conduit, a sponge for knowledge, absorbing her every word below his level of awareness.

"So, through our hair we can communicate with the universe?"

"Exactly," Dr. Karma replied, her eyes lighting up. "Each strand can transmit and receive signals, connecting us to the cosmos in ways we're just beginning to understand. Ancient cultures across the multiverse were aware of this. Take Samson from the Bible, for instance. His hair was the source of his strength, a direct link to divine power. Or consider the Rastafari, who regard their dreadlocks as a symbol of their connection to Jah, to the universe."

She walked over to what looked like a microscope, beckoning Zach to follow. "This is where it gets interesting," she said. Beside the piece of equipment were about fifteen metal trays stacked on top of each other, with crystal slides in racks of about ten. Dr Karma took out a slide from one of the racks.

"This is a hair sample from yesterday," she said, placing it under the lens. "When hair is cut and no longer part of the quantum network, it retains psychic energy. That's why I collect it. Analysing these strands tells us not just about individual health or psychic state, but about the influences at play."

"Negative energies, you mean?" Zach asked, squinting into the microscope.

"Precisely. Hair can absorb negative energies as well. It's

like a record of everything you've experienced, everything you've been exposed to," she explained, her tone serious. "If I detect high levels of negative energy, it indicates manipulation by malevolent forces. It's a way to see how widespread their influence is."

"How are we doing?" Zach asked.

"Not good," she said. "The Darksiders are throwing their entire psychic arsenal at us, and we are fighting back. The residents of Runnymede estate are victims of this conflict, and we cannot and will not leave them to suffer this alone."

Zach paused and thought for a moment.

"I get it! That's why it's important to get as many of the residents through our doors. You're trying to inoculate them from the dark shit being spread on the estate."

"You got it! Got it!" Dr. Karma said, her energy levels rising again. "Do you see why my work is so crucial? What can be measured can be improved. Tracking the data can help my brothers on the Barbershop floor to gauge their coding and programs to balance the effect of the darkside algorithms."

Zach looked down at Sigma1 neatly ensconced in its charging bay, blinking merrily.

"And they bring you your samples for analysis."

The doctor bowed and curtsied.

Zach shook his head in amusement.

He liked her.

"Can I show you something?" The doctor said.

"Definitely," Zach could feel the enthusiasm for knowledge being generated by the Journal and siphoning its way through him. He didn't mind; this was fascinating.

Dr Karma led the way through a small maze of equipment desks, ducking from dangling, curled wires and extendable light fittings until she came to a bank of oddly shaped monitors that had been set in the corner of a room that really shouldn't have corners. That kind of rational world thinking in the irrational world of the Barbershop was a slippery slope, so he reigned in that part of his mind. He leaned on the desk that framed images of eight different aspects of the Barbershop floor. The images didn't give a clear impression of the shop and looked like a dialled-down heatmap. An overlapping colour palette, mainly consisting of orange, red, purple, and blue, made up the digital sketch. You could make out the furniture and distinguish the architectural flourishes that made the place unique, but fine details were much harder to see.

Dr Karma pointed to a screen that showed the front door leading into the Barbershop.

"Have you ever heard of what your people call Kirlian Photography?"

"No, I haven't," Zach said.

"My records say it was discovered by Semyon Kirlian and his wife, Valentina. They stumbled upon a diagnostic tool that revealed the human aura and, if properly applied, could revolutionise human health, but like many discoveries that weren't fully understood, it was discounted. It's another tool we have mastered that allows us to analyse our clients as they come in for appointments."

Just then, the door opens and a man and a little boy walk in. The camera follows them. The little boy's aura is bursting with colours and extends from the child like an energetic halo. The monitor produces a string of data beside the image of the boy.

Dr Karma taps the screen with her finger.

"Little man here is in good health across the physical and psychic spectrums. Not so much for his guardian."

The older man's aura was like a thick grey rain cloud with sporadic bursts of colour. The edges of his aura were tinged with green. A chain of data appeared beside his image, making the doctor shake her head.

"He doesn't know it, but he's been siphoning his life force into his little boy's own," she paused, her eyes squinting with thought. "He needs our help, and we will do our best to protect him. Four more nights before we will know if all of this made a difference."

"Four more nights," Zach repeated, an unexpected shiver puckering his skin as someone had walked over his grave.

Chapter Twenty-Six

Dr Karma had been kind enough to lead Zach to a chill Spot within labyrinthian pockets of reality that made up the Headhunter's back-of-house. This particular zone was a large, comfortable and functional room. If he were going to be trapped anywhere, this would be as good a place as any. Flat-screen TV, huge and comfy sofas, work tables, snack dispensers, and a multi-gym. He couldn't contain the urge to download what he had learned from the doctor, so he sat back and let the Journal work through him. Time flies when you're having fun, they say, and Zach was having fun. Having finished working with the Journal, he sweated in the multigym, showered, and was fed. It was dusk, according to the clock on the wall. His watch was stuck in the early afternoon.

He decided to see if Anthony was up and let him know he was ready to go. He wasn't going to venture out into the perpetual corridors without help, so he called for it.

He felt like one of those aristocrats from the period dramas, ringing their bell for a servant to come running. In this case, it was like an electronic doorbell beside the double doors that didn't make a sound when you pressed it. Within five minutes, his guide's smiling face was pushing the door open.

Now that was service.

"What can I do for you, Chronicler?" He asked. The young man, with curly brown hair and tanned skin, wore a T-shirt and jeans and had a skateboard under his arm. He seemed to be the kind of brother who didn't have a care in the world, even if it was collapsing around him.

Which it was.

"All's good," Zach said. "Can you take me to Anthony's quarters?"

"Sure," his guide said and pushed the articulated doors open towards the corridor, dropped his skateboard on its wheels, and hopped on.

Zach watched as his guide led the way. Sometimes he propelled himself beyond where he could see him, or sometimes looping up from behind and cruising shoulder to shoulder. The corridors shifted in look and length, but the visual parallax did not affect his guide in the least, and in moments, he stood outside an enclosure with a door that Zach recognised.

"Just holla if you need me," his guide said and hurtled away.

Zach was about to walk up to the door and knock, but it pushed itself open as he approached. Stepping back, a statuesque, naked, dark-skinned woman breezed past him. In no rush, she looked over her perfect shoulders, flawless skin and ample derriere.

"Oh, hello," she said, smiling. "Anthony's inside."

Zach nodded, flushing with unnecessary embarrassment.

It may not have been gentlemanly, but he watched the confident sway of her broad hips, the jiggle of her ass and marvelled at her amazing hourglass shape, right up to her disappearance in the fluxing perspective of the corridor. He was forced to conclude that, extra-dimensional beings they may be, but they had acquired the human form to a 'T' and the better habits of humankind, too.

Zach didn't bother knocking this time and walked in.

Anthony sat on the edge of the bed, a white sheet wrapped around his waist, his elbow propped on his thigh with a book in his hand. The warrior had a smile on his face, his lips moved enunciating the words silently, and he obviously enjoyed what he was reading. The scars of his battles were stitched into the dark skin of his chest and back. He looked up, knowing Zach was in the room, and closed the book.

"Zach!" He sounded surprised. "You're early?"

"Just thought we could get going sooner than later," Zach said.

"Don't worry, they'll be waiting for us, no matter when we go out. But I'm glad you're here, there's something you need to see." He stood, and the sheet around his waist fell to the floor.

Zach could only admire in silence Anthony's significant 'attributes' swinging pendulously between his legs.

ANTHONY HAD SHOWERED AND DRESSED QUICKLY, LEAVING his Great coat, the one Zach was afraid to mess with, especially knowing what those bottomless pits of space its pockets contained. It was apparent that they would swing back to his quarters after whatever it was he needed to see. They walked down one of the few corridors with an end and a neat miniature piazza. In its centre was a set of heavy oak doors with a sophisti-cated lock mechanism. Anthony approached it, then leaned in to present his eye to an aperture. After a 'click!' he stepped back and waited for an orchestra of retracting metal to end. He swung the door open into the dimly lit room. Shadows danced across the walls, cast by the flickering torchlight.

"Step in," he said, his tone deeper than normal. "This is Remote Viewing and the Trophy Room all wrapped into one."

Zach walked in just as subdued fluorescent strip lights kicked into operation, reinforcing the eerie luminescence of the walls.

A chill zig-zagged down Zach's back. He attempted to take a step further into the room but hesitated.

He took a deep, shaky breath.

Lining the walls were over a hundred mounted heads - grotesque, twisted, monstrous. They were all contained within a transparent hemisphere, and a smoky atmosphere inside kept them as fresh and lifelike as the day they were dismembered.

"Headhunters...," Zach murmured.

Anthony nodded.

"They may be remnants of my conflicts, yes, but also important tools in our fight against the Darkside."

He strode over to a particularly large, horned trophy, one piercing eye in its forehead, razor-sharp teeth and powerful jaws. "This was an Aatxe demon from the 6th Circle of Umbral. It has an insatiable hunger for human flesh, but it must be spiced with anxiety." His fingers traced over the bubble protecting the head from deterioration. "Slaying it this was no easy feat..."

Zach watched as Anthony silently reminisced.

He stopped at another head and pointed; the light reflected off the concave bubble.

"A Nyrathian Nightmare," he said.

Zach peered at its lizard-like skin and bulbous eyes and suddenly felt tired.

Anthony tapped him on the shoulder.

"Don't look at it for too long. It may be dead, but those lidless eyes can induce an endless cyclical dream state in any human unlucky enough to meet its gaze."

Zach averted his eyes and stepped back.

"My predecessor was the only one of our kind ever to kill this creature, and it has proven a treasure trove of useful data."

"Are humans data too?" Zac asked, standing beside a section of heads that were unmistakably humanoid in appearance.. "I see not just monsters get a place on the wall."

Anthony folded his arms.

"The sad truth is, not every interdimensional creature arrives directly from the Darkside. Sometimes, a human's greed or carelessness can introduce these horrors into your world."

He placed his splayed fingers over the protective bubble of one such head - a look of twisted anguish frozen forever on the blonde man's face.

"We were in a parallel universe to your own a few centuries ago. 43566XT1 to be exact. This unfortunate soul became possessed by a Rayuvian Spectre after stupidly opening a dimensional rift while using a particle accelerator. By the time I tracked them down, the Spectre's influence had progressed too far. There was nothing I could do."

Anthony shook his head slowly. "Harsh as it may seem, I had no choice but to sever the consciousness from the physical form. It was...regrettable, but necessary to prevent further harm."

"Okay, I get it," Zach said. You needed to do what you had to do to save lives, but this feels excessive."

Anthony nodded and smiled grimly.

"When I said they were data, I wasn't jesting," he tapped the bubble with his finger, making the glass ring. "It's not a popular process, but I can access residual memories, knowledge, or senses that remain imprinted within the meat, skin and bones."

Zach's eyes widened.

"Not the most pleasant of processes, but sometimes necessary," Anthony said with a grim scowl on his face.

"That's why we hunt the heads as they serve as psychic conduits, allowing me to sometimes remote view through the eyes of their living counterparts within range."

"Secret weapon?" Zach asked.

"Secret weapon," Anthony confirmed.

Both men left the Remote Viewing room quietly. Anthony pulled the big doors closed behind him and tilted his head toward the corridor leading away from the grim reliquary.

"You ready for tonight?" Anthony asked.

"Do I have a choice?"

"No," Anthony said, sounding pleased with himself. "No, you don't."

Chapter Twenty-Seven

Zach almost rebounded off the wall, his powerful thighs absorbing the kinetic energy, then exploding off the brick into midair. He flew through the space between buildings, both gloved hands like outstretched claws, the ledge he was aiming for hurtling towards him. There was always some doubt in his mind. Would he make the jump, yes or no? At the beginning of his training, that question was a shout, but at this level, it was a murmur, if he could hear it at all. Gloved fingers splayed, his body continuing its forward trajectory as he fell according to gravity, he gripped the concrete ledge, the tip of his feet pressed against the wall below him. He looked back at where he had come from, then looked down at the fifty-foot drop. His heart was hammering in his chest, not so much from the mad dash or crazy leap he had made from one balcony to the next, but because of what was pursuing him.

Rats.

If you could call them that. Thousands of them.

Hundreds of thousands of them.

Coal black fur, oversized claws, molten red eyes and distended needle-sharp teeth.

A mass of ravenous hunger that stank of sewer, excrement and sulfur.

Zach pulled himself up from his precarious position to the safety of the ledge and crouched, looking about nervously for any sign of his pursuers. He checked for the satchel around his neck, then looked inside to make sure the Journal was safe. He looked back from where he had flung himself into the night sky and saw the ever-growing mass of evil red eyes peering at him like a growth he was seeing propagating in real time. That ravenous, confusing, chaotic clump of unchecked hunger would have shredded him for sure, if not for Anthony.

Where was he?

Zach didn't think that even with his skills, he could have overcome the vermin if they had overwhelmed him.

They had separated as soon as Anthony had suspected that the growing chattering sound approaching them in the darkness was a threat that required immediate retreat.

"I'll meet you at number sixty-four, now go!" Anthony bellowed.

He didn't need to be told twice, especially after seeing them approaching in a rolling, tumbling tsunami of black fur and red eyes. The sentient mass of disease and hunger immediately split in two as it saw its quarry scurry away in opposite directions.

Anthony wasn't the most elegant of runners, but even with his body armour, he was quick and powerful. Zach knew he was devising a survival or an attack strategy as they fled.

Trying and failing to calm himself, Zach swung off the balcony onto the security railing that protected the exterior walkway and slipped quietly onto the grey corridors whose sameness weaved its way through every building on the estate.

Zach resisted the urge to crouch and stood up straight when he walked through the common areas. After all, it was just after 21:00, and some residents were going about their business, while others were at home, most oblivious to the war raging around them.

Zach was glad for that.

With his senses almost stretched to snapping, the Chronicler made his way to the rendezvous point of apartment sixty-four, Sixth floor, Palladin House.

The knock at the door made Zach jump from his comfortable position on the sofa. He had got here way before Anthony, and he couldn't calm himself, which made him very nervous. He resisted the urge to catastrophise, but it was difficult not to. If you had seen what he'd seen, you'd have trouble keeping it together, too. Whatever he was feeling, he couldn't make it bubble to the surface for the sake of the two kids. He had already reassured them everything would be fine, but he wasn't so sure now.

The rapid Clack, clack of the door knocker came again, making him uneasy. The confidence in the announcement was unnerving, especially knowing it wasn't Anthony.

The Journal wasn't only attuned to him; it knew who all the good guys were in this drama, and the emotional 'ping' Zach was receiving wasn't infused with honour or determination but chaos and bloodshed.

Fuck that! The door would remain closed.

Zach stood up, wondering what his next move would be. And just to remind him of the stakes, the Journal popped an entry into the screen of his mind's eye.

. . .

ISABELLA AND PABLO GONZALES - THE SYMMETRY PAIR

Gift: Fractal Cognition

The twins don't just solve puzzles—they see them in every-thing. Their minds naturally map the world as fractals, tessellations, and spirals, allowing them to decode complex systems, such as traffic flows, patterns of social unrest, resource distribution, and even psychological loops. Their gift only functions at full capacity when they are together, their cognitive fields synchronising like paired qubits.

Impact: *In the possible future, they could be steering entire cities toward balance. On the estate, they quietly model patterns that could one day restructure society from the ground up.*

"AREN'T YOU GOING TO LET YOUR FRIEND IN?" ISABELLA asked.

Zac blinked, his focus back in the real world.

One part of fraternal twins and mathematical geniuses looked at him with concern. Their single father was a bus driver and was working a night shift. Sylvester had nominated them to look in on the twins with the pretence of community outreach. The families of the surviving gifted unanimously trusted the head barber. The parents or the gifted themselves didn't fully understand what was at stake. They had no inkling of the forces involved. His head hurt when he thought of what was required to keep this war from being talked about on the street, in the local press or online. But somehow this episode would be relegated to a dusty, cobwebbed corner of their collective memory, recounted only by the main players.

Zach looked at the youngsters and smiled.

The influence of the barbershop was obvious to Zach. Pablo's spiky hair was cut short with faded sides and marked into the fine hairs of his scalp with coded programs in the form of sigils that looked like stylish swirls. He wasn't sure if Sylvester or the Journal was drip-feeding his unconscious mind with information about the symbols that were helping to make the children invisible to the Darksider's detection. Isabella would have the code woven along her straight brown hair and more lines of code tattooed on her scalp.

The adversaries had obviously found a way around their defence.

"What did your dad say about opening doors to strangers? Especially at night?" Zach asked.

Isabella laughed, capturing the attention of her brother, who had been engrossed with a puzzle on his tablet.

"But you're an adult," she said. "And father was being protective."

Pablo padded over with a mischievous grin on his face. The resemblance to his sister was more pronounced when he smiled.

"You're not scared, are you, Zach?"

Zach considered whether he should set the little 'shit' straight with the truth —that he was scared — and if he'd any sense, he'd be scared too, but he let it slide. They may be geniuses, but he wasn't so sure about their street smarts.

Clack! Clack! Clack!

Both teenagers looked at him curiously.

"Whoever's at the door isn't our friend," Zach said. "Don't go anywhere near it. Do you understand?"

"You're a scaredy cat," Pablo said in a sing-song voice.

"Are you five years old?" Zach asked with mock incredulity. Pablo's young ego picked up on the barb, and he started pouting. His feelings hurt, because every young boy wants to be older than they really are, Zach weighed in to quash his dissent.

"Nobody goes near that door," he repeated. "Do you understand?"

They both nodded.

"Isn't it nearly bedtime for you two anyway?"

"Not yet!" They both burst out.

"It'll be soon, so get ready. And I'm not reading you a bedtime story either."

Isabella rolled her eyes.

Pablo laughed.

Brother and sister sat back down, pretending not to watch the door. And Zach was pretending it was all cool when it wasn't. If it came to the worst, he could bunk here until sunset and then get the Headhunters crew to look for Anthony. His stomach tightened at the thought. Was it such a good idea after all to split up, but it seemed like the best thing to do at the time? Wasn't the Chronicler meant to be the weak link, and yet here he was, and his protector was nowhere to be seen.

The front door shook as someone on the outside tried to force it open. They were done with the courtesy of knocking; they wanted access, and force would be their next option. Isabella and Pablo stared at the door, wide-eyed and trembling.

Zach caught himself staring, too.

He thought they didn't have the power to enter past the sigil at the doorway.

What if there were no sigils?

The front door vibrated from the force of it being aggressively shaken, and Zach ineffectively thought of nothing better to do but to pull the sitting room door closed.

He needed a plan?

Even if he could contact the barbers, the rules of the game barred them from getting involved. He looked around the sitting room for makeshift barricades. If he were to be trapped here, he would make it as difficult as possible for them to reach the kids. If he could fend them off until sunrise, that would be great.

If he couldn't...

He didn't have much time.

ZACH WAS PLEASED WITH THE BUNKER HE HAD constructed in record time. He had four cook knives from the kitchen that were sturdy and sharp. Water and snacks for the kids. Bedding from upstairs and some more sturdy furniture to help reinforce the main door. The fallback point in the living room was ready. He only had to stave off an attack until sunrise, which he was still not certain he could do. His gut tightened at the thought, and a sense of panic was pushing in from the edges of his awareness that he was managing to keep at bay.

But for how long?

This couldn't be happening to him.

Was this some record for the fastest collapse of a mission in Headhunter history? How to kill your Guardian in two days.

Boom! Boom! Boom!

There was no further need for courtesy; whoever was on the other side of the door wanted in, and the force of those blows would see that happening any time soon. Zach retired to the living room, only glancing back at the furniture he had propped under the door handle of the front door, wondering how long it would take to break through. Quickly brushing that thought aside, Zach began constructing his barricade with the furniture he had scrounged from the small apartment and dragged into the living room.

There was a knocking sound that was becoming annoying, but the twins needed to do something to take their minds off what was coming. He couldn't expect them to be quiet, either. Isabella and Pablo were behind an overturned single sofa seat, with a duvet and pillows serving as the floor and walls. There was not much protection, but they were comfortable. They were old enough to know this was real, just unable to grasp the consequences.

Death would be the least of their worries.

The annoying knocking continued, and Zach tried to block it out.

When he had done his makeshift 'perimeter protection', he leaned against the wall, looking over at his handiwork. It was as good as it could be. Zach felt the knife in his hand and felt how his fingers shook. He was on his own, and he would have to do what he had to do. All he was left to decide was whether he could murder to stay alive. Did this even count as murder, and if his attackers weren't human, then sleepless nights would be his future if he survived.

The persistent Tap! Tap! was infuriating, but he took a minute to listen.

The sound was not coming from the twins; it was coming from the sliding patio door, or was it a window that led out to a balcony six stories up? The tapping was on the outside, muffled on the inside by a thick set of curtains that had remained drawn since he'd been here. Zach moved closer and listened. The tapping made him jump.

There was something out there. Swearing, he made tentative steps to investigate.

Very tentative.

His imagination was running wild as he used his index finger to part the curtain. His heart thumping in his chest, he looked out and saw a figure blocking out a portion of West London, its body and hand knocking on the glass. Zach stepped back, and without completely understanding why, a wave of relief washed over him.

"Anthony?"

Zach pulled the curtain open, flooding the tiny balcony with light from the living room. Anthony stood there, relief on his face. Zach slid the patio door open, preparing to unleash a barrage of questions as Anthony stepped inside.

"Damn, you're alive," Anthony said, his forehead peppered with sweat and his long coat scuffed with grime. "You've got skills. Well done."

Zach ignored the compliment.

"How the fuck did you get up here?"

"I climbed," he said simply as if it were the most natural thing to do.

"Six stories up?"

"That wasn't the difficult part. The challenge was not to let THEM track me up here."

"Why didn't you just bust in?" Zach asked.

Anthony sighed and shook his head.

"The rats are very sensitive to sound, and I didn't want to draw them to my position," he looked around at Zach's interpretation of the Alamo. " I shouldn't have bothered because you've already brought them here."

Zach shook his head.

"I lost them just like you did," he protested.

"My nose is never wrong. I can smell them, and you were preparing for something's arrival."

"Someone's trying to break down the door," Zach said

"Not someone," Anthony said. "Something. It's the rats."

Zach was gobsmacked.

"They can do that?"

"Oh, yeah," Anthony confirmed with a grim smile. "They can be very resourceful when they wanna be."

Three more booming impacts from the front door reverberated in the flat.

"And persistent," Zach added.

"I have a plan," Anthony said, then turned to the twins. "You must be Isabella and Pablo."

They nodded vigorously.

"You look cosy and comfortable here, but I need to get you to bed. Do me a favour. Sit tight for another thirty minutes, and I'll come back for you"

"You coming back?" Pablo asked.

"Of course," Anthony said.

BOOM!

The reinforced wooden door splintered in its centre. If not for the bolts and hinges, it would fold into itself and tumble to the floor in two neat pieces. Zach and Anthony were kneeling in the poky hallway facing a front door that could not take much more punishment. Anthony's fingers were working furiously in constructing a contraption from parts he had extracted from the dimensional lining of his big coat. He kept looking up while he put his plan together, hoping he could finish before the door was ripped off the hinges.

Zach tried to occupy his mind elsewhere. The technology Anthony was using looked early nineteenth-century with some futuristic touches, but Zach guessed it was purely coincidental that it resembled anything from Earth's history, just as long as it worked.

Anthony placed the last of four brackets on the floor and wall. Thick conduits the size of Zach's little finger connected all of them, and what he could only imagine was some sort of control console coiled with wire at his feet.

"You know what I've learned from this shit show," Anthony scowled, not waiting for Zach to say anything. "We never have enough time."

Zach agreed with a nod of his head.

"Who made the rules of this game?"

"That Chronicler is the ten thousand Kromal question."

Anthony jumped from his crouched position just as the front door exploded from its centre, sending chunks of wooden shrapnel across the hallway.

"Get behind me," he roared. In a blink, the console was in his hands.

The door shattered some more, the hinges falling away.

Anthony's hands were glowing mauve, his brows furrowed as he forced his energy into the console and from the console into the equipment. The space between the four brackets shimmered, and a shit-kicking grin of satisfaction appeared on Anthony's face. The rest of the door came apart in spectacular fashion, showering the hallway with wood fragments and metal debris. The silhouettes of the two men causing the chaos stepped through the doorway. Well built and confident, the men strode in, heading straight for them.

Rats, Zach thought. He knew it couldn't be rats.

Satisfied that his need for being right was met, he could calmly return to being singularly afraid.

That's when his world tipped sideways, and he was reminded of who he was and what kind of world he was embroiled in.

Four powerful strides into the hallway, the two men approached with a disquieting synchrony that seemed almost mechanical, their gait too smooth and their faces obscured by the light from the landing. Zach shuffled back, giving himself space between the barrier and himself.

As the two men drew nearer, the air grew thick with a musty, damp scent, reminiscent of earth and decay. He could see better, too, and immediately wished he couldn't.

Zach's eyes widened and he shot a look at Anthony, who was mouthing the words, 'You, sneaky motherfuc...

They were not men at all; their appearances were mere illusions, a tapestry woven from countless writhing bodies. A grotesque parody of form and a nightmare birthed from the darkest crevice of human fear. The men's faces, once seemingly solid, began to undulate and contort grotesquely as hundreds of small, gleaming red eyes peered out from what had appeared to be flesh.

It took everything Zach had not to retreat to the living room screaming, but he knew the Journal was somehow fortifying him. Training his nervous system to cope.

The illusion shattered, and with the shlick! Shlick! Sound of thick, crusty fur rubbing against each other, their bodies disassembled into a chaotic swarm of vermin. The creatures, each a mottling of dark fur, sharp teeth and evil intelligence, poured onto the ground like a liquid nightmare, their intention obvious.

Swarm, obscure and feed.

The hallway seemed to boil with the vermin until they impacted with Anthony's barrier. The air was filled with the sharp, acrid tang of rodent fur, and the overwhelming, instinctual terror of being consumed by this living, moving mass of pestilence was not easy to control, but Zach managed by closing his eyes.

The sound of squeaking, screeching and chattering was too much to bear, expecting the smell of burnt flesh and singed fur as they impacted with the barrier, but that didn't come.

Zach hinged open one twitching eye.

The rats weren't being incinerated at all. They were disappearing on contact with the barrier. Zach leaned forward as they kept coming. It was a crazy feeling seeing them enter the barrier, while his brain was telling him they would be all over them. As smart as they were, the anticipated feeding frenzy was enough to drive them forward without further thought as their kin was being transported to God knows where. He looked over at Anthony, who had his eyes closed, sweating; his focus on channelling his life force into the contraption that was keeping them alive was steady and sure. Zach felt like a dick, wondering how long Anthony could keep that up for while he crouched with two blades in his fists, ready to fight for his life and Anthony's if he had to. He felt ashamed of his minor role, but at the same time, could he be of real use in a fight? Scared and grateful, Zach gave a silent prayer of thanks because, without him, he pictured his lifeless carcass being picked clean by the rats.

IT WAS EARLY MORNING, AND LIGHTS WERE ON IN THE barbershop that never closed. To Zach, it was the most beautiful sight. He adjusted Anthony's arms around his shoulders and locked into his second wind. The warrior had used his last reserves on the Rat trap he had powered with his life force. He may have saved them, but rendered himself vulnerable.

And that scared Zach.

An interdimensional being was putting his life in the hands of a human, even if he was the Chronicler.

Out here, they only had each other, and tonight brought home that fact to him in no uncertain terms.

The rules were clear.

After midnight, only one assigned member of the Headhunters team was allowed to roam the estate at a time. If they needed help in any form, they were on their own. Of course, Zach knew this, but it had more significance when he was propping up a weakened partner across the estate, fearful they would be attacked at any time. He couldn't have been more overjoyed as the Barbershop loomed in the distance, with all its lights on like his lighthouse guiding him into port. He wasn't sure where he got the strength from - Anthony was heavy, but he managed to bring him back to base. The entire front of the Barbershop was open to the elements. It was designed to fold into five sections and then slide to either side. Sylvester and Medusa stood together, and three other people Zach recognised stood on the demarcation line between the shop and the real world. When he reached the finishing line, his strength gave way, tipping Anthony forward into the three pairs of awaiting hands.

For a moment, Zach watched Anthony being laid out on a stretcher and tested.

"Will he be ok, Doc?"

The doctor smiled up at him.

"He gave a lot tonight," Doc Karma said. "He drained himself to some dangerous levels... but I think he'll be okay."

Zach let out a sigh, not realising he had held his breath and turned away. Sylvester came up to him and placed his hands on both shoulders and stared into his eyes through his glasses.

"Well done, Chronicler." His smile was a fleeting one. "Well done. I'll leave you in the capable hands of Medusa. We will catch up later."

Sylvester walked over to Anthony and crouched down beside him while Medusa grabbed Zach and hugged him.

"Let's get you to bed," she whispered.

Chapter Twenty-Eight

T he rhythmic hum of clippers, the occasional laughter and old-school reggae filling the gaps with a feel of Sunday mornings in a Jamaican household offered Zach a temporary reprieve from his troubling thoughts. He wondered how the residents would have processed the terror occurring around them if not for the program being baked into the fabric of the estate, erasing their short-term memories. There would be chaos and panic if that weren't the case. As his mind wandered, he stretched out on his oversized bean bag near the fogged-up front window of the Barbershop, his eyes skimming over a dog-eared copy of the London Metro. The news of mundane world events barely penetrated the fog of dread that had settled around him since the previous night's horrors.

As the door chimed its familiar tune, a gust of cold air swept through the shop, ruffling the pages of Zach's newspaper. He looked up to see a well-dressed older black man entering, the silver accents in his business suit catching the soft overhead light. The man's presence seemed to shift the energy of the room; his confident stride and the crisp tilt of the trilby on his head spoke of a life lived boldly. Beside him was a woman dressed in a simple gingham skirt, a white blouse and her hair wrapped in a colourful African-designed head wrap.

There was something about her that shone. He couldn't judge her age, but she was a stunning-looking albino woman.

Sylvester, mid-fade with a customer, glanced up, and his face broke into a wide grin. "Spokes! Nanny," he exclaimed, setting his clippers down with a clatter. He wiped his hands on his apron as he approached the newcomer, enveloping him in a hearty embrace. Then he turned to face the woman he called Nanny and bowed. She extended her hand, and Sylvester took it and kissed her fingers. She curtsied.

Zach sat in rapt astonishment at Sylvester's sense of practised formality. But the big man didn't disappoint him, and with a snap of his wrist, he spun Nanny into him with a little squeal from the coy woman.

They hugged.

"Yuh devil yuh," Nanny smiled gently, placing her hands on Sylvester's cheeks. "Good to see yuh, Master Sylvester."

"My brother," Spokes said, planting his hands on his hips, his voice rich with a Jamaican lilt. His smile was infectious, reaching his eyes that twinkled with a kind of mischievous wisdom. "You are not pure legend, then, king."

"I'm as real as a heart attack," Sylvester said with a straight face.

"If Nanny hadn't told me about your dilemma, bossman, I wouldn't have known your kind existed."

Snippets of conversation were drifting over to Zach's position, making him neatly fold his newspaper and listen intently to something more interesting than world affairs.

"Can I ask you something, Nanny?" Sylvester looked a bit uncomfortable.

"Of course," Nanny said. "What is that calculating mind of yours brewing?"

Sylvester smiled.

"Do you remember everything about your life in the other realities we've met?"

"I remember everyting and don't you ever forget it."

"I won't," Sylvester laughed.

Other realities, Zach thought. Who are these people? His curiosity must have telegraphed to the group from his attentive posture on his bean bag from across the shop. Spokes looked over, noticing he had caught his attention, he swept his trilby off in an exaggerated flourish in Zach's direction.

Sylvester, constantly aware of what was happening around him in the Barbershop, to the degree Zach thought they were connected psychically, beckoned him over.

He sprang up, not caring how his enthusiasm must seem, and planted himself beside the senior barber. Sylvester put his arms around his shoulders.

"Zach, meet Spokes and Nanny. A new friend and an old friend," Sylvester cleared his throat pointedly. Let's say they are significant players in some very influential circles worldwide. Which is why I called in the big guns, figured they might lend a hand. We need all the help we can get."

Spokes extended a hand, his grip firm and warm. "Heard quite a bit about you, rude bwoy, Chroniclers, right? Keeping the stories alive, that's a mighty task." The dapper Jamaican tsked softly under his breath. "Deh fates spared no expense in settin' you on a treacherous path, youngblood?"

One calloused hand settled on Zach's shoulder, squeezing lightly.

'Take it from ol' Spokes. This burden is heavier than any one soul ought to bear alone."

Spokes flashed another megawatt smile. "Don't fret.

According to the cosmic rules, I, Nanny an deh Bad II de Bone crew got your back."

Next came Nanny, who hugged him, long and hard, then held him at arm's length to look at him again.

"My condolences for the loss of Miss Hortense. She always spoke highly of you."

Zach nodded, his tearducts prickling, and a feeling of sadness formed a knot in his throat.

Nanny paused and then used her intense grey eyes to scan his expression and maybe even the thoughts firing in his brain.

"How is my friend Anthony?" She asked.

The question made Zach raise his eyebrow and take a sudden breath.

"You know Anthony? I thought this was his first time here?"

Zach didn't know how much he could say, but he needn't have worried.

Nanny smiled.

"It is the first time feh him, but I get around a lot and we've met in many places, some sticky situations, and we've become friends."

"Friends? I didn't know he had any."

Nanny laughed.

It was a beautiful sound like tinkling crystals and optimism.

"You know of him in other universes?" Zach's question had an out-of-breath tone to it.

Nanny nodded.

He absorbed the revelation and tried to be cool about it.

"He's demanding," Zach said honestly. "He's a pain in the ass and disagreeable on a good day. But I'd be dead without him."

Nanny put her hand on his shoulder.

"He has a noble heart, son, and I knew you both would work well together."

"She had faith in you, youngblood," Spokes added.

"Thanks, this is all new to me. Strange one moment, terrifying the next."

"Welcome to deh club," Spokes chuckled, his voice a melodious rumble. "We guide where we can, shield against the unseen when necessary. There's more to this world than meets the eye, as you well know."

As they spoke, the usual hustle of the shop seemed to slow, the barbers and customers alike stealing glances towards the intriguing conversation. Spokes shared stories of otherworldly encounters and cosmic battles, weaving a tapestry that depicted a London caught between reality and something altogether different.

"You see, Zach, there's a thin veil," Spokes continued, his hands gesturing as if pulling back an invisible curtain. "Behind it, energies play deh game of destiny. Most people will guh through dem life not knowing the sacrifices made on their behalf so they can live free of the knowledge of these forces."

Zach agreed with the shake of his head. He was once one of these people.

Spokes continued.

"We, like you, work to maintain a balance, lest chaos tips the scales too far one way. Sometimes we win and sometimes we lose. You young blood, the Headhunters and the gifted are losing dis battle. We are here to not just represent but support. Yuh feel mi. We can only follow deh rules and give advice, but as my old lady used to say, *Every mickle mek a muckle*."

Zach's smile at the Caribbean colloquialism was brighter than it had been before. His earlier dread was now mixed with a newfound sense of purpose. He was part of something larger than he could ever imagine. How long it would last, he couldn't say, but he wished to store it away for use when the horrors appear and appear they would.

Sylvester clapped his hands, breaking the spell. "Your time is limited my guests. Let's give you a fresh cut, Spokes and Nanny a manicure. We can talk more privately, out back."

"You're an inspiration my yout," Spokes said saluting him with a clenched fist.

Nanny bowed and said.

"Thank you, Zach. For everything."

Sylvester then ushered his guests to the labyrinthine rooms at the back. Zach glanced around the shop, seeing it anew: a sanctuary, a place of gathering, where worlds intertwined, twisted like the mystical Bantu bumps or cane rows created by the Headhunter hairstylists.

There was an unmistakable aura of ancient power and mystical knowledge surrounding the Jamaican duo.

Especially Nanny, who moved through the world with a casual self-assurance. If even a fraction of what he sensed about the two proved accurate, they may just have been granted invaluable new allies in the coming conflict. He just hoped Spoke's mystical prowess and streetwise bravado with Nanny's mysterious connections would be enough to help turn the tide.

Because after last night's demonstration, it was terribly clear that the forces arrayed against them were only growing bolder and more brazen. And Zach knew deep in his soul that worse things still awaited them in the days ahead...far worse.

Chapter Twenty-Nine

"Where do you lot sleep?" It wasn't meant to be a deep question, unlike the questions he'd asked himself and others about this eternal battle he was embroiled in. Maybe he should have asked Medusa if she slept at all.

The Headhunters looked human and were indistinguishable from his neighbours, except for their distinctive fashion sense. That meant nothing in the world he inhabited.

The personal question didn't have any bearing on the outcome of the war and had no significant ramifications outside of his curiosity. He surprised himself at how interested he was in the more mundane aspects of this circus. It wasn't that he took the unimaginable powers and forces at play for granted. He may not have understood before, but these immutable laws were beyond his control. But the beings that were impacted by it were the real story.

His Journal would agree.

After Anthony was being tended to, Medusa was the one to

escort him through the estate to his flat. That's when he asked the question, his tiredness reducing his inhibitions.

"Where do you sleep?" Zach asked again, this time staring directly at her.

Medusa smiled.

Perfect teeth, dark, dark skin, golden eyes, her smooth face framed by long, luxuriant hair.

"Let me show you," she said. "I can freshen up while I'm there. Come on."

She took Zach's hand and led him into the back of the house and the mind-numbing relative dimensions in space.

As was usual, Zach didn't have a clue where he was being led and would have no memory of the route Medusa had taken even if he wanted to retrace his steps. Medusa had no hesitation winding her way through corridors, sliding doors, slopes and a few stairs. It felt like a brisk fifteen-minute walk, but with time dilation, who could tell? Zach knew he had arrived as Medusa released his hand for the first time and stood with her arms folded beside a door. It was plain except for a symbol that, at first, witnessing it meant nothing to him, then, in a moment, it became clear. The Journal had recognised his query and provided him with a snippet of information that popped up bold and bright in his mind's eye. It was the House to which Medusa's family belonged. A prestigious lineage amongst her people. The Journal would obviously inform him of the details. Details he would appreciate about this mysterious woman.

"What do you think?" Medusa laughed. "Home away from home."

At that moment, Zach was paying more attention to where he was and knew immediately that Medusa was teasing him.

Where he was standing was nothing to write home about. It was like something you'd expect in a large hotel: muted colours, raised ceiling, a pedestrian intersection and a semi-circular string of nondescript doors surrounding it. Zach guessed there were about thirty accommodation units here.

"Everybody bunks here?" Zach asked.

"Everybody, Except Anthony." She said. "The rest of us have our space that we can design to our own tastes." Medusa placed her palm and elegant fingers on the door. It throbbed a golden yellow from deep inside and then slid open.

A scent of calm assaulted him.

"Welcome," she said and motioned him inside. "I hope you like it."

LIKE IT! ZACH THOUGHT THE PLACE WAS AWESOME.

The minimalist decor of the open space was unlike anything he had ever seen. The kinetic sculptures, arranged around the nearly circular floor plan, and the mind-bending art on the walls were created by a non-human mind, you could tell. Beautiful and engaging all at once. There were no light fittings as you would expect in a human habitat. The walls and ceiling emitted a calming, pale yellow luminescence, which Zach guessed could be adjusted according to one's mood.

He sighed heavily.

Taking in a lungful of the sweet-smelling aroma that he was struggling to compare with something familiar, but couldn't. Whatever it was, it made him mellow but alert. His tiredness was leeching away in waves.

But his back was still stiff.

It was bad manners, he knew, but Zach didn't care; he needed to stretch, he was relaxed, and Medusa's bed was too irresistible, even if it was shaped like a crescent. If she didn't want him messing with her mattress, why make her open-plan living quarters so inviting and place the focus of his attention in the middle of the room, teasing him?

With his eyes closed, Zach smiled and stretched. The bones in his back made a popping sound.

It was all her fault.

Medusa had left a trail of her clothes on the floor like sexy breadcrumbs to the bathroom. He could hear the water from the shower, and for a fleeting moment, he was in the shower with her. She had clung onto him from behind, her large wet breasts on his back, and he was reaching behind as far as his hands could go to lather her ass, quite a task, but he managed.

"Comfortable?"

Zach's eyes flew open; the question caught him by surprise.

He had not heard her leave the bathroom, but Medusa stood at the curve of the crescent bed naked; her hair had grown denser and longer since the last time he saw her. She smiled warmly. If he had any concerns about her physical compatibility with a human, he needn't have.

She was all woman.

Her golden locks were not a fashion statement; the pubic hairs between her smooth legs confirmed that, just as the splashes of gold dust on her dark skin weren't makeup but natural.

Zach tried to remain ambivalent and gave up in the first seconds of that ill-conceived idea. There was a slight hitch in his voice.

"Veeery comfortable!"

"I'm glad," she cooed. "But let me try to make you even more so."

Before he could respond, not that his response would have been coherent, Medusa gracefully lowered herself and crawled onto the bed, straddling him. Zach adjusted his position slightly, shifting his shoulders to accommodate her. She leaned forward on top of him, her voluminous hair covering his head like a veil, her breasts on his chest. She rested her forehead on his, her skin soft, her locks soft too and smelling delightfully of the tropics. Medusa gently reached under his arms, her fingers deftly finding the hems of his garments and pulled off his Nike sweatshirt and then his vest. Medusa was a tall woman, and her long legs were powerful. Zach was no slouch in the height department either, but she had some inches on him. Still, when she leaned forward against him, their noses were level. Zach could really see into those deep, sparkling, golden eyes. There was a warmth there. A passion. Her skin was so soft, and the touch was electric, literally. It was a delightful tingling that spread across his entire body. Medusa's breasts and nipples pressed against his chest, and the moist, luxuriant flesh between her legs against his stomach.

He was hard.

She was wet.

Her lips brushed against his ears.

"Kalerem," she whispered the word, and her hair came alive, the strands snaking away from having surrounded them both as if it had been protecting their privacy, retreating like cobras to neatly bundle on her back.

Zach's eyes widened.

"Wow!"

She smiled and kissed his earlobe, then said.

"Turn over."

He did as instructed, and Medusa rose slightly to accommodate him.

Zach had his arms folded in front of him and his chin propped on his arms. He could only imagine what Medusa was doing, and that may have intensified the sensations even more. There was a pleasant warmth on his back. Was that an Akhan symbol she traced on his skin? He hadn't known what that was before becoming the Chronicler. But he was beginning to understand. His shoulders relaxed, and so did the muscles of his neck. He trusted Medusa. This was not just pleasure but protection.

She was blessing him in the same way she had blessed hundreds of people from the estate. She rubbed more symbols into his back as she spoke incantations, each one feeling as if it was penetrating his dermis and impressing upon the eternal part of who he was. After the ritual, her strong hands began working magic not with his chakras but with his tight muscles. The tension and stress were lifting off him in waves. When Medusa was done, he was tingling all over and was sure his body was floating inches off the bed.

"That was amazing!" Zach whispered; his focus had returned to the Goddess on his back. "If this is anything like what you have on offer for the residents, the estate will have a chance."

Medusa lay flat on his back, her head on his head.

"We all have our gifts, and we give everything we can," she said. "But there are some things we reserve for 'special people'. Personal gifts that are unique to the giver."

"Am I special?" Zach asked.

"Very," Medusa said.

Zach was grinning into his arm.

"So, do you have a personal gift for me?"

"I do."

"Can I have it?"

"Turn over."

Zach did what he was instructed.

The gift was tight, wet and kept coming.

Chapter Thirty

"I need you!" The voice that was Sylvester's sliced through Zach's reverie and demanded immediate attention. He had just finished writing in the Journal, feeling light-headed as data was transmitted from his memory to the handwritten script on quantum paper. It always felt good when he downloaded something. He had been chilling after that, taking in the frenetic energy of the shop floor, marvelling at how they were saving the people of this community with one haircut, braid or tattoo at a time. Zach had no doubts in his mind that the Journal had somehow rewired his nervous system to cope with the existential repercussions of his Chronicler duties. How could anyone sleep with that kind of forbidden knowledge rattling around in your head? And yet he slept like a toddler whose soother was dipped in honey and rum.

Coming out of his ruminations, he realised Sylvester had summoned him. He stood up from his giant beanbag, his eyes drifting over to the door that led to the space-time distorting back of house. Sylvester had left his barber chair with the customer still luxuriating in the fine leather and indicated he was going through the tinted glass entrance at the front. Before Zach could reach it, the door had closed, and Sylvester had walked through. Judging by the silhouettes on the other side, he was not alone.

What now?

Whatever was going on, the Darksider that demanded Sylvester's presence was a boss.

The Chronicler took a deep, shaky breath and stepped out of the safety of the shop into the outside world.

THE MOMENT ZACH CLOSED THE DOOR BEHIND HIM, HIS sense of relief was immediate, but was replaced by a palpable tension he could almost taste. Sylvester stood there, his arms folded with his usual composure, gaze locked onto a well-dressed man who exuded an aura of unearned confidence and cold pragmatism.

The Minister of Defence, Lord Alastair Eversleigh, embodied the classic aristocrat—his thin, sharp face adorned with a well-groomed, slicked-back silver hair, and an impassive stare that conveyed both disdain and intellect. His posture, upright and aloof, spoke of an untouchable authority. Behind him, three bodyguards clad in tailored suits, their stance military and watchful, marked them as the Knights Templar, notorious for both their loyalty and their reputation as ruthless killers.

The Journal had filled in the gaps to his woefully incomplete knowledge of the man.

Zach fought to control his reaction, willing the shock to settle within as he tried to gauge the situation.

Lord Eversleigh caught Zach's scrutiny and smiled—a grin that was less human, more predator. "Aren't you going to invite me in?" His voice oozed with mock surprise, although his demeanour said he didn't care.

Sylvester's brows lifted slightly, a trace of amusement softening his otherwise firm expression. "I don't think the shop would appreciate you stepping through its doors knowing your intentions aren't pure. It may... trigger a response. The shop is sensitive like that. Better safe than sorry."

Eversleigh's smile faltered, just for a second, before he inclined his head in mock civility, shifting his focus from Sylvester to Zach, his gaze evaluating, even as his expression remained controlled.

"One of yours?"

Sylvester chuckled, the sound rich and warm.

"No, he's Human. The Chronicler. An example of the best your kind has to offer."

Eversleigh's lips twisted into a parody of a smile, his slow clap echoing with disdain. "Well done, young man. You're still alive. That, in itself, is an achievement."

Zach nodded, his expression unreadable, eyes flicking to Sylvester, hoping the man would clarify this bizarre encounter. Sylvester took a measured breath, his gaze turning colder, more resolute.

The minister put both hands in his pockets with frustration.

"Sylvester, I've limited time and have to chair a meeting in Parliament. Whatever you have to say—spit it out."

"I want you to consider preventing the Day of Reckoning from happening. You've had talks with them; surely, we can find a way to postpone this."

The Minister's sardonic laughter echoed between the buildings.

"Are you fucking serious?"

"Very," Sylvester replied. "The agreement your predecessors made—the sacrifice of innocents—it's barbaric. You're condemning the souls of the Runnymede estate, an entire community, to pay a price for your leader's lack of fight."

Eversleigh rolled his eyes, his patience evidently wearing thin. "Let's not pretend you're new to these games, Sylvester. A few hundred souls in exchange for the safety of millions? It's a fair deal. One I'd make every time."

"A *fair deal?*" Zach cut in. "What's fair about sacrificing people like cattle?"

A flicker of disdain danced in Eversleigh's eyes.

"Spoken like a voter. They're not your concern, Chronicler. This is statecraft—sacrifices must be made for the greater good. Runnymede estate has borne the mark for sixty years, and the ritual keeps Hell's denizens bound. Should they ever truly break free, they would sweep through London, obliterating our world. Our government allows the damned only this one night, to feed on the souls of that estate—an act of containment, if you will."

Sylvester's eyes blazed.

"They are innocents."

"Wake up! There is no such thing." Eversleigh's voice was clipped, resolute. "Every soul carries darkness within it. I merely chose the method by which they atone."

"And what happens when they break your contract? What happens when they find a way to dismantle what you created? They will find a way. Chaos is in their nature."

Eversleigh's lip curled.

"I'm a politician; lies are my stock in trade. Your realm is the supernatural, Sylvester. You deal in forces beyond our control. I, on the other hand, have a responsibility to the stability of this nation. We cannot afford to have your kind meddling in our world so openly. We were content dealing with you on the periphery, in our dreams, in the unseen. But now, to have you in the flesh, threatening our sovereignty? Unacceptable."

"Your arrogance has already caused damage to the very fabric of the Darksiders realms and your dimension. If it were to tear open, there wouldn't be enough bodies in the world to fill the abyss."

"His Majesty's Government is willing to take that risk. The estate has stood for seventy years as a buffer, and it will stand for seventy more. All for the greater good."

"The greater good?" Zach's voice came out almost as a whisper, barely concealing his disgust.

"What your mentor Sylvester forgot to tell you, the pact was formed after the Second World War, when we saw first-hand the horrors that mankind could unleash. Our greatest fear was our own kind until the Darksiders slipped through. They respected and feared the human spirit, and we brokered an arrangement—a containment zone of gifted individuals where the checks and balances of good and evil could play out without jeopardising the whole of Britain. Their price? A regular tithe. Souls. And Runnymede was chosen. Its residents marked, its fate sealed."

Sylvester's jaw clenched.

"Isn't it time for a new way?"

"There is no other way." The Minister checked his watch. "Know this—you are just as bound by this deal as we are. If you disrupt it, if you meddle with the rites of the Day of Reckoning outside of the ancient rules, you and your people will pay. And I'll watch from Westminster as it devours you and anyone foolish enough to stand beside you."

"That's a chance I'm willing to take."

The Minister's demeanour shifted, and his predatory smile returned. "Then, by all means, Sylvester, do what you must."

Eversleigh turned, gesturing for his guards to follow, casting one last, lingering look over his shoulder. "Best of luck, old boy. I hope we never meet again."

Sylvester stood silent, his eyes darkened with something Zach had never seen before—a raw, burning conviction mixed with a trace of sorrow. He looked down at Zach, who met his gaze with newfound resolve.

"Where there's a will, there's a way."

He sounded like Hortense.

Chapter Thirty-One

They were too late; he could feel it. "Shit!" Zach brushed at the fetid air with his hand, disgusted and surprised at how suddenly it appeared into his awareness. He stopped as if to catch his breath and hesitated to make another step. He leaned on the intervening concrete barrier, which allowed you to see across the Runnymede Estate from the sixth floor, but was tall enough for only the suicidally inclined to climb over. The corridor was open to the elements, which should have allowed air to circulate, but the stench was thick and cloying, determined to linger.

The Journal opened his mind's eye and presented him with a high-definition file on the Gifted they were sent to check on.

Selene Moreau – The Bone Archivist
Gift: **Osteomnesia**
Selene can extract emotional and sensory echoes from human bone, reading what the flesh once felt—love, terror, resolve. To her, a graveyard is a library. She works in quiet rever-

ence, piecing together forgotten truths that others would prefer stay buried. Given time, she would have been recruited by a top-tier humanitarian organisation.

Impact: She could revolutionise justice, ancestry tracing, and posthumous healing, bringing closure where none seemed possible.

WHAT A WASTE!

A part of him was screaming to turn tail and flee, but he held the reflex back. The Journal must have helped, because he certainly couldn't have done it alone. He could feel Anthony hovering behind him, his wariness making him even more cautious about moving. His wingman, for once, did not intervene as Zach got in tune with his fears or push past him with impatience. He hung back, protecting his rear and glaring ahead for potential threats. His nostrils flared as the smell assaulted him again. He took out a rag from his back pocket and covered his nose and mouth. He wasn't sure why, but like a scolded child, he looked down at his feet. The grey landing was lit with fluorescent strip lights attached to the ceiling. Some were smashed, some unlit, while others flickered like strobe lights, casting erratic shadows. It wasn't clear, but Zach stood at the end of a trail on the slick, grey concrete floor. It stretched up to flat 721, like a trail of mucus from a giant snail. It ended where Zach stood, and all that was left were huge scorch marks.

He looked to the darkened flat ahead and just let his eyes trace the winding, glistening path from the door to where he stood. Zach rubbed at it with the toe of his sneakers. It had dried hard, and when his trainer made contact, it broke off in wafer-thin flakes. He bent and looked more closely at it. The smell remained unbearable, but he still examined the slime and shuddered at the thought of what could have made it.

"What do you think?" Zach whispered hoarsely.

Anthony's eyes glistened from the dull fluorescent lights, and his demeanour was maudlin. He was already feeling the loss they were about to experience together. The warrior shook his head.

"Dammit!" Zach said, relying on Anthony's experience and preternatural senses to establish what had gone on here. "There could be survivors, right? It could be lying in wait for us to come in. Could it still be in there?" Zach was sounding frantic, hoping for something positive but still terrified.

"It's gone," Anthony said. "Do you think I'm stupid. Making you take point, knowing it was still inside?" He shook his head. "This exercise is for you to see what we are up against and for the Journal to extract the data it needs through you."

"This is fucked up, man!" Zach muttered. "Fucked up."

"I know. But let's get it done and find a way for this never to happen again."

Zach agreed with a grim nod.

Three nights into this adventure, Zach looked a little different from his first night on the estate. He still wanted to travel light. The rats taught him that much, but in his satchel with the Journal was a blade Anthony gave him with a weird shape and the ability to mould itself to the unique shape of the wielder's hands. He also received a head-mounted flashlight from Sylvester, which he slipped over his forehead.

Anthony said nothing and made no move until Zach began to follow the trail of the stinking mucus to the front door.

Zach looked down and expected to see the designs of a protection sigil that had somehow been breached, but the chalk symbols and the archaic script had been rubbed clean.

"What happened?" Zach said his voice carried incredulity even through the flannel covering his nose and mouth. "How could they rub the sigil clean? I thought it would protect the inhabitants from breaches like this."

Anthony pulled up beside him; the smell of his greatcoat was barely registering above the stench, but his consciousness had already been imprinted with feelings of safety and survival when he sniffed the leather bouquet. He couldn't imagine anyone else having his back. Nobody else could.

"A Darksider didn't remove the sigil," Anthony said, crouching beside where it had been rubbed out. "They couldn't."

"So who did?"

"A familiar did this. A Darksider's influence can be powerful enough to compel the feeble-minded to act for them. They were sent to scrub the sigils before the attack happened."

"Who would do that? Isn't that against the rules?" Zach asked.

"Not if the influence is brief. If they can find someone who is unstable, evil or susceptible. It is not an easy trick to pull off even for them, but it can be done"

Zach stood at the threshold, waiting for Anthony, who had walked away to make a call. It still looked peculiar seeing the dimensional warrior making a phone call. He held the mobile phone all wrong, and he was too loud, but he got the job done.

He sauntered back over.

"Clean-up crew is on their way," Anthony said. "Let's get this ugly business done."

THE STENCH HIT THEM FIRST - A THICK, CLOYING MIASMA of burnt flesh and oxidised copper that stood like a wall in front of him. Zach began breathing through his mouth to avoid gagging on the foul odour coming from the hellish space, but he kept on, pushing open the splintered remains of the apartment door.

He took a step in, and the smell suddenly disappeared, replaced by a noticeable drop in temperature. Zach's flesh pimpled as the chill immediately began to gnaw at his bones. The measurement of time and how it flowed was, for the most part, an exact science, but to the human mind, in times of stress, it's entirely subjective. Zach looked at and tried to make sense of the scene in the apartment for what seemed like an age. Everything had slowed down in his perception, and all he could hear was the beat of his heart and the rushing passage of his blood in his ears.

"Mercy ..." Zach whispered, the words catching in his throat.

The scene before them defied description. What was once a cosy flat was now a house of horror, an art installation by a demonic abstract artist whose materials were strips of gore and smeared viscera.

And it was everywhere.

Chunks of flayed meat... hung in ragged tatters from the light fixtures, slowly dripping long runnels of crimson on the floor. In this slaughterhouse, Blood pooled where it could and soaked into fabric where it couldn't. What had once been the bright crimson of arterial spray was now sweeping arcs of black venous blood as it oxygenated over time.

"Why...? Why this?" Zach's mind reeled, unable to process the sheer horror.

Anthony's expression was grim, his jaw set.

"This is how the Darksiders play the game. Human life means nothing to them. The eternal human soul is their prize. This is a mere prelude to what they will be doing to them on the other side."

Zach shivered, the idea overwhelming as it was horrific.

Anthony motioned for him to follow, and they gingerly picked their way through the hellish wreckage. Broken furniture, tattered books, and all manner of detritus were strewn about in a seemingly random pattern. But Anthony's eyes narrowed as he examined the chaos more closely, his breath pluming in the cold from his lips.

"No...something isn't right," he murmured." Not right."

Crouching down, Anthony traced his gloved finger through the thick, congealed blood coating the floor. Zach clenched his jaw and narrowed his eyes, looking down at a vague impression scribbled into the dust. He elbowed Anthony and pointed to the hieroglyphic scrawl on the floor. The warrior glanced at the message and snapped to attention.

"Get behind me," Anthony growled. "You were right."

Zach shuffled around him, his head swimming.

Whispering, he asked.

"Right about what?"

"It's a trap," Anthony scowled. "A goddamn trap that I led us into."

A sudden crash from the bedroom upstairs made them both look at the cracked ceiling. With the practised twist and flick of his fingers, Anthony's great coat billowed open, and for a moment, Zach was witnessing eternity within the folds, a pocket universe confined by stitch and leather. Both his arms crossed, and he reached into opposite sides, disappearing up to his elbows for an instant, and then reappeared with both hands gripping twin sickles with gilded ivory hilts and gleaming bronze blades. Anthony slashed the air in front of him, both blades leaving orange energy trails that remained glowing in the air for seconds as if they were seared into Zach's retinas. The warrior tensed, then slowly and methodically shuffled his feet into a fighting stance with both hands up, almost planting himself into the floorboards. Zach looked on from behind him, both sets of eyes focused on the staircase.

The stairs creaked, and a shadow ponderously descended.

Zach's eyes fell on the horror for a fraction of a second, but it was enough to take a white hot brand and sear it into his memory.

It...had been a woman, once. Maybe the flat's owner. Now, it was an obscene patchwork thing - all exposed muscle, tendon, and bone fused together in a horrific tangle in a viscous glue of blood, bile and faecal matter. It was constructed not just from oddly stuck-together parts of itself but also from inorganic material. Broken glass in its shattered face, cutlery in its open thoracic cavity. Empty eye sockets oozed blackish ichor down a barely recognisable face locked in an eternal rictus of agony or glee.

Contrary to its gross form, it moved with grace, descending the stairs like a dancer. On the last step, it stopped and regarded them both. The thing opened its lipless maw and sucked air into its chest. How it was capable of doing so without lungs was a mystery, and so was the sound that erupted from its mouth.

Zach clapped his hands over his ears, although he needn't have because the creature's wail wasn't frustration or anger; it wasn't a sound at all; it was a psychic attack. The pain made him double over, as it clawed its way into the deepest, most primal receptors of his brain, filling his mind with visions of...

... eternal torment. Infinite, maddening suffering. A kaleidoscope of horrors born from the darkest, most twisted depths of the human subconscious was given horrific, sanity-shattering form.

Zach collapsed to his knees, shaking his head wildly as if his actions would dislodge whatever images had taken residence in his head. Tears trickled down his cheeks as the assault drilled deeper. Hands still pressed to his head, a trickle of blood dripping from one nostril, he looked up.

A blur of motion zigzagged across his vision. It was his only warning, as Anthony spun twice, releasing the knives in lightning-quick succession. The blades glowed molten hot, leaving a trail in the air as both found their targets. The tortured thing staggered back, sitting comically as its ruined and misshapen head toppled from its shoulders, both blades severing the tenuous muscle fibres that held it in place.

The psychic assault ceased as abruptly as it had begun, leaving Zach trembling and sweating on the floor.

Anthony stood over the remains on the staircase, his chest heaving with exertion. "They took the gifted and left her here," he said, his voice laced with disgust and an undercurrent of fury. "The Darksiders murdered her, then trapped her life force in her own flayed, ravaged body, pulling her strings like a puppeteer."

Retrieving his blades, he wiped them on his trouser leg and stored them away in the dimensional folds of his coat. He turned, walked back over to Zach, and extended a hand to help him back to his feet. "We have two more nights, and things will only get worse."

Zach only managed a weak nod, his eyes still glazed from the onslaught.

Anthony rested a hand on the younger man's shoulder, steadying him. " They are pushing back after our successes. We've hurt them." His gaze swept the horrendous carnage once more. "They will keep coming."

Clenching his jaw, Anthony's face hardened with resolve. "We have never got this far with any campaign we've conducted across the multiverse. The Darksiders are worried."

Anthony glanced at the ruined thing lying motionless on the stairs and shook his head.

"We can't do anything more here. Let the clean-up team do its job."

Zach hesitated, his eyes still haunted. "I can't let this happen again. I just can't..."

Anthony kept walking as he spoke, the dimness of the corridor devouring some of his words.

"We may not have a choice... All I know is there can be no quarter given. No compromise struck. We must keep the gifted alive so they can fulfil their destiny, no matter the price we must pay to accomplish it."

With that solemn vow, he walked through the remaining door frame and turned along the corridor. Outside, the night seemed to press in around them, as if the very darkness itself was communicating its malevolent intent. Zach looked around cautiously, nerves frayed. But Anthony wasn't afraid of the dark. He was the one who fought to keep the nightmares at bay.

Zach was thankful he was on his side.

Chapter Thirty-Two

The Chaos Dimension

The spectral hand did not hesitate. It picked up the Chronicler piece and moved it three squares diagonally, tapping on each space, watching the squares light up with a green phosphorescent glow as the hooded figure made the play on The Eternal Game board. A grotesque and twisted piece representing one of Anastasia's unleashed minions was blocking the Chronicler's progress, but it soon disappeared in a granular cloud as the Chronicler piece took that player out of the game.

The phantom opponent remained silent as she always did, surveying the terrain of the Eternal Game, her thoughts hidden. Anastasia grunted at the sight of one of her players disappearing off the board. She gracefully slid up from her chair, her eyes blazing and her feet apart, ready for confrontation.

"You are an insufferable woman, do you know that? There is something about you I have not sensed in my other opponents over the millennia. What is it?"

The phantom player said nothing; her silence, although expected, seemed to enrage her even more. But it wasn't rage but pleasure.

"Why do you favour that Chronicler player so? Do you know I could have had him slaughtered, and I spared him? What would you have done if I had?"

Anastasia strode away from the game to compose herself. In the heart of her shadowy lair, amidst the cacophony of eternal torment, she felt multiple orgasms and smiled crookedly.

It was exhilarating, infuriating, orgasmic and frustrating all at once. An incendiary device of heightened emotions in her chest that made her addicted and her nether regions wet, never disappointed. The Chronicler, who was supposed to be a disposable pawn with no meaningful role to play, was upgrading his significance every day. The Gifted ones were the glittering prizes, invaluable and sought after, and she had culled their number to nearly half. The Overlords would be pleased with that, but she was more ambitious. She cast her eyes, burning with a dark intensity, over at the spectral woman, knowing whoever she was in a past life, this would end how it always did.

"We will be ready for the Day of Reckoning," Anastasia mused aloud, her voice a haunting melody of menace and determination. The room seemed to pulse with anticipation, the air thick with the promise. She was ready to unleash the formidable among her legion of demons, but there were rules.

She looked away from the board and walked over to a stone plinth, atop a stone basin filled with a murky liquid with a mercurial sheen.

Oh, if the rules were different.

She waved her hand over the liquid, and an image swam into focus.

The magnificent Gorgath. A behemoth whose very shadow spelt doom. With skin as hard as obsidian and eyes that glowed with a malevolent ruby red, he was an unstoppable force of nature. Having him in her legions meant victory was a foregone conclusion, but not in this battle.

As the grotesque thought unfurled like a black daffodil in her mind, the images of the Sisters of Despair, a trio of demons whose beauty was only matched by their cruelty, appeared in the waters. They weaved illusions so convincing, so utterly terrifying, that even the strongest minds broke under their spell, but not what was required here.

The water bubbled, releasing a sickly fetid smell as the form of Azakel, a demon of shadows, able to slip through the smallest of cracks, undetected, a master assassin for those who thought themselves safe behind locked doors, appeared in all his glory. If only his speciality were necessary in this case, but it was not.

How beautiful it would be if she could let these three loose on the cattle of the Runnymede estate, but it would not be appropriate.

The Compliance Department had spoken, and they were a cabal not to be trifled with.

She thought of this not as a battle but more of a surgery that required finesse, not a blunt instrument. Anastasia turned back to the board, her mind racing with strategies and contingencies. The pieces moved to plan, and the dynamic shifting of fortunes with each passing moment was anticipated. With each move, she drew closer to her ultimate victory.

Human torment.

She was a general commanding her forces in a battle of cosmic significance, each move calculated with precision to bring maximum turmoil to those gifted with free will.

Beyond time and space, the night air of Runnymede Estate

grew chill, an ominous portent of the terror that was about to descend. The residents, unaware of the nightmare poised on their doorstep, slept soundly, their dreams soon to be invaded by the harbingers of despair.

Anastasia's smile dripped with malice.

Chapter Thirty-Three

"I can barely see them," Anthony pointed to the vague figures hustling through the mist-shrouded street.

"Let's get to them before they break the barrier and try to step out into the real world."

Zach was hurrying beside him.

"What if they do?" He asked.

"They can leave the estate if they want," Anthony thought about it for a moment. "The problem is if they have no intention of coming back. The programming makes sure that never happens. But if it did..." Anthony's tongue licked his lips as he thought some more. "The estate will try its best to stop them, but once they step outside of its influence, all protection would be forfeited, and they would lose all memory of their time here. The Darksiders would pick them off before the day ended."

Zach shuddered.

As far as Zach could intuit from the Journal, the estate's mystical barrier was a boundary designed to keep only the gifted in. Tonight's fog was an added layer of protection, thick and unnatural, a living thing that sought to confuse and mislead. And within it, dark shapes moved—lurking, waiting. The Gifted were tethered to the estate. They could leave, but an almost overpowering compulsion to return after twenty-four hours would force them back. Usually, the program worked perfectly, but this time, an issue had arisen with the coding.

Or had it been tampered with?

He had lived on the Runnymede Estate for five years now, and it was only on meeting Ms Hortense that he slowly began to recognise the true nature of the place he called home. And now, as the Chronicler, his eyes were wide open.

The estate was alive, and it was a bloodthirsty bastard.

"Mrs Fleming! Mr Fleming!" Zach called out to the two parents, who had a teenager between them. "We just need to talk."

The Flemings were trying to flee the estate, driven by fear and desperation. The program was a complex set of instructions that altered reality in ways that made the Eternal Game possible. One of the millions of problems it solved was keeping the Gifted from asking too many questions, particularly the youngsters. Being unable to leave the estate for six months meant that questions were bound to be asked and attempts would be made to leave before the allotted time. Even the adults, whether gifted or directly related to the gifted, had to be tempered, or the rules of the game could not be upheld. But whatever complex code that was written, in this case, the script wasn't working as effectively as it should.

The Flemings shouldn't be out here. They shouldn't have a need to flee.

Zach suspected that they heard him call out to them, but he wasn't sure. They disappeared in a shimmering, rolling bank of fog, their silhouettes contorting crazily as light refracted through water droplets. The estate was playing tricks with them. Creating a thick fog, subtly altering the laws of sound, making it difficult to form coherent thoughts. It was even adding a soundtrack of its own, producing a soundscape that was meant to confuse and disorient. All this was clear to him through the connection he had with the Journal. The Fleming family didn't know what was assaulting their senses. It was the estate they had lived in until something changed, waking them up to the fact that their home was actively dissuading them from leaving its embrace.

Zach thought of something morbid.

"Has anybody ever committed suicide, unable to handle the pressures?" The question was asked as a whisper.

Anthony snickered.

"The Eternal Game is as old as time. They've figured out most of the kinks and loopholes that could grind the game to a halt. The program that blankets this place prevents you humans from taking your own lives. They want to decide when you die. The infinite lines of instructions make sure no one can put a premature end to the game without the powers that be willing it."

Zach shivered.

BOTH MEN WERE MOVING QUICKLY THROUGH THE FOG, which had a sticky residue that condensed on their coats and skin.

"Stay close," Anthony said. "If I lose you in this soup, then we are both fucked.

"Roger that," Zach croaked, his whisper voice embarrassingly high. "I'm right beside you."

He was stuck with him, whether he was happy with it or not. The unseen energies swirling about them were making the hairs on the back of his neck and arms stand on end. He had better things to think about, but here he was still trying to wrap his head around the magic and power that established this game and what it required to keep it functioning. The ordinary residents were in the middle of a war, unable to remember any incidents related to the game. If you happened to be collateral damage, you would disappear from memory. Maybe relatives from outside the estate would still have their recollections, but anything inside the borders, Poof!

Zach couldn't help but wonder what would happen if he didn't make it. Would his dad return from Jamaica and not remember that his son ever existed? Would his father's lady friend still recall him? She didn't live on the estate, but did the reality programming still affect her?

Damn, Maya!

Surely, his girlfriend would remember him?

A cranial itch appeared on the inside of his skull, thinking about the conundrum. Ceasing to exist, all records of him, snuffed out. He breathed deeply, the prickly ends of anxiety turning up to gloat at him.

"Is your head in the game?" Anthony asked.

"Yeah," Zach lied.

They were still moving forward, and Zach was depending on Anthony's tracking skills to keep up with the fleeing family. But if he were having trouble orienting in the fog, they would be lost too. At that moment, it seemed like Zach was reading his mind.

"This isn't working," Anthony announced. "And we haven't got time," he paused for thought. "I'm going to try something."

Zach was open to anything. He had a sinking feeling they would not reach them in time, and that was something he wasn't sure he could accept, not again.

The fog felt like it was pressing in on him, growing thicker and more oppressive.

"What's your plan?" Zach wished his voice wasn't tinged with apprehension.

"Shed a little light on our dilemma," Anthony said.

Anthony picked up the pace and flew open his coat. Zach, matching his stride, could make out the warrior's silent annunciation, his words opening up the void inside the folds of his coat. Then, without hesitation, he reached inside eternity.

"We have to move fast," Anthony whispered, his voice barely audible. "The longer they're out here, the more danger they're in. We haven't got a lot of time," Anthony said. "So listen carefully."

WHEN THE FLARE WENT OFF, ZACH HAD HIS EYES CLOSED following Anthony's strict instructions. He referred to it as a flare, but it was nothing like any fireworks he had ever seen before. Anthony opened his big hand and thick fingers, and what lay on his palm was a kind of multi-coloured seed. It was brimming with trapped energy and was vibrating as if it were struggling to contain itself. That's what he threw into the air. Five seconds after the explosion, his eyes opened. They were back-to-back, and the seed had done its job.

For a moment.

That was enough.

The estate was alight.

In his visual zone, he could see everything. Night had become day, and the fog had become a thin, wispy veil. Zach had been assigned a hundred and eighty degrees field of view, and so had Anthony. Whoever saw the family first had to reach them before the illumination was lost to the fog.

They had seconds left.

His eyes moved up and down, left to right in rapid sweeps.

His brain is processing the familiar and assessing the unfamiliar.

Everything slowed as his eyes and perception narrowed. The seconds seemed to draw out like taffy, and he was absorbing ever more visual data. His pattern recognition capability had amped up. He could feel the deluge of associations being made with such speed and clarity that he wondered if it could slow down.

He could.

It did.

Zach saw the family just as they rounded a corner, using the newfound light to their advantage. He sprinted away from Anthony as the fog began to take hold again. It was back to its familiar thickness as he broke around the corner, seeing no more than two feet in front of him, but their position was seared into his mind.

A tree planted in a brick enclosure was coming up. He leapt, just as it appeared. He took one running step and launched himself up.

A bank of fog was all he could see.

When he hit the ground, he rolled and came to his feet in one fluid motion and kept running. A Skoda should be in his path next about five strides away, or could it be six?

Fuck it!

At four and a half strides, he threw himself into the air and was rewarded with his body smashing into the bonnet of the Skoda. He grunted and rolled off.

He kept moving and crashed into what he immediately knew was the absconding family. There were screams, yelps and a grunt as Zach's elbow connected with bone before rolling away. He scrambled to his feet and watched the family do the same. His eyes were wide and pleading to return to sanity, but instead, more insanity heaped upon them. They didn't know where to look. Their focus was flitting between the mist surrounding them and a young black man with his hands outstretched, trying his best to placate their fears. Mr Fleming's outstretched hand gripped a large chef's knife in Zach's direction. The grimace on his face said he was coiled to strike or die.

The Journal immediately opened up a dossier in his mind.

Toby Fleming – The Narrative Intuit

Gift: Narrative Intuition

Toby instinctively understands the "story" of a person, place, or situation—not the facts, but the arc. He can predict emotional climaxes and see when someone is about to break or transform. His gift makes him a natural strategist, editor of real life, and keeper of legacy. Lunar and Mars colonies will thrive because of his processes.

Impact: *A natural strategist, peacebroker, and keeper of moral trajectory—Toby will understand the heartbeat of a community like no one else.*

"I'm a friend," Zach hurried his introduction with his hands up in submission. "Mr Sylvester sent me," he took a breath. "Mr and Mrs Fleming, Toby, are you okay?"

"What do you want from us?"

"You'll die if you continue down this road."

"We'll die if we stay."

Hearing Sylvester's name seemed to control the panic in their eyes, but the fog was disorienting and had an anxiety-inducing effect.

Maybe that's why they didn't answer his query. Maybe that's why they were still looking into the fog with a kitchen knife extended, his wife muttering.

First, it made no sense.

Then it did.

Mrs Fleming had a dog lead in her hand. At its end, there was no collar, no dog attached to that collar, just a mangled leather strap and a bloody smear left on the concrete. She was muttering the dog's name.

"We just thought, leaving would be the best option," the father muttered." I couldn't just sit back. I had to do something."

Whatever was slithering around in the swirling eddies of the fog had taken their pet, and the Fleming family was poised for it to return. Mister Fleming hugged his wife, and his son Toby, an adolescent, seemed more frustrated than frightened.

"Let's stay together," Zach pleaded with them. "When my partner gets here, we are gone." He tried to get the family to look at him and wanted to scream the question, What were you thinking? That was for another time and place. Right now, he had to get them back to the relative safety of their flat. Zach activated part two of their plan by unzipping a pocket in his trousers and reaching inside. The device he took out felt cool to the touch and was as heavy as a pebble. He threw it around the corner and heard it rattle on the ground, just as he had been instructed, and immediately it began pulsing powerful, bright waves of light.

Anthony could use that to find them. In the meantime, he had to keep them calm and together.

Zach tried to distract them from the immediate danger they were facing by asking questions. Maybe talking would help alleviate his rising fear, too.

His voice was low and gravelly as he directed his question to the man.

"Why now? Why try to leave after two years, knowing the consequences?"

Mr Fleming stared right through him. His eyes were wide with fear, but there was also confusion. That emotion seemed to come and go.

"It felt like... the right thing to do. It said it would be good. It would all be good."

"Who said?" Zach asked.

"Who...," Mr Fleming abruptly lost his train of thought, and that distant stare returned.

The fog swirled around them.

"Who?" Zach asked.

"It felt like a good idea," Toby answered in place of his father. His voice was strong, but Zach sensed an uncertainty about him, too, like he was holding something back. "This was a good time."

There was that word again, 'Good', Zach thought.

"Did someone encourage you to leave, convince you it was a 'good' idea?"

Toby shook his head as if trying to gain some clarity. He ignored the question or forgot what was being asked. He hugged his mother.

Zach was sure that something had overridden the code that had kept them questioning their circumstances. Making them think that they had a choice of leaving the estate when they didn't.

A good way of flushing out The Gifted into the open and picking them off at your leisure.

Throw in a Chronicler to sweeten the deal.

Zach grimaced.

A sudden dog's howl of pain coming from a fog bank ahead of them made him jump.

It seemed to be distant at first, but the yelping came closer. The disturbing sound of the dog in distress, being viciously taunted. It was like an echo chamber, and they were in its centre.

The dog's pleas were agonising.

"Rufus?" Mrs Fleming wailed, suddenly struggling to get free from her husband and run to the agonising sound. "I'm coming," she said, wriggling out of her jacket.

"Mrs Fleming!" Zach screamed, reaching out to her, knowing if she disappeared into the fog, he'd never see her again.

His fingers grasped air, his heart pounding. Regret was already washing over him.

He scrambled towards her, but she had freed herself from her husband and was heading towards the source of the sound.

Toby wrestled her to the ground.

A sudden noise cut through the silence—a rustling, swishing sound of a blade, slicing through the air, followed by a shriek and the thud of something large and moist hitting the concrete. Zach peered into the disorienting, swirling fog in the direction of the sound, but all was quiet.

Then he heard the whistling.

A smile appeared on his face, knowing who would turn up in a minute.

Anthony emerged out of the fog with the amulet around his neck, blinking brightly like a powerful strobe light.

"That was not your dog," Anthony said flatly. "The thing mimicking your pet was hoping to lure you in. Don't do that again."

"My partner," Zach said, introducing him quickly, his relief obvious. "We're getting out of here now."

Nothing more needed to be said. The warrior nodded, his actions aligning completely with the Chronicler's.

"I'll take point," Anthony said to Zach. Then he turned to

the family. "Stay behind me. Grab my coat and hold hands. Do not let go."

They nodded.

Anthony handed Zach the strobing amulet.

"Put this on and swing it to your back. Nothing will come up and surprise you from behind. Hold on to Mr Fleming's belt at all times."

"What about you?" Zach asked. "How are you going to see?"

Anthony snickered.

"You'll need it more than I do. Let's go and stay close."

They pressed on with Anthony at the head, their senses heightened. The fog seemed to close in around them, dampening sound and distorting their perception. Every shadow became a potential threat, every trick of the light a possible attack. What the Fleming family didn't understand was that the two men at the front and back of them were willing to sacrifice their lives to get them back home. Nothing would stop this human convoy from moving forward, not if Anthony had anything to say about it.

Chapter Thirty-Four

Z ach gripped the handle of the shopping bags a little
tighter, his eyes scanning the dimly lit corridor. The
walls were heavy with the scent of damp concrete,
and the only light came from the occasional flickering fluorescent lights, casting eerie shadows that danced across the graffiti-
covered walls. He could feel Anthony's presence behind him,
moving silently but with a tension in his steps that mirrored his
own. At this hour, the estate was teeming with demonic activity, a place where the veil between the worlds was paper-thin.
The almost hilarious thing was that the majority of humans
that the Darksiders rubbed shoulders with would have no idea
they were mingling with beings from a dark dimension whose
intentions were to sow seeds of chaos in the plane of reality
they called home. There may have been some dignity if they
had at least been observers of the game, but they were less than
that. They were disrespected and relegated to mere cannon
fodder. Zach couldn't help thinking that was a good thing, a
necessary thing. That's why walking unimpeded for almost
thirty minutes and not being confronted by some threat was

nerve-wracking in itself. Even the Darksiders couldn't work effectively with that degree of panic. They loved surprise and melodrama. That's why Zach's level of frustration was mounting. Why don't they do what they must? Get it over and done with. Let the night begin.

He looked back at Anthony striding behind him, his eyes were like aquamarine crystals, his head moving from left to right in a practised sweeping pattern.

If his warrior companion's demeanour was any indication of his state of mind, he was frustrated, too.

Come on, you wankers, Zach thought. I know you're watching us make your move.

His prayer. His wish. We're not to be.

Zach felt the thumping bassline as they walked up the concrete funnel of the landing.

Their destination.

Surprise.

He recognised the soulful tones of Reggae icon Dennis Brown from listening to his dad's reggae sets on a Sunday.

Sylvester had sent them to deliver groceries to this gifted individual. He was to be their last outreach before the chaos to come in twenty-four hours. He was one of four survivors, and all they were told was that he was a veteran physics professor named Ras Tobias. The fact that he lived in Esquire Tower near the Wormwood Fields Cemetery was enough to put them on edge.

As they approached the door of apartment 34a, they both felt it—a presence, just out of sight, watching them. The sensation was subtle, like the prickle of static on the skin, but unmistakable. Zach exchanged a glance with Anthony, who gave a slight nod. They were being watched, but if they didn't make themselves known, they didn't care.

They pressed on, reaching the door. It was plain, battered

by time and perhaps the occasional scuffle, but the sound seeping from within was anything but ordinary. The bass of reggae music vibrated through the air, making the floor beneath their feet hum with rhythm. Zach looked down to see an elaborate veve design made in chalk, fully intact, protecting the entrance. He lifted his hand and pressed the buzzer, the sharp sound cutting through the music for a moment before being swallowed up by the bass once more. He pressed it again, and then once more.

The Journal made its introductions on the screen of his mind's eye, before the door swung open.

Ras Tobias – The Harmonic Architect

Gift: Emotional Resonance

Ras Tobias has unlocked what many suspected but could not prove—that **sound***, particularly in music, can tune the emotional fields of human beings at a bio-quantum level. Through precision frequencies layered into his compositions, he can calm rage, heal trauma, or awaken buried empathy. His proprietary technology will be utilised to mitigate tensions and foster dialogue.*

Impact: Imagine urban centres where violence is defused with harmony rather than force; that is the Ras's dream.

A MAN STOOD IN THE DOORWAY, HIS PRESENCE commanding but warm. His grey locks stretched down his back like silver rivers, and a pair of headphones perched on his head, though they did little to contain the music that spilt out into the hallway. He regarded them with wise, curious eyes, a smile lifting the corners of his mouth.

"Sylvester sent us," Zach said, his voice clear but respectful.

The smile broadened on Ras Tobias' face. "Come in, Iyah, come in."

They stepped into the apartment, immediately enveloped by the warmth of the space. It was unlike anything Zach had expected. The air was thick with the scent of incense, a soothing counterpoint to the throbbing bassline of the reggae music that filled the room. But it was the chalkboards that caught his eye, each one crowded with equations—long, complex strings of numbers and symbols that looked like a language of their own. Shelves lined the walls, filled with vinyl records and books, while sophisticated sound equipment dominated the living room, its wires snaking across the floor like roots.

Anthony's eyes widened slightly as he took it all in.

"You're... not your average Physics professor, are you?"

Ras Tobias chuckled, a deep, rolling sound that matched the bass that continued to thrum through the room. "Not at all, champion, not at all. I man, is an Acoustician to be exact. And a Sound System owner too. Maths and music—they're not so different, you know. Both can change the way people see the world."

Zach set the grocery bags down on the kitchen counter, glancing around. The place was surprisingly tidy, given the sheer amount of equipment and chalkboards that filled it. He noted the lack of food in the kitchen, the empty shelves and bare counters. "I've been told you haven't eaten in 24 hours," he said, turning to Tobias. "Do you want me to rustle something up?"

Anthony looked at him.

Zach shrugged.

'It helps me to relax."

Ras Tobias nodded enthusiastically at the offer.

"Yes, Iyah, that would be blessed. Just some steamed vegetables and rice will do."

"Easy," Zach nodded and began unpacking the groceries and preparing the small space. "So, Ras, what are you working on?"

Ras Tobias walked over to one of the chalkboards, picking up a piece of chalk and twirling it between his fingers as he spoke.

"You know dat music is vibration seen—waveforms moving through space. But what if I told you that the same principles that govern these waveforms also govern the universe itself? Every particle, every atom, vibrates, moves in a rhythm all its own, like a cosmic dancehall."

Zach listened as he chopped vegetables, the knife moving rhythmically against the cutting board, the sound blending with the music in the background. Ras Tobias' voice was deep and melodic, as though he was channelling the rhythm of the music itself into his words.

"Quantum mechanics, they call it—a science of possibilities, of probabilities. Everything exists in potential, and it's the observer who decides what becomes real, just by the act of observation. But what if we could guide that potential? What if we could use music—these vibrations—sound to uplift human consciousness, to guide it to a higher state of being?"

Anthony leaned against the wall, his arms crossed, but his attention was entirely on Tobias.

"I thought music did that anyway."

Ras Tobias nodded his head in agreement.

"Hit and miss, rude bwoy. I'm talking about a way to boost your mood and elevate your emotions without your conscious effort, every single time."

"You're saying you can do that using this music?" Anthony asked.

Ras Tobias smiled, a twinkle in his eye.

"I believe so. You see, Reggae is more than just music—it's a message. It's about unity, peace, and resistance against oppression. When you combine that message with the right frequencies and the right vibrations, you can resonate with the very fabric of the universe. You can lift people up, open their minds, and their hearts. It's like tuning a radio to the right frequency— you get rid of the static, and suddenly, everything becomes clear."

As he spoke, Ras Tobias moved to his sound system, adjusting dials and switches with the practised ease of someone who had done this a thousand times. The music shifted subtly, the bassline deepening, the rhythm slowing slightly, becoming almost meditative. Zach could feel it in his bones —the way the music seemed to pulse through him, syncing with his heartbeat and breath.

"Every frequency, every note, has a corresponding wavelength," Ras Tobias continued, his hands moving with the grace of a conductor as he adjusted the sound. "And those wavelengths interact with the world around us, with the people around us. It's all about finding the right combination, the right harmony, to elevate the mind, to clear away the negativity, the darkness. My H.C.E can do that."

"H.C.E?" Anthony asked.

The Ras nodded.

"H.C.E stands for Harmonic Cognition Enhancer. My baby is a revolutionary neuro-acoustic modulation tool that works in tandem with specific musical compositions to stimulate and strengthen neural pathways associated with peace, cooperation, empathy, and emotional resilience. While it nuh override free will or brainwash yuh, it optimises the brain's natural capacity for positive cognitive functions. Positive vibrations, Iyah."

Zach stirred the vegetables in the pan, the sizzle of cooking food mingling with the steady beat of the music. It was hard not to be drawn in by Tobias's words, by the sheer passion and conviction in his voice. This wasn't just theory to him—it was a mission, a purpose.

"But how do you know it works?" Anthony asked, his scepticism giving way to curiosity.

Ras Tobias paused, his hand resting on one of the dials.

"It's not just about theory, Iyah. I've been experimenting, testing the effects of the H.C.E for a while now at Goldsmiths University of London. When you play certain frequencies, certain rhythms, people respond. Their mood shifts, their thoughts clear. Our tests have proven it—people who were lost an confused suddenly find clarity an peace. And it's not just about the individual—it's about the collective. When enough minds resonate together, when enough people are lifted up, it creates a wave, a movement. And that, Iyah, is powerful."

Zach glanced over at Anthony, who was nodding slowly, his usual pragmatism tempered by a growing interest. Ras Tobias played his classic reggae tunes, enlightening Anthony on the artists and the history.

As Zach plated the Jamaican steamed cabbage and rice, he couldn't help but feel a sense of respect for the man in front of him. Ras Tobias was a warrior, just like them, but his battlefield was different to theirs. His weapons weren't swords or reality-altering algorithms, but music and mathematics, electrons and vacuum tubes. And yet, the stakes were just as high—perhaps even higher.

He carried the plates over to the small table, setting them down with a nod.

"Here you go."

Ras Tobias smiled broadly, clapping Zach on the shoulder

as he sat down. "Blessed, man, blessed. It's not every day I get such fine company, and good food to match."

The meal was simple but nourishing—steamed cabbage seasoned with Jamaican herbs, scotch bonnet pepper and a side of perfectly cooked rice. As they prepared to eat, the music continued to play softly in the background, the steady bassline a comforting presence that seemed to ground the room in a sense of peace. Anthony took a seat as well, his usual guarded expression softening slightly as he picked up his fork and sampled some Earth food.

As they ate, the conversation flowed easily, the three of them discussing everything from quantum mechanics to the best reggae artists, to the challenges of life on the Runnymede estate. The tension that had gripped Zach and Anthony when they first arrived slowly eased here, replaced by a sense of camaraderie and connection. They were different, each of them, but in that moment, it didn't matter. They were united by a common goal, a shared understanding of the stakes involved in the world they navigated.

"So, where do you see this going?" Anthony asked, his plate picked clean. He ignored Zach's incredulous look of surprise. "This theory of yours—how do you plan to apply it?"

Ras Tobias leaned back in his chair, a contemplative look crossing his face. "I see it as a movement, Iyah. One that starts small, in places like this, but grows. People are seeking something real, something that connects them to the world and to one another. Music has always had that power, but when you combine it with science, with a deep understanding of how the universe works, you can do so much more. You can elevate the collective consciousness."

"Sounds like you're talking about a revolution," Zach said, a slight smile playing on his lips. He could understand why the Darksiders wanted him dead. He was dangerous.

Anthony nodded slowly, his brow furrowed in thought. "Reggae music?"

Ras Tobias spread his hands, palms up, as if the answer were obvious. "Reggae, jazz, classical—it's not just the genre, Iyah, it's the intention behind it. The frequencies, the rhythms —they're a tool, a way to access something deeper. Reggae just happens to be my way, my connection. But the science behind it, the math, that's universal. It's about finding the right harmony, the right balance, and then sharing that with others."

"So, what's next?" Zach asked, leaning forward slightly. "How do you take this from theory to practice?"

Ras Tobias smiled, his eyes lighting up with a fire that hadn't been there before. "I'm building someting, someting big. A sound system, but more than just speakers and amps. It's going to be a vehicle for dis movement, a way to spread the message, to reach people where they are. Sylvester has been a big supporter. I've been working on it for years, refining both the technology and deh equations. And I'm ready."

They finished the meal in companionable silence. Zach felt a sense of peace he hadn't felt for five days, but it was fleeting.

The test was upon them.

The Day of Reckoning was to come.

In the next twenty-four hours, the rules that kept some semblance of sanity alive would no longer apply.

Hell on Earth.

As they prepared to leave, Ras Tobias clasped each of their hands in turn, his grip firm and warm. "The estate is dangerous, Iyah, but remember—there's always light, even in the darkest places. And music, well, that's the light I choose to shine."

Zach nodded, wondering if that was enough.

"We'll be back," he promised.

Anthony gave Ras Tobias a nod, his usual stoic expression softened with a hint of respect.

"Stay safe."

Chapter Thirty-Five

The Day Of Reckoning

The knock on the door made Zach's gut tighten as if his stomach was intimately connected to the old brass knocker. He took two deep breaths and jumped off his bed fully clothed and as ready as he was going to be for a day like no other.

The Day of Reckoning was upon him, and he was shit scared.

He had woken early, or what could be conceived as early, because the Runnymede estate was trapped in a period between seconds after the hour of midnight, and it would remain that way until the day was done. His circadian rhythms were fucked, and although he felt fully rested, he had a dull sensation of timelessness throbbing in his temple. Breakfast was a no-no; he would be fuelled by adrenaline for hours to come.

Was it day or night?

Did it even matter in this Twilight Zone? He couldn't tell and didn't care. He looked at his smartphone out of habit, placed it on his side table and massaged the screen with the pad of his finger. As the phone's home screen loaded, Zach gasped, swore, and flung his phone onto the bed, stepping back.

A shiver zigzagged up and down his spine.

"Fuckers!" He spat.

The Darksiders had co-opted his phone.

His screensaver was a picture of his mother from the early 80s, all dolled up with nowhere to go, according to his father. It was a snippet of memory he loved to carry with him, and they had defiled it. The image that was mocking him from his phone was a dark version of his mother, her skirt hiked up, a grotesque smile, a tongue licking her lips, on her hands and knees and something naked and hung servicing her from behind.

"Shit!"

He covered the screen and thrust it into his back pocket, squeezing his eyes closed, but the image was already seared on his mind like a white hot brand.

"Fuck you, I'm going to do this."

He slipped into his lightweight jacket and gloves and cast an eye at his windows. The curtains of his room were pulled tightly closed because he didn't want to see what his world had become.

Not yet.

The Journal was under his pillow. Snaking his hand through his unmade bed, his finger found it easily as it hummed like a small motor.

Excited or scared, he didn't know which. Zach just slipped it into his leather satchel. As ready as he was going to be, he exited his bedroom.

All this could have been easier. What was he thinking?

He could have stayed at the barbershop with Medusa. It would have been safer, but he insisted. Sylvester had ensured that an armed cadre remained with him throughout the night. Medusa wanted to be the one to have his back, but he had convinced her to stay behind and prepare for today. Something was telling him he needed to be home for this and ground himself in some way. The reasoning eluded him, but it felt right.

His two minders were in the kitchen playing a weird strategy game that resembled multi-level chess. They both were dressed for war. Their barbershop bibs were replaced with smart-looking leather, carbon fibre and metal armour. They looked up when he approached and respectfully stood.

"How was your rest, Chronicler?"

Zach stopped and placed his hand on the broad shoulders of one of the men.

"I slept like a baby. Have you been up all night?"

Zach looked at both men; they were awake and alert. He just knew what they would say.

"I only wish this shit was over and done."

One man smiled wanly, his eyes sparkling. The other bowed in agreement.

"That is what we are here to do... To end it."

Zach wandered into the kitchen, and both men came to attention without realising it. One man's jaw clenched. He showed an impressive network of muscle along his jawline, while the other flexed his fingers like steel traps. These men were no longer barbers, tattooists, hair stylists, or nail technicians; now, they were warriors, and they were not playing.

"Chocolate," one of them asked, having left his seat and was already standing beside a cup and the kettle.

"That's the least I can do. My appetite is dead."

"Who was at the door?"

"Anthony!"

Zach was surprised. He had naturally thought the warrior would rise when the sun dipped behind the giant grey stalks of the tower blocks, as he had done over the last five days. On the

Day of Reckoning, the rules changed, it seemed. With a mug of chocolate in hand, Zach made his way to the front door. For a moment, he stood looking at it. How many times had he opened it and stepped out into what he thought was the real world? He reached for the door's handle and hesitated. A chill like an inverse electrostatic shock tickled his fingertips. For a brief moment, he pictured himself back in his room, the sheets over his shoulders and the door securely locked. A feeling of comfort didn't get the opportunity to take hold as his resolve reestablished itself. The fear would never diminish, and neither would his purpose. He swung the door open and stared at Anthony's back and his familiar leather greatcoat. Zach needed a focal point to anchor him before he took in the environment around him.

"How are you adapting to the Negative Zone?"

Anthony didn't turn around. Zach could feel his intensity radiating off him.

"I'll manage."

He kept his eyes on the detail of Anthony's coat, determined not to look at the new environment outside.

"Well then, let's finish what we started."

Zach nodded and turned back to the kitchen. He left his half-finished drink beside the sink, the taste of the dark chocolate still on his taste buds.

"I'll wash up when I get back."

If you get back.

He thought to himself.

Chapter Thirty-Six

The air was pregnant with alien energy. Zach had no choice but to experience the sensation assaulting him from this Negative Zone version of the estate. The act of breathing felt weird. He'd never been to an environment that was high altitude before - he had read about it. But this must be the feeling or something close to it. Or was this his mind coping with the overwhelm? Anthony was unmoved by the changes around him, and if he wasn't, then he was in no mood to talk about it. After all, he had more pressing concerns on his mind. Survival being high up on his list. Both men walked side by side, their disquiet palpable.

The gravel crunched beneath Zach's boots as he and Anthony walked through the estate's winding paths. It should have felt familiar—he'd spent his whole life on this stretch of land, navigating the brick-paved alleyways, the narrow courtyards, the rooftops that slanted just enough for mischief. But today, nothing was familiar.

An overcast sky hung low, pressing down like a weighted shroud. It wasn't just a dull grey; it was a dense, depthless shade that seemed to soak up any shred of colour left in the world. Wherever they were, a sun of any sort did not kiss the Earth of this domain. Even the estate's hallmark red-tiled roofs looked drained, ghostly in the muted light. Zach scratched at his arms, his skin crawling as if he'd walked through cobwebs he couldn't shake. The air smelled faintly of rot, something dark and rank that stayed just out of reach, teasing at the edges of your senses.

Anthony strode beside him, unflinching, unbothered by the estate's transformation. "You never forget your first time," he said, glancing sideways at Zach, a hint of a grin shadowed across his face.

"Yeah..." Zach said, lost for words, trying to keep the waver out of his voice. "Smells like ..."

"Rot?" Anthony finished. "It's like life and death are struggling for dominance, and death is winning." His eyes swept over the skeletal trees lining the main courtyard, their leaves long gone. "Trapped between one second and the next. Limbo, or close enough."

The words dropped between them, heavy and unsettling. Limbo. A crack in time itself. It made sense, in that twisted way all things made sense in this world. Only the Gifted were awake, the ones who'd somehow earned Headhunters' protection. At the same time, the vast majority —his neighbours, his family, people he'd known his entire life—lay trapped in slumber, vulnerable.

The two men stood outside of Mrs Hunt's flat, relieved that the door was still on its hinges and colourful protective sigils surrounded the entrance. He couldn't go about today's grim tasks without making sure the old lady was okay. This service should be every resident's right, but sadly, the reality was somewhat different.

Anthony looked at Zach.

"Mrs Hunt is well prepared?"

Zach nodded, his heart pounding in his chest.

"I'm just making sure."

Anthony picked the door lock, and both men entered.

THE BUILDINGS GROANED UNDER THE WEIGHT OF CHAOS. Within the transdimensional pocket, the unnatural silence of frozen time wrapped the estate like a suffocating shroud. Homes flickered between their mundane forms and something warped, elongated shadows, cracked walls that bled black ichor, windows that reflected otherworldly realms instead of their surroundings. The air shimmered as though struggling to hold itself together, rippling with each howl of a Darksider.

The demons were a grotesque parade of chaos, their forms ever-shifting but always terrifying: talons sharp enough to rend steel, glowing eyes radiating cold malice, their twisted shapes sometimes bipedal, sometimes crawling like beasts. They prowled and floated through the estate, slipping through walls and doors like smoke. Residents in their cursed sleep moaned faintly, clutching at their chests in some distant recognition of their imminent doom.

From his vantage point, people were dying, and Zach could only watch in horror. He was so wired that when Anthony closed the door and stepped over the protective glyphs of Mrs Hunt's flat and stood behind him, he nearly jumped out of his skin.

"Are you okay?" Anthony looked concerned.

"No, I'm not fucking okay," he snapped. "I'm glad Mrs Hunt is protected. But me..."

"You're doing well, Zach," he slapped him on the back. "This place was not meant for humans in three-dimensional space, and here you are. You're stronger than you think."

Zach thought about it.

"The Gifted will be safe at Headhunters, right?" Zach's voice was barely a whisper. The environment seemed to demand it. He tried to imagine the many people who had sat in the pristine leather chairs, hair braided in precise patterns to ward off the Darksider's reach, a spell woven into every twist and coil. He'd tried to imagine the sigils tattooed into skin and shuddered at the thought of the vast majority of residents without.

Anthony's face softened, a rare thing under the circumstances.

"The Gifted we will protect with our lives. The rest ..."

He shook his head.

"You and I will do our best."

A sudden shiver shot down Zach's spine, prickling and persistent. He glanced at the community centre, where he'd spent late nights - before the demonic assaults - with friends, now a bleached, hollow shell. He almost heard the whispers, the faint echoes of voices that felt like they should still be filling that space but were locked out of reach, like the trapped residents. "So they're...they're just lying there?"

Anthony's mouth tightened, a flicker of something hard in his eyes. "You saw Mrs Hunt. She's lying in her bed, helpless, if she hadn't protected herself. The estate is easy pickings without our programs. And the majority are unprepared." He rolled his shoulders, cracking his neck like he was gearing up for a fight. "That's why we're here."

Zach clenched his fists, trying to focus on that simple truth. They'd come to keep everyone safe - or at least the ones they could reach. But the weight of it, of every step they took through this hollowed-out, twisted version of home, pressed down on him with every breath.

"You don't...you don't get used to it," he said, almost to

himself. "Feels like the place is—" he hesitated, searching for the right word "—fighting itself."

Anthony nodded, then paused and closed his eyes. When he opened them again, they glittered blue.

"Let's go. I think the boss needs us."

THE RUNNYMEDE ESTATE SHIMMERED AS LINES OF esoteric code altered perception and muted reality into shades of silver and twilight. Every brick, every door, every streetlamp looked dull and lifeless, caught in the between-space. Inhuman howls and snatches of dark laughter echoed in the strange stasis, chilling Zach's blood as he kept his eyes sharp, scanning from doorway to doorway.

Next to him, Anthony, with his impressive height and the heavy, dreadlock-styled mane he wore loose tonight, moved quietly, his presence both reassuring and ominous. Together, they followed Headhunter protocol, scanning for anyone left wandering outside or who hadn't made it into the safety of the barbershop. By day, these warriors were specialists in trims, fades, nail art, or a quick fix to a mangled tattoo—but on the Day of Reckoning, they became something else entirely.

"Over there, two o'clock," Anthony pointed with a quick flick of his head.

Zach glanced in the direction and spotted two rare figures - not gifted but immune to the sleep spell—a mother clutching her child, eyes wild with terror, edging along the walls as if that would somehow conceal them from the demons roaming free tonight.

"Shit," Zach whispered, then louder, "Ma'am! Over here!"

The woman glanced at them, face stretched in horror as she hesitated. Her child, wide-eyed and silent, clutched her leg tightly.

"Quickly!" Anthony urged, moving toward them with Zach at his side, both men forming a protective front.

Just as they were about to reach the woman, a shadow peeled itself away from the darkness, revealing a Darksider with unnaturally long limbs, a smile too wide for its face and a mouth filled with jagged razor-sharp teeth. The demon wore a distorted approximation of a human form that, at any moment, could revert to a more comfortable, familiar and gruesome shape.

Zach, without thinking about his own safety, ran towards the woman. The machete Anthony had given him was out of its sheath and in his hand.

The woman stumbled into Zach's arms, and he awkwardly pointed the blade towards the creature as it lunged. Then, playfully, the Darksider stopped in its tracks and laughed. Dancing on the spot like a sadistic marionette.

Anthony stepped in, throwing his hands up. They glowed briefly with a soft blue light. The demon stopped in mid-prance and eyed him.

Anthony was in no mood.

"I'm game if you're game," Anthony growled at the creature. "But if you step to me, I'm going to make you wish you'd invited a friend."

The demon chuckled, its voice a twisted sound like a crackling radio. "Just a matter of time. You can't save them all, Headhunter."

The Darksider faded back, but not without giving them a parting grin that made Zach shiver.

"You good?" Anthony asked, casting a glance toward Zach.

"Good as I can be," Zach muttered. He moved to the mother and child, gently guiding them. "Let's go. Follow me. Keep your eyes on my back, and don't look anywhere else."

The woman nodded, clutching her child close, and they

moved quickly through the eerie stillness toward the barbershop. Zach could feel the woman's terror pressing against him, like her fear was a real, tangible thing clinging to the back of his jacket.

"How many more are out here?" Zach asked, his voice quiet but tense.

"A few. And some are probably still hiding. It's a big estate," Anthony replied, his voice carrying that steady confidence Zach could always count on. "They'll survive if they make their way to the shop. At least they're mobile."

In the distance, the barbershop lit up the depressing landscape like a lighthouse. Its avant-garde architecture never fit with the brutalist design of the estate in the first place; in this dimension, it was the very antithesis of what this place stood for. Its futuristic, red-and-white striped pole spun on the outside, flickering with a soft, protective glow that sent out wards across the immediate area.

Another Headhunter, a wiry man, his leather-metal protective garment decorated with splashes of demon gore, appeared from the side street and waved them over.

"Got three kids stashed in the bus shelter," Sean reported. His face was streaked with sweat, and his eyes darted, restless. "One of 'em's pretty banged up. Couldn't leave 'em."

"Of course not," Anthony said, clapping Sean on the shoulder. "Where are they? Let's get 'em inside."

Zach glanced at the sky, which seemed frozen in perpetual dusk. "Let's move. If we stay out here much longer…"

As they made their way to the shelter, Zach could feel the stares of creatures watching from nearby windows and darkened corners, hidden yet present, knowing they had time on their hands, savouring their freedom and not rushing the gourmet meal of human souls and human flesh. It wasn't long before they saw the kids, huddled together, faces pale but determined.

They escorted the group past a play area. The swings' frame was grotesquely twisted, the chains and seat dragging on the ground. The see-saw snapped in the middle, and the benches melted into strange shapes.

"What is it with demons and defacing public property?" Zach muttered under his breath.

Anthony laughed.

Zach couldn't wait to step into the shop; the oppressive atmosphere outside lifted, just a little. The familiar hum of magic filled the air, buzzing against his skin like a low-grade current, protective and alive. Inside, the air was thick with incense and the subtle hum of clippers, the smell of lavender and rosemary cutting through the lingering decay outside. Faces turned toward him—some relieved, some exhausted, all united in a grim determination that matched his own.

Chapter Thirty-Seven

"I've said this countless times before, and you'll bear witness to me saying it countless times more. But for the few who haven't heard this speech, here it is."

Sylvester took off his glasses and ponderously cleaned the lens, placing it neatly back onto the bridge of his nose.

"I'm proud of you all."

His tone grew darker.

"The forces of evil have free rein for the duration. The residents are in the 'Deep Sleep' and we don't have the numbers to prevent them from taking souls."

Sylvester stood on a stool, looking out over the serious faces that made up the crew: barbers, hairdressers, nail technicians, and tattooists. Then there was the back-of-house crew, engineers, and scientists who played their part in the Barbershop's smooth running. They were all here.

"I know you're resting and taking sustenance to go back out there. I need your attention for a moment. Mr Fitzsimmons and Mr Mupato have arranged for seven teams to patrol the seven houses. Report to your team leaders. Our hands may be tied, but we will do our best."

Zach stood at the back, not needing to see Sylvester's face to know he was worried. Worried more for the community and the crew than for himself. And for what he knew of this day, he had a right to be. The Day of Reckoning would be their D-Day, and Sylvester was rallying the troops. Zach looked around for Medusa and saw her golden locks at the very front, absorbing the excitement and fear from their leader.

"People are going to be scared and confused in the moment, people are going to die and be injured, we must do our best to aid and support them. They don't deserve this; they never asked for this, but they are a part of the game. Care for them."

Zach had his Journal open in the palm of his hand throughout everything Sylvester said. His pen was hurrying across the blank pages, recording this historical moment. What else could he call it? A conflict that has been ongoing for a millennium, spanning multiple universes and realities. And he was a witness to it and a player. That feeling as the Journal bypassed his conscious mind to control his output was exhilarating. It felt as though he was a separate, benevolent entity, keenly observing an unusual story unfolding. All his human senses, as well as the others, which he would never have been familiar with if not for the Journal, were required to compile this document, which was of such importance to this conflict. Would the final reader of the Journal appreciate the horror, blood and sweat that went into the manuscript? Would they be able to use it to their advantage the next time these two forces clashed in some far-off reality? These were questions he may never be able to answer. He had faith that what he was doing was significant.

Leave deh world bettah than yuh found it, his old man *always told him.*

In some ways, he has tried to live some of his life by that maxim. For the last five days, he had certainly made a difference, and his father would be proud of him. But there was more to do, more sacrifices to make, and he wondered if he could handle it. What more could they throw at him?

As soon as that thought blossomed, Sylvester called over to him.

Chapter Thirty-Eight

"I have something very important I want you both to do. I've been planning this in secret. I had doubts whether I should go ahead with it." Sylvester looked at both men intensely. The eyes behind his glasses were sparkling. "I've decided we must."

He had shed his usual Headhunter barber apron, replacing it with a leather/metal amalgam that looked flexible and rugged, a clear sign of the change in the situation. His razors and scissors were no longer in sight, replaced by a chunky blade with a bejewelled hilt strapped to his chest. The sounds of activity were everywhere around them. The salon was on a war footing, and like everything else today, nothing felt the same.

Zach and Anthony moved in closer, all three of them shuffling around to create some space in the frenetic activity around them.

"In the past, this ongoing nightmare, we had no choice but to see it through," Sylvester squeezed the shoulders of both men standing beside, his voice lowered and tired. "We've always had our hands tied as we had to adhere to the rules of The Game, the circumstances we found ourselves in."

Anthony took in a deep breath.

"How does knowing this help us?"

"My friend," Sylvester twisted his head to look at him. "There is something special about this dimension. Can't you feel it?"

Anthony shook his head.

"We have no time for details, but Spokes and Nanny posited the idea. We have nothing to lose and everything to gain. Chronicler?"

Sylvester looked at Zach.

"You and Anthony must escort Ras Tobias to the piazza. This will be an interesting entry into the Journal."

Anthony was no good at whispering. He might as well have spoken to everyone in the room.

"He's not here? Shouldn't he be fully secured with the remaining Gifted Ones?"

Sylvester inhaled deeply.

"Under normal circumstances, maybe, but this time we have plans. Ras Tobias knows what to do; follow his lead."

Anthony chuckled, a humourless, grim and calculating expression.

"The Darksiders ain't gonna like it."

Sylvester thought about it for a whole second.

"I don't give a rat's ass, take their heads for our trophy room if they try to intervene."

"Sylvester said to show you, not tell yuh, young bwoy."

That was Ras Tobia's cryptic answer to Zach's question and only part of what had him worried.

The professor was humming.

How could anyone be in the mood for optimism in a world like this? How?

Zach imagined that Anthony's alien psychology could adapt to places like this.

Tobias, on the other hand, was a human. He was gifted, yes, but what made him special was his intellect, not his adaptability.

He knew something Zach didn't.

Both Sylvester and Ras Tobias had planned this. The Rastaman knew what to expect and was confident with it.

His humming was pissing Zach off, but he restrained his impatience.

All three men were carrying duffel bags. They had made their way from the professor's flat to the ground floor, then across a terrace area that was open to the elements, surrounded by the brutish grey architecture of Runnymede. Looking up, Zach shuddered at the slate grey sky filled with flying things, skittering creatures defying gravity and scuttling along the walls.

Hell on earth.

Ahead of them were the stairs leading up towards the piazza. Anthony was taking point and carrying the largest bag, with one hand free and his greatcoat unbuttoned. The relativistic physics within his dimensional coat was cooking. Sometimes his gait would cause his great coat to flap open, issuing twirling tendrils of vapour from the worlds within as it met the cool air, obscuring the warrior like a stage magician. The professor was carrying two aluminium impact cases between them. Zach had another bag slung over his right shoulder. The satchel containing the Journal was slapping on his thigh when he walked. And to complete the ensemble, he gripped a sword, or should he say the sword held him in his right hand. Anthony had retrieved the wicked-looking blade from the dimensional folds of his great coat at the beginning of this adventure. At first, Zach had thought it was alive, and maybe it was in some form or another. Six snake-like appendages wrapped around his wrist as soon as the skin of his palm made contact with the hilt. Warm to the touch and gritty like sandpaper, it constantly needed to be encircled with your fingers. He would never be without a weapon in battle. As reassuring as that may be, his fear kept him on a razor's edge. Their little unit moved quickly and remained tight as they hurried up the stairs from the lower levels to the piazza. The familiar sight of a circular garden, a dribbling fountain and concrete benches had not changed much in this world. Two telephone booths, relics of a pre-cell-phone era, had been retconned into a defibrillator and an information kiosk, and remained as if they were still in the real world.

"Where to?"

Anthony's question needn't have been asked; Zach could see exactly where they were going. There was a section in the far right-hand corner that was covered in a green tarp. Zach had noticed it a few days ago but had never given it a second thought.

"Yuh see it?" Ras Tobias pointed to the area.

Anthony lifted his head, his brow furrowed. He quickly looked to his left and right, then raised his hand as if to block any further movement forward. Zach could only see his back, but watched his shoulders lock and his arms sway outwards with his fingers dangling.

"Keep low," the warrior's voice rumbled. He crouched, laid his sword down at his feet, and placed the case he was carrying beside it.

A spine-tingling screech that was partially heard and

partially felt in the base of your skull made Zach pay attention. The order to get low was beginning to make more sense.

There was something on the tarp, and they were angry at being disturbed. He heard and felt the flapping wings as three amorphous shapes took to the air. They were humanoid, their skin stretched taut over wiry muscles, glistening with a damp sheen, almost as if sweat and oil were seeping directly from their pallid, greenish flesh. They had been perched on the tarp, their colour blending in perfectly with it, and had taken flight upon seeing their approach. Even in the open space of the piazza, the flapping of their wings created a relentless, hollow thud in the stillness, echoing off the grey concrete; each beat grew louder, closer, pounding like a throbbing headache.

Zach could feel Ras Tobias's weight on his back as they squatted. The professor had one trembling hand on his shoulder, and his breathing was even. They both were in the shadow of Anthony's great coat when the warrior reached into eternity and pulled out something for the occasion.

He swung the Crossbow that appeared in his big right hand, across his chest, a bolt already in its groove, arms extended, and he fired without hesitation. Zach looked up beyond Anthony's coat and saw the bolt leave the crossbow like it was rocket-propelled and pierce the snarling face of the first flying demon. Its head exploded, the momentum carrying the body over their heads, landing in a tangled heap behind them. Zach watched the carcass flapping as if it were still clinging to life.

Ras Tobias closed his eyes and mumbled a prayer.

Seconds had elapsed, and Zach swung his head back to Anthony. By this time, the ear-splitting screech had grown more intense and was met by another bolt from the crossbow streaking its way towards its target. The creature tried to evade the bolt, veering left then right, chattering with glee, revealing rows of jagged razors for teeth, black and irregular, dripping saliva in its maw, thinking it had won. But the bolt followed it like a demon-seeking missile burrowing through its chest and exploding out of its back, incinerating its wings in the process. It fell from the sky, a flaming fallen angel, crashing into the flagstones, bouncing once before demolishing a trash can as it came to a messy stop.

Anthony didn't have time to load the third bolt in the crossbow before the final winged horror was upon him.

"Shit!"

He tried to use the crossbow, furiously swinging it like a club, hitting nothing but air. The creature pulled back in mid-swoop, its powerful wings bellowing air over them that carried a putrid smell of rotting meat and sulfur. It lunged again with razor-sharp claws from its feet and arms, snatching the crossbow out of Anthony's hands and raking a ragged track along the tough hide of his great coat. Still hovering over them, screeching and threatening, Anthony shrugged off the initial attack, standing his ground and reaching down for his blade. He didn't have to reach far. Zach flipped the weapon up into the air, and Anthony reached out and snatched it. Zach jumped to his feet and positioned himself at Anthony's back, brandishing his sword. The winged creature didn't care for their camaraderie; it wanted to spill life-giving blood and came at them again. It was so close its breath stank, claws slashing and teeth snapping. Anthony moved like a dancer, backpedalling from the attacks, waiting for an opportunity and finding none. Zach played the role of a compliant dance part-ner, letting Anthony's movements carry him without resistance. Ras Tobias had to read that dance and nervously keep in their shadow.

Zach almost screamed out as Anthony let his hands fall to his side as if he had suddenly decided that this was all for nought and he was giving up. The sword was loosely in his hand, but he was dragging it on the stones. The creature foolishly thought it was a sign of capitulation and lunged. Anthony's sword was a blur as it seemed to leap into his hand, and he marked the air with an 'X', slicing the creature's arms and wings cleanly off, and then, in the same movement, a horizontal stroke removed its head.

Zach's eyes watered as he covered his nose from the vile smell that immediately exploded from the exposed innards of the dead creature. Anthony stepped back from the spewing gore pumping out of the stump between its shoulders. The warrior looked around, almost unconvinced he was done. When he was satisfied, he walked over to Ras Tobias, offering him his hand and helping him to his feet.

"This better be worth it, Doc?"

The Rastaman looked around uncertainly and then focused on the green tarpaulin.

"It's more than worth it, Iyah."

Anthony nodded.

"Are we still good to go?"

Anthony kept his hands on the Rastaman's shoulders when he asked the question.

Ras Tobias tried to look taller and forced a smile. He reached down and picked up his aluminium cases.

"I man, was born feh dis."

All three dragged the tarpaulin free, revealing towering speakers and a DJ turntable.

Chapter Thirty-Nine

Before a single dubplate was spun or a Reggae tune had an opportunity to slide through the speakers, specialised vacuum tubes exploded with a …

Pop! Pop! Pop!

Immediately, the sounds snatched Zach's attention from focusing on the shadowy fringes of the piazza to the Rastaman's audio setup.

"What?" Zach asked

"No! No! No!" the doctor wailed, dancing on the spot, fists clenched, his face a mask of anguish.

Anthony was quickly by the Rastaman's side, looking concerned.

"You okay?"

"I've been better, big man, much better." Ras Tobias had his hands on his head. "Fire bun!" He mumbled the words, looking at the twirling tendrils of smoke curling up from a tray of vacuum tubes. "One of deh handmade vacuum tubes in deh synthetic synaptic frame just burn out. Jah, Jah, know. This is not good."

Zach could feel the panic in the doctor's voice and felt his body tense.

Bad news. He knew it was coming. Zach prodded the bear.

"Why don't you just plug in a replacement?"

"I can't young bwoy. The replacements are at the flat. In my haste..." The doctor's voice tapered off, and a sinking feeling followed.

The Rastaman's voice gained amplitude for what he had to say next, but it was born of desperation, not common sense.

"I man will go..."

"No, you won't!"

Anthony and Zach said it together.

Anthony shook his head.

"No way. Sylvester would have my head. You have to stay with the Sound System. Nobody else can do this. I'll collect the replacements and get them back here."

Zach felt sick because he knew what he had to do. During the five days he worked with Anthony, he had never seen him make a strategic decision that seemed illogical—a decision Zach had to call him out on. There was a first time for everything.

"Bro, you know that's bullshit, right?" Zach pointed to the outer edges of the piazza. The Darksiders were beginning to take notice. It was only a matter of time before they would begin attacking like white blood cells recognising an infection. Who would be best suited to keep them at bay?

Not him, that was for sure.

Zach looked steadily at his comrade-in-arms.

"I've got to go. Only I can do this. If I stayed with the doctor, it would be suicide. This is the only thing that makes sense."

Anthony nodded.

"No heroic shit. Stay away from the Darksiders. Get in and out, you got me?"

"In and out," Zach nodded his understanding and attempted to hand back the Gorgon - the blade Anthony had loaned him.

Anthony looked at him and the weapon with disbelieving eyes.

"Are you sure you want to do that?"

"Don't worry, I know I haven't got your warrior skills, this decision is purely common-sense. If this is going to work, I need speed and freedom. The Gorgon is a luxury I can't risk."

On Anthony's command, the sword unravelled its metal coils from around Zach's wrist. Receiving it, he deposited it into the folds of his great coat. What replaced the short sword was a handful of glowing orbs that were the size of marbles. He handed them to Zach.

"If anything gets too close, throw them in their direction. Shield your eyes and prepare to be deaf for a few seconds. Understand?"

Zach took them and rolled them into his satchel.

Anthony called the doctor over from the jumble of electronics, his two turntables, a mixing board and a MacBook Pro.

"Zach needs to know exactly where the replacements are in the flat. Time is everything."

The Rastaman stood between them, looking nervously over his shoulders at the encroaching shadows.

"Dat's easy young bwoy. Listen carefully." Rass Tobias dangled the house keys in front of him.

THE SCRAPE OF CLAWS ON SLATE NARROWED HIS FOCUS TO a pinpoint.

Zach didn't look back—he never did. The creatures were behind him, tearing over the Runnymede rooftops like smoke with bones. One missed a ledge and shrieked as it fell, but two more kept coming, faster than any living thing ought to be.

His shortcut was meant to be a quicker and safer option to the flat.

He was wrong on all counts.

He vaulted a rusted gutter, tucked into a shoulder roll, and sprang up running.

"Yuh foot know deh rhythm before yuh mind catch up..."

Hortense's voice rose in his memory as clear as if she ran beside him, her eyes intense, her tone calm.

A year ago, he was all knees and elbows, complaining about scraped palms and cracked ribs from endless parkour drills on the estate's ruined arches and crumbling cornices.

She'd sat watching him with those dusk-colored eyes.

"These walls were meant to keep others in, but not you. Everyting here is yours to use, to bend to yuh will."

A rooftop tile cracked underfoot—Zach adjusted mid-stride, momentum flowing through his limbs like water over stone. He leapt, caught the edge of a gothic dormer, swung wide and landed in a crouch.

"Dem will try to contain yuh," she had said, tapping his chest. *"But yuh is deh wind an' fire when yuh run. Dem make walls, but yuh make paths."*

The creatures were gaining again, voices clicking like cracked teeth. One flung itself toward him—a mass of shadow and limb—but Zach twisted sideways, catching the narrow balcony railing.

Hortense's voice wove into his concentration and muscle memory.

"Deh estate ain't just concrete and steel but memory. It is a map."

He could *see* it now—not just where to go, but how. The architecture of Runnymede wasn't just a battleground. It was a language, and Hortense had taught him to speak it with his body.

Zach ran the curved spine of a buttress, arms out like balance incarnate. Below, the estate gardens twisted in shadow. Ahead, the final rooftop angled steeply into the hazy grey sky with an expanse between.

"*Yuh will rise,*" she'd said, long before he knew what his role was in this drama. "*An' when you rise, deh world will rise wid yuh.*"

He reached the roof's edge. One deep breath. One last step. And he flung himself out into space. He heard the scream of his pursuer tumbling over the edge, felt the wind catch him mid-flight, and for a moment, Zach wasn't running for his life.

This was his life.

He tucked and rolled as he landed on the flat roof.

It felt good.

Not being chased but Free running through this hellscape that was once his home was a release for his pent-up anxiety. His fear was dialled back, adrenaline was pumping through him, muscles were firing, and his reflexes were sharp.

The more he ran, the better he felt.

The estate was like some lunatic's canvas; every wall, ledge, and rooftop harboured danger or death. As he defied gravity, leaping from structure to structure, his brain calculated speed, depth, height, and width, while a more active part of his consciousness prepared for what could lunge out of the shadows at him. In the meantime, he was five minutes away from the Rastaman's pad, every surface touched by his hands or feet providing him with a boundless array of movement possibilities.

This was what he was good at, what Hortense had encouraged him to master. It had saved his life on numerous occasions.

How did she know it would play a part in his survival? How did Hortense know anything?

Zach looked up at Esquire Tower and squinted his eyes. Ras Tobias's flat was in striking distance now. Three flights of stairs, and it was the closest to the exit of the steps to his apartment. Zach sprinted up the first set of staircases and sensed the depressing gloom further up. He stopped, breathing evenly, much more in the tank, but fear slowly threatening to leech out the remainder of his energy. He peered up at the remainder of the stairs leading into the unknown, and he hesitated. Subtle twin sensations he would have easily missed if not for his heightened performance - a faint musky smell of rotting meat and an almost inaudible sound of scratching.

Zach patted his leather satchel slung tightly around his neck. The Journal snugly inside, a reassuring presence. He slowly stepped back from the next flight of stairs and took stock of his surroundings. The concrete staircase was partially open to the elements. For every half level, there was an opening with a grill. As fate would have it, the grill on this level had been smashed out.

That was Zach's way up.

He slipped through it without hesitation, familiar with the wall's surface structure, and he carefully scrambled up the remaining two storeys. His back to the estate, three storeys up, he couldn't get back into the stairwell. All the grills were solidly in place.

He could go up to the fourth or fifth floors and check if vandalism had given him a means of access, but that was a big 'if'. Something else was bugging him, too.

Those stairs and the thick gloominess that clung to the rails and the grey concrete floors.

No, thank you.

He didn't want to have anything to do with it.

Zach flexed his fingers, his gloved hand solidly gripping the hand and foot holds that were the convenient 3D abstract art features of every high-rise building on the estate. He breathed deeply, and instead of continuing upwards, he remained on the third floor and started moving horizontally across the face. If he couldn't enter via a grill, there may be another way. So he kept moving until he came to the end of the protruding design. Peering around the corner, he could see the balcony that would allow him access to all the flats on the third floor.

He needed to swing himself around the edge with enough momentum to catapult himself towards the lip of the balcony. Just above him was a handhold he could use for his swing. Of course, it wasn't easy to get to, so he'd have to stretch for it. Then he'd slip his fingers in the crevice and use that point to swing his body like a pendulum.

Okay, it could be done.

Zach breathed deeply, ignoring how high and exposed he was and rehearsed the manoeuvre in his head. He talked to himself as his mental movie played. A reminder that he could do this. When his mantra abruptly ended, he gave himself no further time to ponder. He let gravity nudge him and exploded up and forward, his leap strong enough that both hands firmly gripped the lip of the crevice.

This was the tricky bit.

He shifted his body, ensuring the grip on his left hand was strong, and then released his right hand. His entire body weight was suspended from one arm, causing him to swing. Zach took advantage of the angular momentum by adjusting his body to improve the swing. He could do it one more time ...

At the top of his last swing, he let go...

For a brief moment, he was weightless, thinking the Gods

of physics could revoke their laws in this twilight zone, but they didn't.

Zach fell in an arc, as any falling object should and slammed into the balcony, his greedy fingers finding purchase. With no time to celebrate survival, he pulled himself up, vaulting over the balcony's barriers. The muscles of his arms were burning as he demanded more from them.

Relief was interrupted as his heightened perception was bitch-slapped out of kilter with an eye-watering stench and dissonant whistling sounds.

"Oh, shit!"

Zach hit the hard concrete floor and rolled as three feline forms loped out of the darkened stairwell and bounded towards him.

Chapter Forty

Anthony flashed the gore off his blade and watched the splattering cast off form arcs of viscera on the paving stones. He wiped the remainder on his pants, glaring at the steaming carcass of the creature he had just dispatched.

Anthony looked over at Ras Tobias, his cans over his ears, the headphones frame resting at the back of his neck due to his voluminous locks. He'd easily disposed of and frightened away the inquisitive Darksiders that came sniffing around their setup. But when the doctor turned on his speakers and began his set, all bets were off; the creatures from the Chaos dimension would attack them from every corner of the estate.

There was no way he could stem that tidal wave. They'd be overrun in moments.

What if Sylvester was wrong?

What if the Ras was wrong?

Then the honour of a warrior's death would be his, and no better way to ascend to a higher plane than this.

The doctor must have seen the warrior staring through him because he gave a nervous thumbs-up that interrupted his reverie. Anthony nodded respectfully and turned his attention back to scanning the perimeter.

Who would have believed that the human Zach would be the one who could turn the tide of this one-sided conflict?

The Chronicler had surprised him on every front. He had merged with the Journal in a way they had never seen before. He was tough, brave, and prepared for this battle, although he was unaware of it. Too busy comparing himself to others - a human foible.

Did the Chronicler understand the significance of returning with the valves and watching the doctor prove or disprove his theory? No matter how this ended, the mere possibility that they had a potential tool to fight back with was intoxicating.

Completely out of character, Anthony found himself fervently praying the Chronicler would return.

THE FIRST HAIL OF SPIKES AND THE SMELL OF SHIT STRUCK Zach's armour and miraculously missed his face and neck. The impact stunned him, knocking him off his feet, but he regained his wits quickly. He had contorted himself in mid-air, his senses screaming at him as he leapt the barrier, only to be ambushed by the creature's attack in mid-air. He landed awkwardly, rolling as his body slammed into the ground. Ras Tobia's front door was on his right, just as he had planned it. Zach faced off against two of the creatures, trying to impale him. In the fractured seconds, his eyes took in their positions, and his mind struggled to understand what they were. They walked on all fives - that's right, fives? Feline-like but scaled like a dinosaur.

Their gibbering barks were aggressive and sharp. Their skulls were armoured and swept back, but what made Zach's balls shrink like a prune was their prehensile tails that were whipping left and right with the intelligence of a cobra.

The spikes were coming from an orifice in its tip.

Without thought, Zach rolled sharply to his right, banging his head and elbow as he manoeuvred, but not caring. The spikes rattled into the concrete where he had been, penetrating the surface with the accompanying waft of excrement. He scurried backwards, slamming into the wall beside the Rastaman's front door. His back was literally against the wall.

At least he was where he was supposed to be. Zach had nowhere else to go, nothing to do but stand up and become an unwilling target as the feline, scorpion hybrids slinked out of the shadows and squared up on their prey.

Does time always seem to slow down in life-and-death situations like this? Or was it the Journal helping him to level the playing field? Whatever it was, time dilation had occurred, and from his perspective, he needed to evade and escape, finding another way into the flat later or die where he stood. All three of the creatures had shot their spikes, and a cloud of fast-moving death was heading his way.

Fuck! His mind screamed.

Zach prepared for explosive action as his window of opportunity slammed shut.

Then the still, small voice of clarity spoke.

'Hey dummy, try the door.'

Zach reached out to the handle with an inelegant sweep, falling into the door and feeling it push open. A cacophony of impacting spikes rattled into the door frame above him.

He was thanking every deity he could recall.

Still on the ground, he tucked and flipped awkwardly past the door and into the darkened hallway of the Rastaman's flat.

The smell of food lingered.

On his back, he used the flat of his feet to kick the door closed with all his might. He heard the security lock click into place.

One second.

Two seconds

Three...

The creatures slammed into the door, barking and howling.

Zach just lay there, eyes wide, breathing heavily.

He gave himself a minute and tried to sit up.

He couldn't.

It was as if his legs and arms had been suddenly sapped of energy. He couldn't raise himself. Shifting his weight, he tried to rock himself onto his shoulder, but he couldn't muster the effort required. The satchel with the Journal inside felt warm on his chest, but his immobile body was getting cold.

Damnit!

A spike had penetrated the armour or caught an exposed part of his body. He hadn't noticed it because of the adrenaline rush.

What else could it be?

He was going to die right here, having let down Sylvester, Medusa, Anthony, Ras Tobias and every tenant on the Runnymede estate.

His passing would break his father's heart. The grief Maya would feel made his chest achingly hollow.

'I gave it my best shot,' was all he could say to himself.

The world was closing in on him, squeezing his perception into a deep, dark pit. The edges of his awareness were slowly being painted in black, and soon there would be nothing.

"I'm sorry," Zach repeated. The muscles of his jaw were seizing. "I wanted ... to give the estate a chance... at ..."

Those were the last words before darkness took him, but not before another voice in his head said its piece.

"Don't worry, Chronicler, I'm not done with you yet. You have more information we need to share. Much more."

Chapter Forty-One

Ascream tore out of Zach's throat as he emerged, spluttering and coughing from a liquid darkness he thought would drown him. When his eyes sprang open, and his flaying arms and legs realised where he was, he lay frantically looking around, slightly embarrassed by his panic.

Get a grip, Zach mi bwoy.

A metallic taste lingered in his mouth, and throbbing points of pain all over his body, as if he had lain on a bed of nails, reminded him he was still alive. His vision blurred before snapping into stark clarity, then dimming again. Patches of dark blood were smeared across the floor around him, and the flat was eerily silent, save for the low ponderous hum of the refrigerator.

Zach took a deep, nervous breath, his throat dry.

He sat up in the darkened corridor, his mind struggling to piece together a timeline of events that ended up with him on his ass in a tenant's flat. It was slowly making sense.

The Day of Reckoning.

Sylvesters plan.

Ras Tobias is missing a piece of equipment.

His head was pounding.

Out of habit, he looked at his watch, knowing he couldn't trust anything it was telling him anyway.

Why wasn't he dead?

Zach tried to get up too quickly, and his head spun. He remained in place for a while longer. The overall sense of being crucified by multiple executioners was concentrated on his neck. Instinctively, his hand came up to the area of his throat, and his fingertips found the foreign object jutting out. The offending spike that had penetrated his skin was still in place. Zach shuddered, pinched the spike's prickly shaft, and yanked it out, flinging it to the ground with disgust; a faint faecal whiff accompanied the action.

Zach pushed himself up to his knees. He moved slowly, like an old hinge rusted over—careful, deliberate, fragile. Every impact wound hurt, and he debated lying back down. Just resting. Just closing his eyes. But a gnawing fear chewed at his insides.

Stop fucking about.

He had to get out of here. He had something important to do.

Taking a deep breath, he tried again to right himself, this time leaning on the wall and bracing his legs. He was able to maintain that position for a moment.

The question came to him again.

How long had he been unconscious, and why wasn't he dead?

Zach risked standing with his back against the corridor wall, propped up and unstable. Cautiously, he reached into his satchel that was still around his neck and stroked the warmth of the leather-bound journal inside.

It was humming, and the vibration it sent through his fingers and into his body was not just pleasurable but therapeutic. He could feel it warming him, repairing him.

He took a tentative step.

His world had stopped revolving.

Thank you, Journal. Whatever you did. Thank you.

Zach walked over to the front door and looked through the peephole's concave lens. The three creatures were silently prowling outside on the landing. They must have heard him or sensed his presence behind the door because all three of them pounced on it, their paws frantically clawing at the metal.

Zach turned away, his thoughts immediately settling on Anthony and Ras Tobias.

Moment by moment, the picture in his head was gaining clarity, and his sense of urgency ramped up. He was still a bit shaky, but he had to go. Zach dashed into the doctor's bedroom, kneeled and reached under a bed that smelled of weed and potpourri. His fingers touched the aluminium case he was looking for. Pulling it out, he popped the latches and peered in at eight custom-designed vacuum tubes, their bases colour-coded and embedded snugly in protective foam. Closing it, he slung the case over his neck and tested the straps.

There was no way he would exit the flat via the front door. Zach had to make his exit through the balcony and down the side of the building. He walked through the front room towards the sliding patio door that overlooked the back of the building. A set of thick curtains that stretched to the floor blocked what would have been a view of a grass lawn and a well-kept communal garden below.

Zach pulled it aside, slid the glass door open, and an acrid cloud of burning rubber drifted by, making him cough. He dragged himself to the barrier and peered out. The garden was trashed, and the grass lawn looked as if small munitions had exploded across its surface.

He shook his head.

From the third floor, a fall would be fatal.

So, don't fall.

The Journal was enhancing him; he knew that, but he was still weak. And his sense of balance ...? Well, Zach would only know that when he tested himself.

He took one more visual snapshot and allowed his parkour-experienced brain to map out the best route to the pathway below. Touching the straps of both the items slung around his neck, he leapt on the barrier, holding onto a pipe, his first touch point.

Easy does it.

He turned to look back at the room just once—the blood smears in the corridor, the front door being assaulted by the creatures on the other side, the clutter of Ras Tobias' old life.

Zach paused, bracing his forehead against the cold, damp wall and gripping the pipe. He sucked in sharp breaths, then began his upward ascent.

As soon as his feet touched the ground, Zach took a breath and gained his bearings. The grass verge was no longer green but a sallow, desiccated brown that was alive. Something was moving underneath the diseased soil, and Zach didn't want to see what was undulating deep beneath it like circling sharks. He kept to the concrete path until he was away from the shadow of the tower block, and then he started running, his mind already conjuring scenes of Anthony and Ras Tobias dead or dying.

Zach kept moving, knowing he would soon face the true

reality of his situation. He was making good time and not drawing attention to himself.

His only focus is on Anthony and Ras Tobias.

Hustling through a walkway at the root of a tower block, he could see the stairs that led up to the piazza in the distance—a mixed emotional bag of hope and despair, struggling for dominance. The winner would have to wait as a whisper of air—cold as ice—brushed the back of his neck.

Zach's pace immediately slowed, his knees weak. An inexplicable feeling made him aware that he was in the presence of a primal evil, and that made him stop, then freeze like a statue, defeated, shoulders drooped, breathing heavily.

"Leaving so soon, Chronicler?"

That voice. *Her voice.*

His head snapped around. She was there, standing horrifyingly majestic in what could have been a projection, but Zach's very fibre was telling him she was here, on the Runnymede Estate.

Anastasia.

The demoness had transported a piece of hell with her, a life-size diorama of her repugnant lair, wanting not to forgo the luxuries of her station, maybe. The entire cavern of a room, with floating orbs for light, a massive hearth at the back fueled by bones and excrement, her attack dogs snoring at her feet, was translocated to a floating stage on the estate. In that tableau, she stood before a table that was hewn out of a black, glistening rock. Atop the surface was a multi-level crystalline board game with five platforms, each intricately designed with game pieces of black or white scattered over the surfaces. To one side was a huge empty chair; on the other was a woman in dark grey robes seated on a stool. The woman's form was ephemeral like a ghost, and you could see through her to the walls behind. It took some effort for Zach to drag his eyes away and focus on the real threat.

He fleetingly wondered why.

His fear sat thick and vile in the walkway as he pressed his back against the wall. The three times he had seen her, there had been enough distance between them that his nightmares lasted only days. With this kind of proximity, he'd be seeing her in his sleep for a lifetime. Her form towered, seven feet of grotesque elegance—a nightmare wrapped in the illusion of beauty. Her dark skin was smooth, except for the edges of her face, where human beauty gave way to horns that merged with fissures glowing with a blood-red light, pulsing beneath the surface. Her eyes were sharp, black voids within black pits, swallowing every flicker of light in their path. Blackened horns curled backwards from her temples, ridged like tree bark scorched in hellfire.

Her lips curled in a mockery of a smile, serrated teeth peeking from beneath. "Tsk. You look worse for wear, Zachary. Did my pets treat you poorly?"

Zach pressed his back against the wall, one hand on the railing for balance. She hadn't moved, yet her presence pushed down on him like the weight of the whole damn sky.

Don't show her you're afraid.

"What do you want? Get it over with." His voice came out hoarse, barely audible.

She tilted her head. "What do I want?" Her grin widened. "Oh, Zachary. I think the better question is: what do *you* want? To crawl back to that fool Anthony and Tobias? To cling to some threadbare hope that you'll stop what's coming?"

Zach clenched his jaw.

"If you're here to kill me, then do it. I'm tired. I'm not in the mood for your speeches."

Her laughter echoed off the surrounding buildings, sharp

and mirthless, vibrating through the air. The shadows at her feet rippled, shifting like liquid snakes coiling around her ankles.

"Kill you?" she said, voice dripping with condescension. "No, Chronicler. Killing you now would be...unwise. Fortunate for you, God's and men are bound by rules."

She spat out the words as if they disgusted her.

Zach's fingers tightened around the railing until the rusted metal bit into his palms. "Not what you imagined?"

Her smile vanished. Silence stretched between them like a taut wire ready to snap. Her enclosure floated closer. The way it moved set every hair on Zach's body on edge—it was unnatural, wrong. Like a spider crawling across silk, no sound, no effort.

If he could push himself into the wall to provide space between himself and Anastasia, he would. The demoness was close enough that he could feel the unnatural chill radiating from her; she skewered him with her eyes.

"You know Zachary," she whispered, the power of her words carried heat not only to his skin but searing his mind too. "I respect you. You've been tested and you've come through battered but better."

Forcing himself not to but failing, Zach stared into the swirling depths of her eyes, feeling the full weight of what she was—an ancient, powerful, immortal, corrupted energy wearing a woman's skin. And yet—he saw it. Just beneath her venom. A flicker of something else.

Admiration.

"A man like you could be a king of the shadows in my world, control armies, and have the privilege of warming my bed. But you chose this worthless route." Anastasia's smile was wistful as her mind considered the possibilities.

"There are a few things that I regret in this game on the Earth plane, and one of those regrets is not focusing more of my resources on gutting you, Zachary. Stringing your entrails over these buildings, your head on a pike and your dick slung around my neck. Ah, well."

"So-so-sorry to disappoint." The words almost stuck in Zach's throat, but when they did manage to squeeze out, they had been sapped of all sarcasm.

"Don't be sorry. It may still be possible, Chronicler, but unfortunately, it's not in my hands. So tread carefully."

The ghost woman, who seemed to be preoccupied in silent focus, turned away from the board game and looked over at him.

Their eyes met, and the volume of Anastasia's words tuned down.

Time stood still.

Zach almost slid down the wall.

Hortense?

His eyes widened, his heart pounding in his chest.

What the fuck?

Hortense, his mentor, smiled at him and took up a piece from the multi-level board game. Anastasia's mouth was moving, but no words registered, and Zach was no longer Zach; he was the game piece in Hortense's hand.

He was the piece.

And for a moment that lasted forever, he understood the part he had to play and how he had fulfilled his destiny. He could see the myriad possibilities that were available, good and bad. Knowing he had agency. The Journal absorbed it all, recording this encounter with relish, filling his host with a feeling of well-being, a much-needed buffer against Anastasia's awful presence.

Recognising Zach's attention had shifted, she reached out and grabbed his face in one clawed hand; her sharp talons bit into his jaw. Immediately, Zach snapped back, staring, his senses scrambled for a moment. Her touch was cold; her skin was unusually soft, with a disturbing vibration underneath, as if colonies of hungry maggots were trying to break free.

Zach flinched but couldn't pull away.

"You are lucky to be a part of the game, Chronicler." Her breath stank of ash and rot. "Your soul would have been a pleasure to taste. No matter, we will take our fill, and your little band of misfits cannot stop it."

"Not a good idea to count us out." Zach's jaw clenched as he fought Anastasia's aura from grinding him into a fine powder.

If you closed your eyes, her laugh was carefree, like that of a human woman who enjoyed chaos and mayhem.

The reality was so much different.

When she released him, he hit the railing hard as he frantically made space between himself and the demoness; his vision sparked white for a second as pain tore through his ribs. When his eyes refocused, she watched him, her diorama moving away, its form blurring at the edges, and she had already turned to the game on the table, her back to him, losing interest.

"Hurry back to your friends, Chronicler. You don't want to miss the grand finale, do you?"

Her form, Hortense's calm, spectral demeanour, and the diorama folded space around it. It folded again and then folded once more before vanishing entirely.

The silence that followed was delicious. Zach slumped against the wall, revelling in the relief of Anastasia's absence. His legs trembled beneath him, and he massaged his face with a rough hand.

He shuddered a deep breath.

Composing himself and checking his cargo, Zach started trotting again, then running, and this time, he wouldn't let anything stop him from getting to his friends.

Chapter Forty-Two

The temperature dropped, and the depressing hues of the piazza seemed to dull even further. The music had not been given an opportunity to lift moods, and never will if Zach doesn't return. So in the chaos, the sound system remained silent. All Ras Tobias could offer as he tinkered with the equipment - a way to occupy himself against the inevitable- was crackling interference through the speakers, as an oppressive presence descended upon the scene like a squall. The old Rastaman thought it was his own depleting faith that was manifesting itself in this horrid vibe. His opinion changed as he looked over to Anthony, whose eyes narrowed and stance became more defensive than usual because he, too, could sense the upcoming storm.

The architect of this contagious feeling of wretchedness stepped into view, emerging from the shadow of a crumbling archway. Mr. B—Beelzebub himself. His appearance was immaculate, as always. He wore a sharp three-piece suit, the fabric so black it seemed to drink in the light. A blood-red tie hung from his neck, and a pocket square matched the crimson lining of his coat. His skin was flawless porcelain, his eyes glowing faintly like embers in a dying fire, and his facial tattoos pulsing.

In his hand, like a petulant child with a teddy bear, he dragged an enormous sword. Its broad surface was etched with fiery runes that seemed to shift and writhe. The Nephilim sword radiated a malevolent energy, each drag leaving a trail of heat shimmer and cutting a track in the ground. The blade was longer than he was tall, and seemed impossible for any man to wield such a weapon.

But Beelzebub was no man.

The gibbering masses of Darksiders on the fringes fell silent. Tobias stared at the horned prince of Hell, then looked over at Anthony with panic, fear, disappointment and stunned disbelief.

The warrior tried to reassure him with a calm sway of his hand, but then balled his fists and cracked his knuckles.

Ras Tobias groaned.

Beelzebub's gaze swept across the piazza, his lips curling into a smile that held no warmth.

"Well, well," he drawled, his voice smooth and dripping with malice. "It looks like you were making plans for a show stopper?" He shook his head. "You win some, you lose some."

His eyes locked onto Anthony, and the smile widened. "Don't be shy, Anthony, step forward. You know you've always wanted this to happen. I can't believe it took so long."

Anthony nodded his head in agreement.

Ras Tobias couldn't believe what he was seeing. Why would you want to challenge such a thing?

He would be alone.

Zach had not made it.

Dis was fuckery!

He wanted to protest, but Anthony had already fixed him

with an uncompromising stare and a no-nonsense screw of his lips.

"I'm sorry, you never got to try out your theory, Doctor. The world needs you, but we tried. All I can do now is deliver some pain to that motherfucker before it's all over. Do what you do best."

Ras Tobias nodded, not sure what to make of that.

Anthony smiled and turned away, and met Beelzebub's gaze with steely determination.

"Been waitin' for this."

Ras Tobias wanted to tell Anthony not to provoke it, not to give it anything it could use against him, but imagined he would not pay him much attention. All he could do was stand behind his turntables, transfixed by the battle to come.

A dangerously crooked smile crossed the warrior's lips, and his eyes glowed pale blue. Anthony flicked open his battered greatcoat, the folds shifting unnaturally, hinting at the impossible arsenal within the stygian darkness that lined it, and he dug deep inside. His arm disappeared up to his elbow into the impossibility of a universe in his jacket, and he came out with what looked like a thick, long, broken blade that he lay at his feet. Anthony then searched inside his jacket six more times, finding differing pieces that snapped together with a spark to create an oddly beautiful yet deadly work of killing art that looked like it could sever a limb by merely being in proximity to it. Balancing the completed sword in both hands, he then let it fall, catching it by the hilt and deftly spinning it twice in a blur of motion.

Beelzebub chuckled, the sound reverberating like low thunder. "I would expect nothing less. Let's make it memorable."

He raised his sword, its runes flaring to life. The crowd watched in silence, the air thick with anticipation.

The air shimmered with malevolent energy. The old

piazza-turned-arena thrummed with the weight of the gathered crowd. Shadows danced across the cracked concrete walls as firelight flickered in sconces. The Darksiders—a hideous, sanity-twisting cohort of unspeakable things watched in tense silence, their faces lit with anticipation.

Then she appeared above everyone. The accoutrements of her lair lay behind her with what looked like another person, a wispy, ephemeral thing, seated behind her. Under different circumstances, his senses would interpret what he saw like a television broadcast, but the Ras knew this was real —a piece of hell scooped out and on display on Earth.

Ras Tobias wasn't sure his heart could take much more. He would kill for a spliff but could not take his eyes off this new addition to the conflict. He wasn't sure he could call her beautiful; 'horrifically striking' would be a more fitting description. A horned sister, tall, athletic, dark-skinned, with piercing eyes, exuding a magnetism that Ras Tobias could feel tugging at him from where he stood.

Deh bitch!

That was the name he gave to her after invading his dreams on many occasions, trying to sway him from his purpose.

When his focus fell on Anthony again, he had walked out into the middle of the piazza, staring down Mr B's blazing crimson gaze. The demon was no bigger than Anthony himself, but his slight form was generating the power of an infernal nuclear bomb under his skin. He hefted his gargantuan cleaver —a weapon so massive, the laws of physics were being rewritten where he stood. Its jagged edges glinting, the scent of sulfur hanging heavily in the air.

"Last chance, Anthony," his voice reverberated across the piazza like it had been issued from a dinosaur's diaphragm, not a man's chest. "Kneel before me, and I'll make it quick."

Anthony smirked, his knuckles tightening on the hilt of his

sword. "Quick has never been my style, B. You should know that."

Ras Tobias couldn't help but believe in this warrior's swagger. But even he knew Anthony was up against an adversary that could end him.

And all he could do was watch.

Watch and wait.

Chapter Forty-Three

"Fuck! Fuck! Fuck!" The swear words hissed through Zach's teeth as he looked on to see a circle of Dark-siders surrounding the Piazza. There was no music, and he couldn't understand why a soundless sound system had the power to take them away from their evil duties. But here they were, a large, excited cohort of the obscenities from the Chaos Dimension, stomping, growling, mewling, roaring their approval or disapproval; he didn't know which, towards what he thought was Anthony and Ras Tobias.

This God-forsaken hell he found himself in would continue to put obstacles in his way, and he would continue to keep pushing against them. What more could he do? If it were to end here, he wouldn't do it without a fight.

Zach clutched his leather satchel to his chest and gripped the aluminium container. A doppelganger of panic gave him a heart-pounding pause.

Chill, bwoy, you have everything; nothing is forgotten.

Okay! Okay! Now, what to do about this demonic cordon?

As tired as he knew he should be, his mind was still surprisingly sharp. It felt like he had injected three large cans of Red Bull into his bloodstream. A dull ache was on the periphery of his perception, held at bay by his adrenaline. He followed the circle of bodies that had formed around the Piazza, ducking low and keeping a discreet distance from any of the rowdy creatures, who were more interested in what was happening within the circle than being aware of his actions outside of it. In minutes, he made his way around to the back of the makeshift amphitheatre, positioning himself behind a Mercedes van.

He checked both sides.

Desolate.

No man nor beast.

It made no sense.

The climb to the piazza from his position was about fifty feet. The wall was covered with creeping thick vines. An easy leap for these creatures, if they wanted. But instead, they were gawking from the open sections of the Piazza.

If there were a later, Zach would solve that mystery. At this moment, a rare opportunity had presented itself, and he wasn't about to squander it.

No way.

He scurried from behind the van and sprinted towards the wall, his footfalls louder than he would have liked, leaping at it as if he were being chased. As soon as his hands gripped the fibrous creeper, Zach launched himself upwards and began a furious climb to the top of the wall.

ZACH STOOD ALMOST TRIUMPHANTLY ATOP THE WALL, looking down on Ras Tobias and the Sound System. He almost fell off his perch with relief.

He had made it.

Then his eyes surveyed the scene beyond from his vantage point, and he understood why all eyes were on the Piazza.

Anastasia was high up in her alcove, like a dark empress, surrounded by her subjects. Below, Mr B and Anthony were at battle, and his warrior friend didn't seem to be doing so well.

'Ras?"

Zach tried to sound calm yet forceful, but it didn't work. Ras Tobias had split his focus between watching the fight and tinkering with the Sound System's electronics. He knelt, his hands working furiously to reconnect DIN connectors to his analogue setup. His dreads swayed like thick ropes as he turned around at the voice. Wide flashing eyes said it all until he recognised him, and his features softened with relief, and the fear evaporated.

Zach jumped onto a nearby crate, clutching the case to his chest and wincing as pain shot through his side.

"Blessed love," Ras Tobias jumped to his feet and embraced him in a clumsy and desperate hug. "You made it, bwoy." He shook his leonine head in disbelief. Tears in his eyes. "Jah know, yuh made it."

"What now?"

Ras Tobias stepped back suddenly, all business, a flicker of hope igniting in his eyes. He snatched the components from Zach's trembling hands, his fingers opening the case and hurrying over to an open cabinet near the turntables. He slid to his knees and deftly took out two Vacuum tubes, reached into the belly of the cabinet to plug them in. "Hold faith now, Zachary. This machine is gonna sing like Jah-Jah angels when mi done!"

He slammed the cabinet door shut.

. . .

ANTHONY AND MR. B WERE CIRCLING EACH OTHER IN THE distance. Each was eyeing the other for weaknesses. Anthony feigned an attack a few times, but the demon was undisturbed. No one wanted to make the first move.

Not yet.

Even with the tension just beyond, Zach's eyes were on one thing: Ras Tobias and the towering stack of speakers, cobbled together electronics and the Rastafarian's ingenuity.

"What do I do now?" Zach was wringing his hands, watching as Tobias began flipping switches and twisting knobs. "They're fighting out there, Tobias. Anthony...he can't hold him forever. And the Darksiders—they're everywhere!"

Tobias gave him a sharp glance. "Then we nah miss, rude bwoy." He pressed a button, and the stack of speakers let out a low hum that vibrated through the ground. "Music is power, my yout. Vibration stronger than any curse. This here? Dis system? Is not just for playin' tunes. It's a weapon."

Tobias grinned, teeth flashing against his dark skin.

The hum deepened, a bassline so rich it seemed to crawl into Zach's chest and take root. Tobias' fingers danced across the soundboard, adjusting sliders and dials with the precision of a man born to wield the sound.

With trembling hands, Ras Tobias picked up the microphone and tapped it with the palm of his hand. The sound came back crisply through the speakers. He brought it up to his lips and cleared his throat.

"Testing, testing, 1,2,3!" The Ras tilted the microphone slightly. "Testing!"

Zach watched him with his breath held.

Chapter Forty-Four

Ras Tobias stood before the towering sound system, his fingers curling around the microphone. Darksiders loomed at the edges of the piazza, their spectral forms pulsing with malevolent hunger. Zach stood beside him, tense, his blade ready. Anthony, in the heart of the Piazza, faced Beelzebub, the weight of the battle pressing down on him like a storm cloud. And yet, in that moment, time seemed to hold its breath.

Tobias exhaled, closing his eyes for a beat, then lifted the mic to his lips. His voice was deep, rich like the earth and echoing across the estate.

"Deh Philistines seh music is just sound. Just entertainment. But Babylon a twist deh truth Iyah. Music is more than entertainment; it is rhythm, more than melody—it is vibration. And vibration is life itself."

The air hummed as if the estate itself was listening.

"Long before words, before weapons, before walls and borders, we spoke in rhythm. Our heartbeat, di drum. Our breath, di wind through di trees. Our African ancestors, dem

315

know it - sound could heal, sound could lift di weary, could call down fire from di sky or bring peace to a man's soul."

His amplified voice was reacting oddly against the brutalist architecture. It echoed in places, got louder in others and then sounded as if it was being whispered just beside you. Tobias' voice resonated, a wave rolling over the fugue-stricken residents. Fingers twitched. Heads stirred.

"But dem know deh power. Dat is why dem silence yuh, why dem fill deh world with noise but no meaning. Why dem take deh voice from deh people, deh joy from deh dance, deh unity from deh song? Because when we sing together, Runnymede is strong. When we move as one, we are unbreakable."

The Darksiders hissed, shifting uneasily. Some took their eyes off the unfolding battle before them to pay more attention to the human voice infringing on their entertainment.

Ras Tobias didn't require their attention. Soon, they would give it to him of their own volition. He placed the microphone back in its cradle and fixed the headphones over his ears. He looked over to Zach and threw him a headphone.

"Put these on, king."

Zach caught them and did as he was told.

His hands trembled as he placed them over his ears, watching the Rastaman's hands hovering over the turntables, mumbling lyrics to himself. Then he switched the Harmonic Cognition Enhancer to on, and Zach knew there was no going back now.

Chapter Forty-Five

Mr. B moved first, his actions a blur, his sword swiping in a perfect arc, the blade's vast surface creating a shadow that was part metal and part malignant aura. Anthony was prepared, but the speed of his strike caught him off guard; he limboed backwards, and the stinking overcurrent of the blade whistling overhead ruffled his coat, making him even more aware of the power he was dealing with. If the edge of that beast of a sword caught him, that would be his end.

Mr. B's return swing came fast. Too fast.

Anthony adjusted his position, sliding closer to his opponent, his sword already up, needing closer proximity to Beelzebub to cause damage. He blocked it, and sparks flew from the impact of metal on metal. The force was such that Anthony skidded over the flagstones of the piazza. Pain blossomed across his arms, sharp and immediate. His vision blurred, but he rolled instinctively as Mr B's sword came down again, pulverising the flagstones where he'd been.

Anthony sucked in a ragged breath and expertly rolled to

his feet, his sword in a fighting position. He pulled the sword back over his head, gripping it with both hands and threw it. Flying end over end, it spun like a guillotine, the whistle of metal slicing through the air as it banked towards Mr B's neck.

The demon's reflexes were lightning fast, and it adjusted. Instead of the flying sword decapitating him, it bit into his shoulder, flying off to be caught by Anthony, who was within striking distance of Mr B. His smirk disappeared, and his surprise was evident.

"Not so tough up close, huh?"

Anthony struck at his thigh, his torso and arms, slicing through the material of his suit and grating against his demon-enhanced skin. Unsatisfied with the possible damage, he tried to force the point of his blade up into his armpit, but it penetrated only fractionally.

It still hurts.

The demon bellowed.

Mr B tried to shake him with flashing elbows and legs, but Anthony was moving like a gymnast, ducking, diving, rolling in one continuous fluid motion. Anthony swung himself up and onto the demon's broad back, his blade pointing down into his neck. But he had been too close and for too long. Before he could plunge it into the granite-like vertebrae of his spine, an iron grip clamped over his ankle.

With a roar, Mr. B reached back, grabbed a fistful of Anthony's coat and rammed him unceremoniously into the ground at his feet.

He felt something snap. Anthony tried to make himself more pliable for what he knew was about to come.

The demon picked him up again, looked at him in detail and hurled him across the piazza. He hit the ground hard, arms and legs flaying as he rolled to a chaotic stop near a dustbin. His vision swam as he struggled to rise. That's when he felt the liquid pain of a dislocated shoulder.

The world tilted. Voices from the crowd blurred into a cacophony, a chaotic roar punctuated by jeers and gasps. Anthony shook his head, trying to clear it. His left arm hung uselessly at his side.

Keep moving.

He rolled just as the sword smashed down again. He rolled again. The flagstones exploded into dust and debris from the impact of the giant sword. His ears rang, the impact leaving him momentarily deaf. He staggered to his feet, coughing, the dust cloud allowing him a reprieve.

'Don't let me come in there and get dust on my suit, Anthony. You've already tried to disfigure this Savile Row classic. My tailor will not be pleased."

The suit he had cut to shreds was once again in fine form.

Anthony ignored his taunts and concentrated.

He felt the tingle of the sword somewhere near and demanded it come to him, and it did. He raised his arms, and it spun into his hands, glinting with an eerie blue light.

"Ready to go again?"

The sword tingled in his hand.

Chapter Forty-Six

Sting and Shaggy's voices echoed through the speakers, loud and clear, introducing a Reggae set that would shift the power dynamic in this hellish landscape.

Morning is coming, morning is on its way, morning is coming, it's Revelation Day.

Morning is coming, morning is on its way, morning is coming, it's Revelation Day.

Then the words of Dennis Brown - The Crown Prince of Reggae — flowed through, vibrating solenoids, entangled with background rhythmic structures based on the Fibonacci sequence so deep and soulful that it was impossible not to feel its influence.

Love and hate can never be friends.

Oh no, Oh no.

Here I come with love and not hatred.

Surely goodness and mercy shall follow I, all the days of my life ....

Dennis Brown faded, and The Itals poured from the speakers, rich and layered, wrapping their words in Ras Tobias' harmonics that were actively influencing the Prefrontal Cortex of all sleeping humanity.

Inna dis yah time.

Man yuh hafe mind

You get carried away by captivity

Carried away by captivity

Inna dis yah time.

Zach blinked, his pain momentarily forgotten. The sound that was coming through his headphones was regulated, so the sonic power wasn't affecting his hearing, just buffeting his body. The music was alive. The vibrations rippled through the air, twisting and curling like smoke, but with a strange weight to them. He could almost see it: the way the notes tangled with the darkness, pushing it back, forcing it to retreat.

Ras Tobias had transformed.

This was what he had researched, theorised and was now putting into practice.

Six songs into his set, and the effect was subtle.

Zach looked out, and he could see a small selection of the Darksiders looking disoriented, stumbling about.

He looked to Ras Tobias, but he was too focused on his craft. He was a maestro; his movements were fluid and confident, and he flipped the vinyls to a playlist he had in his head. He checked the levels on the HCE while he cued up the next track. The speakers roared louder, the rhythm and the bass like a wall of sound.

Another tune cued up and spilt into the ether —deep, rolling basslines accompanied by the rhythmic strumming of guitars—a riddim steeped in roots reggae history. Burning Spear's "Marcus Garvey" coursed through the estate like an electric current, thrumming along the walls and seeping into every crevice. When the last chord died away, there was a breath, a vacuum almost.

Then, suddenly, it was filled with words.
There's a natural mystic flowing through the air.
If you listen carefully now, you will hear.
This could be the first trumpet.
Might as well be the last.
When Bob Marley began, the Darksiders screamed.

Chapter Forty-Seven

Anthony smashed his shoulder into the wall with such force that chunks of red brick showered to the ground. He could feel the ball and socket joint slotting back into the groove, and the torn muscles around his injury were beginning to heal. Knowing that did not reduce the pain he felt, and the scream that erupted from his lips as he violently set his bones back in place. His back was to his adversary, but he would put Dracnar's on Mr B's broad, shit-kicking smile at his distress and from the demonic audience cheering, he knew he was right.

Before turning back to face Beelzebub, Anthony dramatically flexed his neck, shoulders, and arms. He grimaced at the pain, but he would embrace it. Would the extra seconds he was giving himself help?

The demon was making patterns in the air with his broadsword. A sword that was no longer the behemoth he had been wielding earlier. The energy trails it left were forming glyphs that served some purpose he didn't wish to know.

Big or small, Anthony didn't care.

He ran at him.

Anthony was picking up speed when the speakers behind him gave off a reassuring hum that spread across the piazza. He missed a step but gained back his composure. A smile that shouldn't be allowed spread across Anthony's features as he attacked. It meant either of two things. Ras Tobias had decided to go out in a blaze of glory, or Zach had managed to survive and had returned.

The Chronicler had returned!

He had no choice but to believe it was true because he needed every advantage, every encouragement he could get.

They clashed.

A shockwave rippled out from the point of impact. The force was such that Anthony thought the sword would break apart, but the pieces that made it up held.

Barely.

His speed was waning; he didn't know how long he could keep up this pace. While Beelzebub seemed at ease, even as the fight shifted and the deadly dance of movement and counter-movement became more brutal. Anthony lunged at him, tried to force him to make a misstep, but the demon was nimble, evading every strike. And when he did decide to engage, Mr. B matched his every strike effortlessly, then swung back in wide, devastating arcs. Anthony's footwork was impeccable too; he weaved between the blows, each narrowly missing, the air itself seeming to crackle with the force of the strikes. Any one of them could kill him, but he wouldn't let that happen.

He couldn't.

Anthony found himself moving with the flow of the Reggae music, but the rabble surrounding the piazza watching the fight was getting more agitated, or was it excitement? Then, out of character for the arrogant Lord of Flies, he saw him grimace.

What?

Mr B screwed up his lips. If he were human, you would think he was in pain. Anthony wondered if he had actually seen that—a glitch in his armour. Drumbeats rippled out from Ras Tobias's speakers, and Mr B shook his head to clear it and then composed himself as if nothing had affected him.

Anthony rejoiced in his heart. The music was potent and a voice unlike anything Anthony had heard before on his transdimensional travels.

Honest.

Reverent.

Truthful.

He could feel the power with every word.

Hear the words of the Rastaman say.

Babylon yuh throne, gaan dung, Babylon yuh throne gaan down.

Seh, I hear the words of a higher man say.

Babylon yuh throne, gaan dung, Babylon yuh throne gaan down.

Anthony let the chanting carry him. He slashed low, his arms hacking at the demon's legs, hoping to shred tendon, skin and muscle, but Mr B levitated backwards like he was a figure skater on ice. Anthony shifted tactics, leaning back; he hurled the sword hilt over the blade and watched the super-fast blur tilt and yaw towards the demon's chest.

It did not connect.

In the very last moment, Mr B lashed out with his blade, a sardonic grin on his face, sending Anthony's sword twirling into the flagstones, ending up vibrating with its point buried deep.

Anthony dived towards it, tucked into a roll and stretched for it, his psionic call not strong enough to pull it free from where it had been wedged into the flagstones. He scrambled for it, but Mr B's body checked him with blistering speed, sending him tumbling away in a cloud of grit and dust. Mr B stood over Anthony's blade, yanked it out of the ground and broke it in two, throwing both pieces in opposite directions.

The demon roared, head thrown back, both arms flexed and fists pumping. It swayed, almost swooned and then caught itself, regaining its rock-solid stability.

It was too late.

Picking himself up from the ground, Anthony saw it and knew the music was affecting him.

The demon's composure had been flawless so far. His fighting technique is impeccable. Three missteps within moments were the beginning of a failure he could take advantage of.

Anthony leaned back, reaching into his great coat, visualising what he needed, his eager fingers grasping into the folds of time and space until they found what he was looking for. He pulled free a long, glowing staff. He slammed one end of the staff on the flagstone, and it sparked like flint.

By this, Mr B was focused again, angry and charging him. His smile disappeared, and his arrogance was replaced with concentration. There was chaos everywhere; the screams coming from the demon rabble that surrounded them were not excitement but agony. Anthony glanced over to see Ras Tobias, head down, hands furiously moving, his body swaying, then jumping on the spot as the music flowed through him. Zach was beside him, battered but alive. He wanted to scream his pleasure. He wanted to laugh at the plight of the Darksiders who, by this, were writhing, squirming and flailing all around, but he was too busy staying alive.

Mr B's footfalls sounded like thunder, and the ground shook as he came for him. The demon swung and lunged in one impossible manoeuvre, just as Anthony planted the staff against the ground and vaulted up and over, twisting mid-air to land behind him. In one fluid motion, he twisted the staff, and a blossom of blades and spikes erupted from its end. Anthony drove it into Mr. B's back, the weapon flaring as it pierced demon flesh for the first time.

Mr. B howled, swinging blindly, his fist snapping Anthony's head back and sending him flying again. The halberd remained embedded, crackling as it burned. The demon reached back, dislodged it from his back and with what could have been his non-dominant arm, hurled it in Anthony's direction.

It was a blur with the force of grudge, envy, hate and chaos that Anthony couldn't defend against. His javelin slammed into him, piercing and pinning him to the ground.

Anthony gasped, the pain fogging his reasoning, snatching his voice away and propelling him into a pile of shattered masonry and steel rebars. He tried to free himself and thought about how pathetic he must look like an insect on display. The pain was registering like a gong; as much as he tried to compartmentalise it, the strategy made no difference.

He had to get free.

He may have a chance.

Then he had none.

Mr B appeared. The demon's blade was already swinging, his stride eating up the distance between them like a freight train.

He couldn't get away.

Anthony had been on the brink of death before, severed arm, deatomised leg, ruptured eyeball from pulsed lasers to name a few, and his physiology could repair him to as good as new given time, but a decapitation.

That was game over.

Anthony couldn't flee but shifted his position and raised his arm to protect himself. He grimaced, the pain of his pierced and smashed internal organs shifting as he did, made him swoon. The Demon's blade lopped off his hand with ease, sending it spinning away, but thick steel rebar and bricks impeded the coup de grâce of separating Anthony's head from his shoulders. As the warrior screamed, with bones broken and unable to hold it in, a cloud of shattered brick obscured him from the force of Mr B's strike. The demon's smile faded as he realised Anthony was broken but not dead.

Not yet.

Mr B's gross smile returned as he shrugged, missing his head with the sword and swung it again.

Chapter Forty-Eight

Z ach was trying to keep his eyes peeled on the diversity of grotesque forms that surrounded the piazza; the shadows that had been boisterously celebrating, waiting for their champion to destroy Anthony, were no longer so jubilant. Those same creatures who had thought this would be easy sport were now writhing in agony. Their forms shimmered and flickered, as if the music was tearing at their very essence.

"Yes, Ras!" Zach shouted, his voice cutting through the audio. "It's working. It's fucking working."

Tobias gave him a quick nod, sweat beading on his forehead. He switched tracks; the bassline grew heavier, and the tempo sped up.

No one rememba old Marcus Garvey.

No one rememba old Marcus Garvey.

The words from *Burning Spear* were a battle cry, the melody a call to arms.

Zach had the Journal in one hand and a pen in the other. He did not need to concentrate; his hand was moving lightning fast over the pages, the information being noted bypassing his conscious mind straight to the paper. He briefly wondered how momentous this moment truly was.

Others be the judge of that.

Out in the distance, Zach could still see Anthony and Mr. B locked in combat. They were little more than blurs, their movements too fast and too fierce to follow. But the music was doing something—it was disrupting the programming and unravelling the dark lines of code that the Hellbound had woven around the estate.

"I need to do something," Zach shouted, thinking out loud.

Tobias didn't look up. "Do nothing, my yout. Dis is where you need to be. Protect deh Sound System. Anthony will look after himself."

Zach saw the sense in that reasoning, feeling ill-prepared to protect anything, not even himself.

A test of his uncertain courage was beginning to appear.

The first figure appeared from the shadows, stumbling towards them. It was a woman, her face pale and her eyes sunken. She moved like a puppet, her limbs jerking unnaturally.

"Ras..." Zach said, his voice tight.

Tobias glanced up and swore under his breath. "What now?"

Zach wasn't sure how to answer him.

More figures followed, dozens of them, all moving in the same eerie, mechanical way.

The residents?

God, look at this!

The Runnymede residents had been in the crossfire since this nightmare had begun. Lambs to the slaughter, trapped in a trance-like state, induced by the Darksiders who had the pick of the slumbering souls.

That had changed.

Zach's hand was at his mouth, his eyes glistening with emotion. They arrived in various states of dress, clumping around the big speaker boxes. Some wore sleepwear—old T-shirts and sweatpants—while others were adorned in more traditional attire: bright Ankara prints, embroidered tunics, and colourful headscarves. Despite the chaos, many bore a quiet dignity, as though the music had reawakened not just their bodies, but their spirits.

A young boy wearing Spider-Man pyjamas clung to his father's hand as they reached the piazza. The father hugged his son, a group of women linked arms, and an old couple held hands. The air buzzed with energy, a collective hum of awakening souls.

The music.

What else could it be?

As far as Zach knew, they were supposed to remain in that sleep-like state until the twenty-four-hour period was over and the Darksiders had their fill.

"The residents."

Zach sounded bemused.

"It's the surviving residents."

Tobias corrected nodding his head.

"Deh music—is calling dem back. It's waking dem up."

Zach's eyes widened. "I don't understand?"

"In simple terms yout, dem brainwaves are in sympathetic resonance with my Harmonic Cognition Enhancer. It's disrupting the pattern deh Darksiders have in place." Tobias' fingers flew across the soundboard, adjusting sliders. "We need more time fi break dem all free."

The approaching crowd grew larger, their lifeless eyes fixed on the sound system, the source that was drawing them in. Fearlessly, they had walked past the remaining Darksiders who had encircled the Piazza. It seemed their appetite for human souls was less important than their need for survival. Zach grabbed a metal pipe from the ground, his heart pounding. "They're all coming here. I'll hold them off."

"No!" Tobias barked, his voice uncharacteristically sharp. "Let dem come. Deh music will do its work."

"Are you sure?"

"Trust mi!" Tobias snapped, his gaze never leaving the soundboard. "We have nuthin to fear."

He turned a knob, and the bassline deepened, the vibrations rolling through the air like thunder.

The growing crowd absorbed the sound, absorbed the words of Sizzla Kalonji, and absorbed the raised amplitude of the carrier wave impacting their ears and brains. Hesitation rippled through them, their movements faltering. Some of them blinked, their eyes clearing for a moment before clouding over again.

"It's breaking through!" Zach said, his voice rising with hope. "You're doing it!"

Tobias didn't respond, too focused on the task at hand. He was playing another track now, something slower but no less powerful. The melody was haunting, the lyrics speaking of redemption and freedom.

And then it happened.

Zach had already placed the Journal in his satchel. He had stopped counting at two hundred people, and he was standing amongst them as they made a slow march in pyjamas, shorts, tracksuits and naked, congregating around the Sound System.

Men, women and children.

A woman in a dressing gown fell to her knees, and Zach ran over to help her up. When she stood again, she was humming.

Humming to the music.

Others followed, swaying and humming. The oppressive

weight of the Darksiders' influence was lifting, replaced by something purer, something human, until everyone in the crowd was humming.

"It's working..." Zach whispered again, his voice filled with awe.

The earth moved for him.

Literally.

The source of the mild tremor made him tremble. A massive Darksider emerged from behind the wall at the bottom of the incline.

The creature stood shaking its head from the effects of the music, a towering brute of hardened sinew and plated bone, its skin a leathery expanse of ancient scars and ridged flesh. It took another uncertain step, and then it seemed the instability plaguing it passed. It walked towards them, roaring with frustration. Its jagged, tusk-like protrusions curled from its jaw like fangs, framing a mouth that seemed not for speech, but for grinding bones and the tearing of flesh.

"Tobias!" Zach shouted. "We've got a problem!"

Zach gripped the steel pipe in his hand and ran towards it, not knowing what he would do, but knowing he had to do something. The thing was striding up the shallow incline, heading towards the Sound System and the crowd.

It would be a massacre.

The creature was born for war, prepared for battle.

Its armour was a grotesque fusion of bone and battle-worn metal, its pauldrons studded with jagged spines, its belt adorned with an ornate, skull-like carving—whether decoration or warning, Zach couldn't tell. Every movement it made was measured, deliberate, the gait of something that had walked through a thousand wars and come out the other side battered but victorious.

Zach swallowed.

The Rastaman glanced up, his expression grim. "Can you keep him occupied. I man have a plan."

"How do I do that?"

"Yuh will tink of someting."

Zach shook his head and scooped up a brick on his way. He flung both at it noncommittally. The brick glanced off its broad shoulders, while the pipe smashed into its head.

The Darksider turned and blinked its molten red eyes at him. It was having trouble focusing, but in a moment it became lucid enough to charge, its movements swift and predatory. Zach exploded into action, sprinting towards a set of concrete stairs with impressively thick wrought-iron guardrails that led down to the next level. He took to the air and, with a move that was a nine-point five in Parkour difficulty terms, threaded the needle. He dove through the guardrail, feeling the cold of the creature a fraction of a second behind him. He grabbed another section of the pipe and allowed his angular momentum to catapult him up and away from the point of impact.

The metal guard rail squealed, snapped in two places and uprooted from its concrete anchors as unyielding Darksider flesh ran into wrought iron. The Darksider looked dazed as it tangled itself in what remained of the stairs' railings, uprooting some of the structure from out of the concrete, but the rest holding it fast for the moment. Zach shot a look over his shoulder to Tobias, his body language screaming, 'Whatever you're going to do, do it now.'

Tobias saw it and understood.

A directional speaker was pointed towards the creature. It emitted an odd, short-lived, yet piercing whine. Zach felt the volume rise and could almost see the waveform expand outwards from the source. The words of the legendary 'Freddy McGregor' came clear and strong.

In this time of confusion

People are preparing themselves for Armageddon
Without even knowing
They're keeping fit
Fit for the fire.

The bass thumped, and a wall of pure energy shook the ground beneath Zach's feet, making him lower his centre of gravity in a crouch.

The Darksider let out an earsplitting scream, its form flickering and distorting. The music was tearing into him, note by note, vibration by vibration, pulling its molecules apart.

And then, with one final, gut-wrenching howl, it disintegrated.

Zach bent over, breathing hard, then looked up. He walked over to Tobias, and they both turned to watch the battle between Anthony and Mr. B. The two figures were locked in a final clash, their powers colliding in a blinding explosion of light and darkness.

And then, as the dust settled, only one figure remained standing.

Mr B.

Zach and Tobias exchanged crestfallen looks.

But the music didn't stop.

Tobias kept playing, his hands steady on the controls.

"Not over till deh last note play, my yout. Not over till de last tune."

And so they played, their music a beacon of hope in the darkness, a weapon against the forces that sought to destroy them. And the residents swayed and hummed.

Chapter Forty-Nine

Mr B's mouth fell open. The shotgun appeared in Anthony's only remaining hand, as if by magic, positioned under his chin. Mr B's swing was already committed and came down with such force that Anthony couldn't stop it but only deflect it.

That placed the shotgun on the demon's chest with the dangerous end under his chin.

Not perfect.

He twisted his wrist up, readjusted his aim.

Then pulled the trigger.

The blast was deafening, demon flesh and bone vaporising, grotesquely rearranging Mr B's 'pretty boy' features, sending him two steps back. The demon was genuinely stunned that the pellets tore into him.

It was the music.

With what was left of his mouth, he roared.

His face was a mess, but Mr B was using his other senses to navigate as his demon physiology began the regeneration process. Still, the music disrupted and derailed his foul nature.

Anthony fired again.

He staggered back.

Chunks of demon flesh and gore, splashed on the ground.

Anthony fired again.

The force took him off his feet, landing him on his ass.

Anthony wondered if he was hallucinating.

He could see the weaponised sound waves radiating outwards from the Sound System, flowing around some objects and reflecting off others. But when they reacted with Beelzebub, the waves acted like solid things, slashing, stabbing, and gouging into his person. His fellow Darksiders - the rabble who had been cheering him on, the ones who had encircled the piazza had fared worst, and their number had almost thinned to nothing.

The music had decimated them.

Mr B was struggling to get up from the third shotgun blast—wave after wave of Reggae music was smashing into him.

Anthony grinned through blood-streaked teeth.

His coat was torn, his face bloodied, and one arm hung uselessly at his side. He flung the shotgun down and, with his one good hand, he reached into his coat for what could be his last time. Feeling the tingle of his fingers, he reached into dimensional space and pulled free a fistful of a glowing orb. He slammed it on his chest, and the device sparked to life with a high-pitched whine. He painfully sucked air into his lungs, lifted his remaining arm that felt like lead and awkwardly threw it.

He had enough swing to propel it into a decent arc and watched it land and roll beside Mr B's feet. He could only look down with his ruined face from the shotgun blast, as the orb knocked on his boot.

Then it detonated.

A shockwave of heat, sound and light radiated outwards with Beelzebub at its epicentre.

"You're done," Anthony croaked to himself. Then with more gusto, for no one left to hear. "You're done motherfucker!"

Anthony peered through the cloud formed from atomised concrete, chemical reactions and hopefully demonic flesh.

He blinked and narrowed his eyes, and a wave of despondency overcame him.

A silhouette was shuffling through the gloom, the musical sound waves causing the mist to swirl in small vortices.

Mr B.

"Not today."

The demon was naked, his well-endowed dick swinging between his legs, his designer suit vaporised, his pale skin slashed from flying debris, and his body art not so vibrant. All his wounds were dribbling ichor. He fell to one knee, then to the other.

He started crawling towards him.

Chapter Fifty

"Enough of this!" Sylvester's powerful voice echoed across the battleground. He stood dressed in his body armour and his blade. His sharp eyes swept over the aftermath, lingering briefly on Anthony's broken body and then onto Anastasia high up in her floating diorama.

Puck, Medusa and three others stood close by.

Sylvester motioned over to where Anthony was pinned, and three of the sombre group ran to the warrior's side while Medusa and Puck stood on either side of their leader.

The head barber looked at his pocket watch and looked up at the floating diorama, his words directed at her.

"Call in your lapdog, Anastasia. You and I know this is over."

The night was heavy with the scent of burnt ozone and shattered illusions. The Runnymede estate, once a playground for the Darksiders' dark harvest, now stood eerily quiet. The program was broken. The people, ordinary souls who had no idea they had been prey, would return to slumber until the day's end.

Her piece of the Chaos Dimension that had been levitating above the proceedings descended, and she walked to its very edge, hands behind her back, ruby eyes fixed on Sylvester's.

She started clapping, her powerful hands sounding like the reports from a shotgun.

"Well played, well played." She nodded. "I imagine you think you've made a difference here somehow? But you haven't."

Sylvester smiled.

"Oh! It looks to me like my crew and I have just handed you and your minions their ass."

"Boastfulness does not befit you, Sylvester; leave that to me."

She scowled and shifted her attention to Mr B, who was still on all fours, her eyes bubbling molten red.

"Pathetic!" Anastasia shook her head. "You squandered a perfectly good opportunity to teach these creatures the reason why they do not deserve free will. But instead, I think you may have given them...hope." She turned to look at the table, at her spectral opponent, at the Eternal Game, then she turned back to the pitiful-looking Beelzebub. "That is very disappointing. Very disappointing. You will make amends for this, mark my words. Until then, get out of my sight before I reduce you to bite-sized pieces for my hounds to snack on."

Mr B lifted his head and snarled but didn't argue. He tried to stand, using his sword as a crutch, but couldn't. Small feathery patches of skin sloughed off his body and floated away as his demon-flesh continued to be assaulted by the music. With a pained grunt and a mathematical equation in his demonic tongue, space folded into itself, leaving a singularity that bobbed in place like a glistening black pearl and suddenly vanished from existence.

Sylvester placed his hand on the shoulders of Puck and Medusa, feeling the tension in their alien muscles.

"Wait for me."

As he walked over to his adversary, Sylvester could feel the eyes of his team watching him with concern, but they did not intervene. His weapon felt heavy in his hand. He sheathed it in the holster on his back and stood before her floating domicile. The demoness should have looked content with all the creature comforts within her chunk of hell. But she had been bested, her plans thwarted, the quantity of souls she was anticipating anemically thin. He folded his arms and peered into the nook. He looked at her briefly, then looked over to the game table just beyond her and the spectral woman sitting silently at The Game. The pieces were spread around the four levels. Sylvester smiled at the woman who nodded at him.

Anastasia stood at the threshold of her lair, poised but undeniably defeated. Her minions were dust, her grand design unravelled. Yet, she held herself with the icy grace of one who had played this game before and would play it again.

Sylvester tilted his head slightly. "You know why I'm here."

Anastasia exhaled slowly. "Yes." Her voice was smooth, but there was a tremor beneath it. Not fear. Something deeper. The weight of inevitability.

This was the part of the game that was older than either of them. A ritual beyond brute strength, beyond cunning. This was the formal close of their round, the moment where one power yielded and another stepped forward. It was not a conquest. It was the cycle.

Anastasia extended a hand toward the open doorway of her lair. The space beyond it shimmered with an otherworldly darkness, a living void that rejected the uninvited. Her eyes met Sylvester's.

She began the incantation.

"Night accepts the one who stands in twilight.

Shadow yields to the one who bears the blade of dawn.

Step forward, traveller, but know this:

No one crosses this threshold unchanged."

Sylvester watched her for a moment before responding, his voice carrying the weight of old rites and deeper truths.

"Darkness is neither enemy nor ally.

It is the river through which we pass.

I step forward, knowing I will return.

I cross, knowing I will carry something back."

The air rippled. The threshold no longer resisted him. He stepped inside.

The lair was a distortion of reality—rooms that twisted in on themselves, doorways that led to places that had never been. But Sylvester had no time for distractions. He walked straight over to the table.

The Eternal Game.

It stood at the centre of a room that should not have existed, bathed in the glow of something that was light and not light. A woman sat before it—her form translucent, shimmering, trapped in an endless limbo.

Representations of her had been here longer than any of them. Longer than the war between Sylvester and Anastasia. Longer than the cycle itself.

Sylvester approached, his movements slow, reverent. He understood what had to be done.

The spirit lifted her eyes to him. They were filled with the exhaustion one feels when sharing a stage with eternity.

"You came," the spectral woman whispered.

"We couldn't leave you here, Ms Hortense, after all you did for us. Your spirit deserves to be free."

He studied the game board in front of him. It was a construct of three levels, each representing a distinct layer of existence that comprised human existence. It was here that the cycle was decided. Here, the spectral woman was bound, forced to play and bear witness to the endless struggle for dominance between the forces of good and evil.

Sylvester inhaled deeply before beginning to write his code of release verbally. One that had been passed through generations of those who walked the line between light and shadow.

"The board is set, but the game is not forever.

What was bound may yet be freed.

What was trapped may yet cross over.

The watcher need not watch forever."

The spirit shuddered, her form flickering. Anastasia had kept her here, knowingly or unknowingly, by virtue of her own power and with Anastasia's defeat, the time had come for the spirit to be released. But it had to be done properly.

She lifted her hands, mirroring his words.

"The players move, but the pieces are not their own.

We are all bound, until we are not.

I have watched. I have waited.

And now, I am unmade."

A wind rushed through the chamber, though no doors or windows existed. The spirit's form began to dissolve, its particles of light drifting upward and dispersing into the unseen. Her eyes closed in relief.

The conflict was over.

Until another dimension. Until another time.

Sylvester exhaled, rolling his shoulders. The tension that had gripped the estate, the weight of the game, was lifting. But he knew better than to think it was ever truly over.

Stepping away from the game board, he made his way back through the lair. The walls no longer twisted, the pathways no longer fought against him. The ritual was complete. The exchange had been made. The spirit was free, and with her release, this round of the game had come to an end.

Anastasia met his gaze, her expression unreadable. She was beaten but not broken. Defeated but not destroyed.

"You played well," she said, her voice cool.

"So did you," Sylvester replied.

Anastasia turned, stepping into the darkness. She would rebuild. She always did. That was how this worked.

The Chronicler watched from the sidelines, already composing the words that would record this moment. The people of Runnymede would remember nothing but whispers and fragments of nightmare, never quite sure why they felt the way they did, only knowing that something had shifted in their lives.

The music played with Ras Tobias at the helm.

The Headhunters had won this round.

But the game would never truly end.

Chapter Fifty-One

The air felt too still, as if the world was holding its breath. Runnymede Estate was quiet now, the fractured skyline pieced back together, the shadows that once danced between the buildings gone. Zach stood before the barbershop, his body aching, his mind a whirlwind of exhaustion and reflection. The building, with its futuristic aesthetic and perfect signage, still stood defiantly in place, though Zach knew it wouldn't be for long.

Sylvester leaned against the shop's doorframe, the lenses of his glasses dusty. His once-imposing frame seemed a little smaller now, his shoulders carrying the invisible weight of their bittersweet victory.

"Chronicler," Sylvester said, motioning for Zach to follow him inside. "There's somethin' you need to see before we wrap this up."

Zach hesitated. The thought of stepping back into the barbershop, a place that had been their command centre during the chaos and his respite on ordinary days, felt heavier than he expected. But he forced his legs to move, trailing behind Sylvester into the brightly lit space.

Inside, everything looked just as it had before the Day of Reckoning began - clippers and scissors on the counters, jars of blue disinfectant lining the shelves. Sylvester led him to the wall at the end of the shop, to a large decorative mirror that stood from ceiling to floor. He had never recognised it before.

"Look at it and tell me what you see?"

Zach positioned himself in front of it, his reflection clear one moment, and the next, the mirror was a doorway into another world. Stood at this new entrance were rows and rows of floating names shimmering faintly, as if they carried some lingering magic. There were dozens—maybe hundreds. Some names Zach recognised: neighbours, friends, others he may not have known, but one and all were the beating heart of the estate.

"They're gone," Sylvester said, his voice heavy. "Wiped clean from this world. No birth records, no bank accounts, not even a scrap of paper to say they existed. Darksiders' way of cleanin' up after themselves." He tapped the plaque lightly with his knuckles. "But they'll stay here. On this wall. In our memory."

Zach's throat tightened. "They didn't deserve this."

"No," Sylvester agreed. "But they deserve to be remembered. That's where you come in."

The Headhunters leader pointed to Zach's satchel.

Zach pulled out a thick, leather-bound journal. It was old, its corners worn and its spine cracked, but it hummed with an energy that made the hair on the back of Zach's neck stand on end.

"The Journal is our record," Sylvester continued. "Every mission, every soul saved—or lost—it's all in there. It's how we secure and pass on what we've learned."

"Keep it safe. I have a feeling we will need its secrets in the future."

Zach frowned. "Next Chronicler? What are you saying?"

Zach looked down at the Journal, running his fingers over its cracked leather cover. The thought of carrying this legacy—of being responsible for something so much bigger than himself—felt overwhelming. But he nodded.

"I'll protect it with my life."

Sylvester clapped him on the shoulder. "I know you will."

OUTSIDE THE BARBERSHOP, THE HEADHUNTERS WERE gathered, their faces a mix of relief and exhaustion. Anthony sat in a wheelchair; the final battle had taken its toll. Despite his injuries, there was still a spark in his eyes, a quiet determination that told Zach the fight could never break him.

Nearby, Puck paced back and forth, his small frame radiating restless energy. Medusa leaned against one of the structural struts making up the frame of the barbershop and smiled at him. The strands of her golden locks meandered, as if she were underwater. Zach had said his goodbyes to her earlier, the memories of her body entangled with his, her screams and passionate whispers as she climaxed, flashed through his mind.

Zach approached Anthony, crouching down to meet his gaze. "Guess this is it, huh?"

Anthony nodded. "For now. You did good, kid. Better than I expected."

Zach smirked. "Don't sound so surprised."

Anthony chuckled, though the motion made him wince. "Take care of yourself out there. Protect the Journal, we're going to need it."

"I will," Zach promised.

He moved to Puck next, who grinned up at him. "Well,

look at you, Mr. Chronicler. Don't go gettin' all self-important on us now."

"I'll try not to," Zach said, laughing despite himself. "Take care, Puck."

The dwarf nodded, his expression softening. "You too, young Chronicler."

Finally, Zach saw Medusa approaching.

"This isn't goodbye forever," she said, her voice low. "You know that, right?"

Zach shrugged. "I guess not. But still..."

He trailed off, unsure of how to say what he wanted to. Instead, he stepped closer, his hand brushing against hers. For a moment, she didn't move, and then her fingers curled around his.

"Be safe," she said.

"You too."

She kissed him deep and for what seemed like an age, then she pulled away, her sentient hair flickering in what almost looked like a wave as she joined the others.

THE HEADHUNTERS STOOD IN A LOOSE CIRCLE IN FRONT OF the barbershop, their gazes fixed on Sylvester. He nodded to each of them in turn, and they entered the shop.

With his back to him, Sylvester turned, addressing Zach one last time.

"We're proud of you, Zachary."

Zach swallowed hard, watching as Sylvester placed his hand on the barbershop's door. The building shimmered, and the sound of rocks being dragged over rocks echoed off the surrounding buildings, as if the barbershop's foundations were imploding. Its edges growing hazy, it slowly began to fade.

He took a step back, his heart pounding as the barbershop

began to dematerialise. The sound of it grating through time, space, and dimensions suddenly stopped and piece by piece it disappeared, leaving nothing but an empty lot behind.

Zach hadn't realised he had taken the Journal out of his satchel and held it in his hands. As he stared at the empty space where the barbershop had been, three apertures on the spine of the Journal opened.

His hand tingled as the Autonomous Data Retrieval Drones came flying in from the estate, filled with data. As he kept the Journal steady, they hovered and locked into their enclosures. They began downloading information immediately.

Zach clasped his hands.

There was work to be done.

THE END

About the Author

Anton Marks' first novel began a trend of bestsellers that would transport readers to the ghettos of Kingston, Jamaica, in **Dancehall**, futuristic London, **In the Days of Dread**, government agents in **Bushman**, the futuristic world of vice in **69**, and the supernatural with the thrilling **Bad II the Bone** series. A young adult Sci-Fi/Fantasy series entitled **Joshua N'Gon: Last Prince of Alkebulahn,** will be dropping the third book under the name *Anthony Hewitt* in 2026. Also, check out the Urban Fantastic Shorts, such as **Messiah**, **Chauffeur** and **Omega Point**, which are shorter offerings in the Supernatural and Sci-Fi genres. Sign up for the Urban Fantastic Newsletter and be the best you can be: **bit.ly/Linklist1**

Friends don't allow friends to read bad books, so please leave a review and share the love.